Less than Meets the Eye

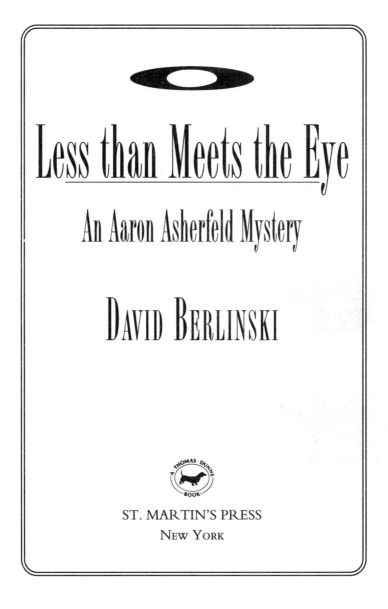

Less than Meets the Eye

An Aaron Asherfeld Mystery

DAVID BERLINSKI

A THOMAS DUNNE BOOK

ST. MARTIN'S PRESS
NEW YORK

Design by Ellen R. Sasahara

LIBRARY OF CONGRESS CATALOGING IN PUBLICATION DATA

Berlinski, David.
    Less than meets the eye/David Berlinski.
        p.   cm.
    "A Thomas Dunne book."
    ISBN 0-312-11298-X
    1. Private investigators—California—San Francisco—fiction.
    2. San Francisco (Calif.)—Fiction.   I. Title.
PS3552.E72494L47   1994
813'.54—dc20   93–45281
                                                CIP

First Edition: November 1994

10   9   8   7   6   5   4   3   2   1

For my Victoria

Contents

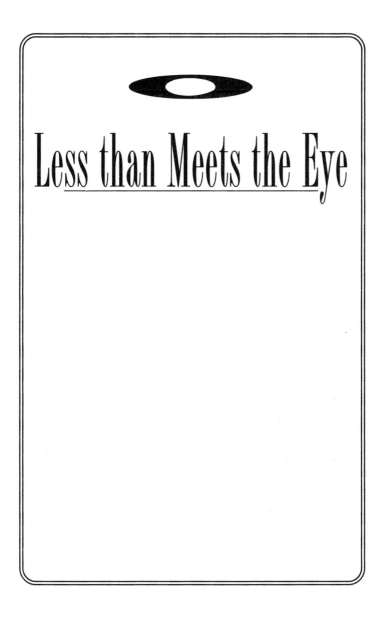

Less than Meets the Eye

The dean of the faculty called me on Monday. The head of the Gay and Lesbian Student Faculty Alliance pushed me over her fat feet on Wednesday. By the time I finished with the university I had earned a doctorate in disgruntlement. It's kind of a post-graduate degree. It didn't take me long to get it and I didn't much want it once I had it.

Body Parts

IT WAS A BRIGHT, cloudless day, the kind we get in northern California between winter rains. I drove down the Peninsula from the city with the window open. Here and there, the sharp smell of sage drifted into the car. I had a tape by Marvin Gaye on the stereo. Marvin was singing about grapevines. He was pretty upset about something. I could tell.

I got off 280 at Sand Hill Road and drove east alongside the university's lush golf course, the rain-washed grass sparkling in the sunlight. Someone at the sixteenth green was going through that elaborate twitch that golfers go through before they putt a ball. He kept hunching his shoulders and reorganizing his feet on the lawn and taking mincing little swings with his club. He looked like an imbecile. No game is as dumb as golf. Polo maybe. I parked illegally in front of a boarded-up fire station and walked through the Union and out onto the main campus. A few students were sitting on the Union's concrete deck, sharing their food with the bright-eyed glossy grackles that swooped down from the trees and strutted brazenly across the table tops. The air was absolutely still.

I followed the footpath past the post office and over to the campus fountain. The fountain itself was turned off, but its blue-bottomed reflecting pool was filled and the air above the water

1

shimmered with iridescent sparkles. A few young mothers were letting their leashed toddlers toddle to the edge of the water. A cocker spaniel stood with his front paws on the fountain's concrete retaining wall, itching to go over the top and scared to jump. He kept his paws on the wall and cocked his head around, looking for help, but when I bent over to give him a boost, he decided he had better things to do than go swimming and headed purposefully up the steps that led back to the bookstore. I followed the dog. I figured he knew what he was doing.

At the top of the steps, two girls were manning a table. One of the girls was short and blonde and chubby and had upturned nostrils. The other had a tiny face half-hidden by her lustrous brunette hair. The girls had mounted a dozen or so photographs of women in various poses on a large white cardboard panel that they kept propped up on their table. The photographs had evidently been ripped from fashion magazines. Some of the women in the pictures were pretty; others could have stopped a beating human heart. On top of the photographs, someone had scrawled These Pictures Oppress Wymyn with a red magic marker.

Miss Piggy was presiding over a petition. It called for photographs that oppressed women to be banned. It encouraged women to make their voices heard. There were exclamation points after every sentence. Every other word was in italics. It seemed that provocative pictures of knock-out women were a terrific problem.

I stepped back to look at the photographs.

"They look all right to me," I said.

Tiny Face shrugged her tiny shoulders. "It's that they oppress women," she said, looking past me toward the reflecting pool.

The largest photograph on the panel showed a woman with a swan's neck having her hair pulled from the back by an exotic looking man with olive skin.

Miss Piggy leaned over to tap the photograph with the tip of her finger. "Look at that," she said decisively. "I mean, that it's all right to be violent against women."

I looked at the picture again.

"You're probably right," I said.

The two girls didn't seem especially eager to have my endorsement. Neither of them looked much as if they had ever had their hair pulled back by exotic men with olive skin. Or anyone at all.

I walked on slowly through the radiant sunny campus; from time to time, a bicyclist would sweep past me, silent as the sun.

When I came to the bell tower, I stopped to look at the machinery. It was supposed to be a pretty big deal. The bottom of the tower had a series of glass panels that let you see the gears in action. The whole thing seemed to be warming up for an absolutely sensational set of chimes. One gear was moving slowly, dragging another gear after it. It was all very complicated and impressive. I waited for something to happen. The gears kept shifting and ratcheting, but no chimes chimed. After a while, the gears stopped moving too. The bell tower was probably making a statement; everybody else was.

The dean's office was in the university's inner quadrangle; the place is the size of Tiananmen Square and about as much fun to look at. There's a church with colored frescoes on one side of the thing; the other sides have departmental offices and classrooms. The offices are faced in stucco with doors of old blackened wood. The roofs are made of curved Spanish tiles. Everything is supposed to look very authentic and everything looks about as authentic as a Taco Bell stand. The quadrangle itself is paved with small red and black sandstone tiles. An army of illegal immigrants must have gone blind putting the tiles into the ground. I could just see the university's coordinator of construction surveying the work from a golf cart. *Yo Juan, you missed a spot here.*

A brass sign mounted on the door to the dean's office said Dean of Faculty, but the dean's name was inscribed on one of those Lucite tags that are designed to slip into a frame. Being a dean didn't seem to be a lifetime job. I ran my fingers over the gold-plated letters of the sign and pushed open the heavy black door and let myself into the empty waiting room. A sign on the secretary's desk said Gone Fishing. It showed a little boy sitting by a stream with a straw hat over his eyes.

I could hear the dean himself on the telephone in his own office. He was grunting affirmatively.

Suddenly he said loudly: "I *knew* those farts had their heads stuck up their asses." Then he resumed grunting.

I sat in the secretary's comfortable orange chair and rested my feet on her desk. I didn't think she'd mind.

After a while, the dean barged out of his office; he looked at me as if he had surprised a burglar.

"Asherfeld," I said, standing up.

He was a rumpled man of medium height. He had a round head with coarse black thinning hair, a snubbed nose, and small bright blue eyes that seemed to glitter when he moved his head.

"You called me."

"Right," said the dean. "Hold on a sec, I'm up to my ass in alligators."

He rummaged around his secretary's desk for a minute or two more, pawing through various papers, making a mess.

"Hell," he finally said, "I don't know where it is."

"Me either," I said.

"Hell," he said again, "if you don't know where it is and I don't know where it is, it must be lost."

There was no arguing with that.

The dean straightened up and smiled. I shook his hand. It was like mopping the back of your neck on a warm day. "Come on in," he said.

I followed the dean into his office and sat opposite him at his desk. There were papers everywhere, even on the floor, and books lying scattered on every surface. The room was sunny but the place looked vaguely dirty, as if the dean didn't wash his hands all that much.

"It's like a zoo out there," he said.

I nodded sympathetically. It was his office that looked like a zoo. Out there, it looked like a morgue.

"Trying to get out a mission statement for this gay and lesbian studies program. I'm telling you, it's a bear."

"Gay and lesbian studies?"

The dean had commenced pawing through the papers on his own desk. "Gays in history, gays in literature," he said.

I chimed in: "Gays in science."

"Yeah, gays in science."

"Like Einstein."

The dean looked up from the mess he was making. "Einstein was gay?" he said. "I didn't know that." He seemed pleased.

"Absolutely."

"Just goes to show you."

"Just goes to show you," I said.

I was hoping the dean would remember why he had called me.

"Listen," he said abruptly, "you ever hear of this Richard Montague?"

He had stopped moving papers on his desk and sat with his hands folded together.

I said: "Nope."

"No reason you should," said the dean. He looked at me with his head tilted slightly, as if he were listening for distant chimes. Then he said: "Take a look at this." He pushed a manila file folder toward me with his pudgy index finger.

There was a resume inside the folder for Richard "Buddy" Montague. The thing ran to more than fifteen pages. Buddy had evidently been worried that someone somewhere might miss one of his accomplishments. A professional glossy of Montague was paper-clipped to the last page of the resume. It showed a youngish looking man straddling a chair in a theatrical pose. He had thick curly hair, very bright merry eyes, and heavy sensual lips. He looked smart, arrogant, vital and alive.

I closed the folder and rested it on my knee. "What about him?" I asked.

"Son of a bitch is dead," the dean said explosively. "One day he's healthy as a horse, next day *boom!* they're wheeling him out of his house on a gurney."

I opened the folder again and looked at Montague's round merry face.

"It happens," I finally said.

"Asherfeld," said the dean, "the man was thirty-eight years old. HIV negative. We're not living in Bangladesh."

I raised my eyebrows and shrugged my shoulders. "What can I say? Only the good die young. You didn't call me down here to tell me that."

The dean chewed reflectively on his lower lip. "No," he said thoughtfully. "You got that right."

"What did the medical examiner say?"

"The medical examiner said that *apparently* Montague died of

5

natural causes. He won't go any further than that and he won't sign off the case."

"Any reason to think otherwise?"

The dean leaned back in his chair and put his feet up on his desk. He crossed his legs and began kneading his calf through the leg of his pants.

"A couple of months ago, there was this graduate student who made certain threats against Montague."

"What kind of threats?"

"Actually, he threatened to cut his heart out and eat it."

"Pretty sensitive about criticism, was he?"

The dean tilted his head and rolled his eyes upward. "He was one of these Rasafrastrians. You know, dreadlocks and all? These guys can get pretty touchy. Seems Montague was just sitting on his thesis."

"Probably asked that it be written in English," I said.

"Yeah, well, no one took it seriously at the time," said the dean.

"And Dreadlocks? I'll bet he's having a tough time finding another friend on the faculty."

"Oh, he's around," said the dean vaguely. "That's one problem."

"There's more?"

The dean pressed himself back into his reclining chair.

"Montague had a pretty substantial grant from the National Science Foundation," he said tentatively.

"You're worried about the money."

"Not worried," said the Dean, *"concerned.* The president is very, very sensitive about any hint of fiscal impropriety."

The president of the university had recently billed taxpayers for his wedding and the fruitwood toilet seats he had added to his mansion.

"Regular Scrooge," I said. "Anyone'd realize that reading the newspapers."

The dean didn't say anything. He just looked at me with his glittering eyes.

I said: "So you want to know why Montague died and whether he took the money with him. What else?"

The dean seemed as if he might be embarrassed.

I helped him along. "You're giving away troubles today. What's next?"

A small wave of color had spread over the dean's face.

"Troubles is right. I might as well lay it all out for you."

"Might as well," I said.

"There's a rumor going around campus that Montague's body was mutilated."

"Mutilated how?"

The dean's face commenced to glow. "It was his penis," he said. "It's supposed to be missing. That's supposed to be why the medical examiner won't sign off on the case."

I shuddered involuntarily.

The dean pulled at his earlobe. He was glad to have gotten that off his chest. "I don't know how the story got out," he said. "Now you got rumors flying around everywhere."

"Hard to believe," I said. "You'd think the university be able to take a little case of ritual mutilation in stride."

"Gays think it was a deliberate provocation, women's group think someone took it as a symbol of the patriarchy, conservatives got some other bug up their ass, it just goes on and on, and the hell of a thing is no one knows it's true or not. Montague's body was cremated after the autopsy."

"All this and multiculturalism too? Any parent be thrilled to have a kid here."

"The university's a pretty special place. It has its own rules."

"You're right," I said. "But I'm not part of it. I don't have to like it."

"Fair enough," said the dean.

"I'll make a few inquiries," I said.

"Terrific. Give me something lay the rumors to rest. You'll keep me posted?"

I said that I would.

"Great, great," said the dean. He was eager to get rid of me.

"I'll send you a bill. Don't worry. It won't cost as much as all those fruitwood toilet seats."

The dean nodded agreeably. I got up and walked toward the door. He coughed as I was opening it; he must have remembered something.

"Asherfeld," he said.

7

I looked up.

"You got it wrong. I mean about only the good dying young."

I waited by the door.

"It's the other way around," he finally said. "Only the young die good."

Calls for the Dead

AFTER I LEFT THE DEAN, I walked over to the philosophy department. I don't know what I expected to find. The office was at the end of a corridor behind another one of those heavy black Spanish doors. I could hear someone clacking away at an electronic typewriter inside. The professor's offices were all closed; there was no one in the small lecture room that gave out onto the corridor. I figured the philosophers were at home, resting up from all that brain work.

I stood in the entrance to the lecture room for a moment, my hands still in my pockets, smelling the chalky smell of the place. Schoolrooms are all alike and like the ocean, all of them make you sad.

After a while, I stopped looking at the empty room.

There was a large cork bulletin board mounted on the wall at the end of the corridor. Someone had fixed a list of courses to the cork with a red pushpin. I stopped to read the list. I wanted to see what I was missing. I could have attended a seminar in feminist analysis. The neatly typed blurb said that the course would present a "gendered account of Derrida's hermeneutic discourse." I was in favor of that; I thought it was a terrific idea. The collection of small snapshots alongside the course list showed the members of the philosophy faculty looking out at the world. The men appeared to be suffering from allergies. A lot of them had tremendous moustaches. The women looked tense and unhappy; there was something bitter in their eyes. One square was white and empty.

The clacking of the electric typewriter stopped, flooding the gloomy hall with silence. There was a *ka-chunk*. The door to the philosophy department office opened. A stout young woman poked her head out of the doorway. She saw me looking at the faculty photographs and flowed calmly into the hall.

"Can I help you?" she asked pleasantly.

She was dressed in a multi-colored shift; she had a very pretty face with lovely clear skin and chipmunked cheeks and calm blue eyes.

I tapped at the place where Montague's photograph should have been.

"Pretty shocking," I said.

The young woman folded her arms around her bosom and hugged herself.

"It's just awful," she said. She looked at me closely.

"Were you like a friend or something?"

"Or something," I said. She nodded and smiled her mysterious fat-woman's smile.

From the inside of her office a cranky voice called out: "Violet, I need you."

Violet rolled her pretty blue eyes. "There's brownies in the office if you want," she said.

I shook my head.

"Listen," she said, "there's a memorial meeting on Wednesday. If you're like involved, you might want to go."

"Violet!" shouted the cranky voice again.

"Call the office if you want to know where it is."

I said I just might do that.

Violet flowed back toward her office in that calm, water-moving way she had.

I had lunch at a Palo Alto restaurant called The Good Earth. It was a place that celebrated fruits and nuts. The hamburgers were made of soya instead of meat. Every dish was covered with lentils or with sprouts. The waitresses were rooted to the ground like bison.

Afterwards, I used the telephone on the counter of the restaurant to check my machine. One of my wives had called to complain about her new husband. "Honest to god, Asher, I think he's gay," she hissed. "He's one of these gays who's gay and just doesn't *know* he's gay. I mean, when we're in a restaurant I see him *tracking* these men. I mean, he keeps *staring* at their behinds. I mean it is so *obvious.*" I tried to remember the man she had married. I thought he might have had a little black moustache. My wife had described him as a real man. *"He* doesn't think with his penis, Asher," she had said.

Downtown Palo Alto wasn't exactly thronged with people when I finally left the restaurant. There were a few teenagers loitering about a diet Mexican restaurant and a few elderly parties were shuffling up the street in that out-of-place way that elderly parties have of shuffling up any street in California. The store selling elaborate mountain climbing equipment was empty. So was the store selling sewing machines. It wasn't a bad street and Palo Alto wasn't a bad town. It was just quiet and empty and vacant. It had nothing luminous but its light.

I walked down University Avenue with the winter sunshine splashing on the back of my neck until I came to one of those little urban parks that people who plan cities think are so sensational—a couple of uncomfortable benches, a man-made waterfall flowing down a metal screen, a few dwarf trees with wire baskets at their base. I sat on one of the benches and looked through Montague's folder again. I wanted a sense of the man. It wasn't easy. He had been a whizz at something, but it wasn't something I knew anything about. He seemed to have had the knack of always being in the right place at the right time; I thought he might have been the sort of man who thinks of good luck as an entitlement, like lower taxes. He had never been married and he had lived in the Oakland hills, not on the Peninsula.

A young girl ambled into the park with her even younger brother in tow. That younger brother was absorbed in eating an ice-cream cone. She sat the little slug down on a bench and sat herself down sideways next to him, one narrow leg drawn up, her arms around her leg and her head resting on her knee. She was dressed in shorts and a halter. She had copper colored skin and delicate thin wrists and thick chestnut hair and she was sending enough come-hither musk into the air to power a battleship.

She couldn't have been more than ten.

I got up after a while. I thought I might as well drive out to

Oakland and have a look at Montague's place. It seemed better than going home. Some days anything does.

Come Hither shot me a final piercing come-hither look as I crossed the bench in front of her.

"You are such a pig," she said, turning her attention to her brother.

I took the Bayshore Freeway to the Dumbarton Bridge and scooted over to Oakland just before the rush-hour traffic began, filling the car up with gas as I drove. I didn't need the radio. The health food made music all on its own.

For the most part, Oakland sprawls over the valley floor on the east side of the Bay, but off to the northeast, the city ascends a series of rugged green hills folded like elephant skin over narrow canyons. There are great views there and fantastic properties. The views are free, but the properties are a kind of secret among the rich.

Montague lived on the top of one of the hills; he must have known the secret.

I took Ashby up past the old Claremont Hotel, with its crumbling porch and tottering gazebos, the white front of the building scorched by fire, and past the turnoff for the children's park at Grizzly Peak; I turned by the 7-11 at Paco Verde and drove upward on a narrow blacktop through green winter meadows and California oaks all bunched in copses. After a few miles, the blacktop gave way to gravel. I could see all of San Francisco behind me when I took the last curve, and the Pacific, blue in the blue distance.

Paco Verde deadened at a chain-link fence. The dirt road beyond looped around a final copse of oaks and then ran up the side of the hill. I got out of my car and eased my back. A lizard scuttled out from underneath a rock as I straddled the fence, and then scuttled right back underneath again. The light hurt my eyes.

Montague's house was on the very top of the hill; it couldn't have been more than a few hundred yards from the fence, but it was completely hidden by the turn in the dirt road. It wasn't a big house—no bigger than an aircraft carrier, say. It had views of San Francisco, the north Bay, the Peninsula, points south. It was all on one level and very modern, with a large granite deck in front and a lot of glass and exposed steel beams.

There was nobody around and no one made a sound except the insects rustling in the grass.

I stood in front of the house and thought of how terrific Montague must have felt every time he walked up here; wherever he was now, the views couldn't have been as spectacular.

When I got back to the 7-11 at Paco Verde I called Skyview Realty on MacArthur Boulevard and asked for the agent on call.

"This is Terry," someone said in a big hurry.

I described Montague's property and asked Terry whether she had a listing yet.

"We sure do, Sailor," she said. "Is this for yourself?"

"No," I said. "I'm working for Mr. Hong Fong Wong. That's Hong Fong Wong as in Wong Shipping."

"I see, I see," said Terry. She was tremendously impressed.

Terry agreed to show me the property; she said she'd meet me right away; she said hang on, Sailor; she said she'd be there in a jiff.

I hung up and went into the 7-11 and asked Mr. Pimples behind the counter to make me a slushee. I took the stuff outside and leaned against the wooden rail in front of the store and sipped at the cool, evil-tasting liquid. It was like sipping benzene. The afternoon was growing long.

Terry was there within five minutes. She roared up in a silver Mercedes 450SL; she must have traveled faster than the speed of light. The vanity plate on the car said GR8D8. Terry rolled down her window.

"Hi there, Sailor," she said. She spoke English as if it were a tonal language. "Come on aboard," she sang out.

I got in the car and took a closer look at her as I fussed with the seat belt. She seemed to have a hard young curvy body, but the skin on her face had been stretched tight, with only her large ears left to hang mournfully from her skull like bell ropes. Her hands were coarse and ragged and old. They looked like claws on the steering wheel.

"So you're with Fong Shipping," she said, "that is *so* exciting."

I said it was pretty exciting.

Terry gunned the car just as we were approaching the first blind curve on the gravel portion of the road. She must have thought it was pretty exciting too.

"And you were just *driving* along and you just *happened* to see the property," she said. "That is so *remarkable,* it is such a *coincidence.*"

I said it was pretty remarkable and a real coincidence.

"You are just going to *love* this house," she said. "Did you know that it's move-in? It is completely furnished."

I said I didn't know.

Terry gunned the car some more up the steep hill toward Montague's house. She drove as if owning a Mercedes gave her rights to both parts of the road. I guess it did. We didn't meet any other cars. She kept her nose in the air as she talked; she wasn't taking any chances on letting me see anything droop.

All the way up the hill, she sing-songed her way through a monologue. She said she had had it with negative thinking. She said she realized she really was a can do person. She said she guessed she was one of those women who loved too much. She said she was in search of her inner child. She said she was learning to deal with codependency. She said she was still looking for someone to light her fire.

She was pretty hard to discourage.

She gunned the Mercedes up to the chain-link fence and stopped in a cloud of dust. As she yanked on the emergency brake she said: "I have been *dying* to show this property to someone *special* for I don't know how long."

Then she rolled down the window and breathed the dusty air dramatically. She swivelled her head toward me.

"So tell me, Sailor, you still looking for that special someone to light *your* fire?"

I said: "I'm a widower."

Terry blinked her blue-shadowed eyes at me rapidly.

"I am *so* sorry," she said. She didn't seem sorry at all.

"Not to worry," I said as I opened the door. "The jury believed my story, thank god."

Terry eyed me from her seat.

"Tell you what," she said. "There's a lock box at the front of the house. Why don't I give you the key, wait for you here?"

She had stopped singing her speech. There are worse things in life than not having your fire lit.

I took the key from her clawed hand and tried not to look into her eyes.

The front door of Montague's house gave out directly into the living room, which must have been thirty feet by thirty feet. The steeply pitched cathedral ceiling had bubbled skylights cut in each side; the floor was polished bleached oak, arranged in an elaborate herringbone pattern. The place was furnished with stuff that was a whole step up from expensive. There was a red oriental rug on part of the floor—the worn looking kind that costs ten times more than anything that looks good, and a sectional sofa covered in pale blue silk, and a couple of geometric chrome and leather chairs, and a white cherrywood desk with silver inlays.

It was the sort of room that needed Wynton Marsalis on the stereo; it was the sort of room that needed lines of cocaine on the glass and chrome table; it was the sort of room that needed a half-dressed blonde named Kimberly sitting on the pale blue sofa.

I didn't think it was the sort of room that needed a professor of philosophy.

The telephone answering machine on the expensive white desk was blinking. Calls must have come in after Montague's death. There was no reason anyone should have noticed.

I pressed the message button. The machine whirred and clicked obediently.

The first message was from the pool maintenance company. Someone wanted to talk about microorganisms in the pool water. "What you got there, you got algae coming up the sides your pool in one maybe two months," said someone for whom algae was like the masque of the red death.

Then there was a message about a conference in Sarajevo that Montague was supposed to attend. The speaker was obviously calling from abroad. He couldn't speak English and didn't seem to realize that he was talking to a machine. "Hallo. Here is Havel. I haff message for you," he rumbled, rumbling on until the machine cut him off after sixty seconds.

The last message began without a salutation. Someone with a

thin tenor voice said: "Richie, listen up. You there? You there, Richie? Do yourself a favor, pick up your phone, Richie."

I left the machine blinking and walked through the rest of the house. It was obvious that a cleaning service had been through at least once. Montague's personal effects were gone from the bedroom—no clothes, no linens, no books. The place already had a large empty feeling.

Terry was sitting tensely in her Mercedes when I got back to the chain-link fence. Her elbow was resting on the window ledge, her hand shading her eyes. She started the car before I reached the passenger side door. She wasn't taking any chances. I slid onto the warm leather seat.

"How'd you like it?" she asked, turning the Mercedes into a graceful backward arc, away from the fence.

"The *feng-shui* is all wrong," I said. "There's bad luck written all over the place."

Terry gave me one of those queer awed looks that superstitious women get; she said, "You have no idea," and compressed her lips. She didn't say anything more.

Fat Man's Cough

I WOKE UP EARLY the next morning. I showered and shaved before the sky outside my bathroom window had filled with light. I splashed cologne on my cheeks and sprinkled talcum powder on my toes. I dressed in a grey suit and a red tie with little blue dots. I drank my coffee and watched the television on my kitchen counter sitting in my shirtsleeves, my suit jacket behind my chair, the thing just raring to get going and start the business of impressing people.

A muscular oaf was cheerfully working his way through an exercise routine on channel 2. The program was called Body By Max. As Max lectured the camera, his assistant, a dazzling young woman in a spandex leotard, stood at his side, smiling grandly.

Max was getting his calves in shape. He stood there on the television stage, his grinning assistant grinning, and pushed himself up in the air from a board, using only his toes.

I waited until he had finished his last set before calling Leland Sturz in Oakland. I wanted to make sure that Max really got those calves of his worked out.

A bored sounding woman with a New York accent answered the telephone.

"This Leland Sturz's office?" I asked.

"That depends."

"On what?"

"On who's calling."

"It's his broker. Tell him I got a terrific deal on frozen pork bellies."

"Very funny."

"All right. Tell him I want to donate my torso to medical science. I need to know if it's okay one of my wives keeps my head."

"That's even funnier."

"I give up," I said. "Tell him it's Aaron Asherfeld. Tell him I need to speak to him about Richard Montague. Tell him I'm working for the university."

"He's not going to be too happy about this," she said dubiously.

"It's a hard world," I said. "Tell him anyway."

I left my telephone number and hung up.

The telephone rang almost immediately. Someone coughed. It was a large wet cough.

"You this Asherfeld?"

I said: "Yup."

There was another of those fat man's coughs.

"Look, I don't care how many smooth silky sons of bitches come out of the woodwork, I'm not signing off on that report until I'm good and ready."

"Fine by me, doc," I said. "But you're giving your speech to the wrong guy."

There was a pause on the line. I could hear Leland Sturz's stertorous breath come wheezing through his lips.

"This here's someone named Asherfeld, isn't it? You called me just now?"

He sounded doubtful, as if he were worried about having dialed the wrong number.

"This is Aaron Asherfeld," I said. "I don't care if you never sign Montague's autopsy report. Sit on it for years if you like."

Sturz directed an enormous wet cough into the receiver and said: "You working for that fat little fellow who sweats a lot?" He meant the dean.

"The dean doesn't tell me what to think."

"That a fact?" said Sturz. He didn't sound angry anymore, just tired of it all and distracted. Then he said abruptly: "So what do you want?"

"Some of your time."

There was a pause as Sturz thought the matter over.

"Yeah, yeah all right," he finally said. "Doris'll set it up."

In a minute, Doris came on the line. It hadn't been exactly like waiting for Elizabeth Taylor.

"Dr. Sturz said you're to meet him the doctors' cafeteria, seventh floor County Medical. He said to tell you he'll meet you there at 11:15 sharp. He said to tell you you can have fifteen minutes."

Doris hung up without waiting for an answer.

I spent a few minutes tidying up my apartment and then I spent a few minutes standing by my living room window. There was still fog hanging over the Bay in white wisps. The hills of Marin behind the Golden Gate were fuzzy and indistinct in the soft peach colored morning light.

The rush hour had come and gone by the time I got onto the Bay Bridge. Traffic was whooshing along. A long white stretch limousine swam up in my rear-view mirror, swung around, and accelerated past me, smooth and silent as a shark. The bumper sticker on the green Audi in front of me said Think Globally: Act Locally. I tried to figure it out. I decided it didn't mean a thing. You were always reading things like that in California.

I drove into the doctors' parking lot at the County medical building in Oakland just as someone on KPFA was explaining that AIDS was a CIA plot.

The uniformed Korean surveying things from a little booth by the entrance looked at me closely.

"You doctor?" he asked.

"Astral podiatrist," I said.

"How come you don't got doctor's card?"

17

He pointed at the windshield.

I looked at him directly, with my hands shading my eyes.

"This is a loaner from my brother-in-law." I said. "The Mercedes was carjacked over in East Oakland. Probably being driven by a drug dealer right now."

"Them people plenty bad," said the attendant without much interest; he waved me into the lot.

County Medical is one of those enormous sandstone buildings that the WPA put up in the thirties; California is full of them. Drug dealers head there after the deal goes sour; so do teenage girls who figured they were fat and panic when their water breaks. It's a terrific place to go if you have a bullet in your liver or gas gangrene that you got from living on the streets; anything less serious, you're better off reading the *Merck Manual*.

The medical examiner's office occupied the top three floors of the west wing; autopsies were conducted in the basement by the pathology staff. The medical examiners were strictly brain workers, like philosophers. They needed to be high up.

The admitting office on the ground floor of the east wing was already packed with people; the place had the close smell of some horrible odor being covered up by disinfectant.

A large dishevelled woman who had been waiting for her number to be called swung her wheelchair in front of me as I edged down the aisle.

"You know where legal aid is at?" she demanded peevishly. "I've had it with this here waiting."

"Don't bother," I said, edging past her. "Those guys are probably all out chasing ambulances."

"They better not be sick," she said bleakly.

I cut through the waiting room and over to the physicians' tunnel that led directly from the east wing over to the west wing.

The doctors' cafeteria on the seventh floor wasn't very crowded: I spotted Sturz right away. He was sitting alone at a steel and formica table, morosely eating a bowl of something that looked like corn chowder.

"Dr. Sturz?" I said politely.

Sturz looked up at me without much curiosity and then glanced down to the name tag on the lapel of his white laboratory coat.

"Last time I looked," he said slowly, and resumed spooning his chowder.

I sat down on a metal chair opposite Sturz. "We have an appointment."

Sturz continued slowly to sip his chowder.

"That a fact?" he said.

He was a tall man, well past middle age, with a large conical head, shaggy grey eyebrows, and a potato nose; he had very narrow shoulders.

"I'm not disturbing you?" I asked. "I mean, if you want to be alone with all that corn chowder, I'll understand."

Sturz looked up at me. He might have smiled slightly. It was hard to tell. He stopped eating for a moment.

"What can I do for you, sonny?" he finally asked.

I slid down on the metal seat so that I could stretch my legs underneath the table.

"You could tell me what caused Richard Montague's death."

"Heart stopped beating," said Sturz.

"Why?"

"No idea," he said.

Sturz sat upright in his chair, his spoon clutched childishly in his right fist.

"Sometimes it happens. Man's heart stops beating." He lifted his heavy left hand into the air and snapped his fingers, making a plopping sound. "Just like that."

"Just like that," I said. "No underlying coronary artery disease, no myocardial ischemia, no spasming in the coronary artiers, no barbiturates, blood chemistry normal?"

Sturz looked at me with his old dog, heavily hooded eyes.

"You a doctor?"

"No."

He snorted happily.

"Didn't think so," he said. "There was postmortem lividity the base of the man's neck. It's in my report."

"Meaning what?"

"No idea."

"Mind if I read your report?" I asked.

"Of course I mind. Material's confidential."

I pushed my chair back, making a scraping sound on the

scuffed linoleum, and leaned forward, resting my wrists on my thighs.

"One more thing," I said.

Sturz waved his spoon in the air. "What's that?"

"There's a rumor going around that Montague's body was mutilated. Tell me anything about that?"

Sturz lifted the corners of his lips by a fraction.

"No," he said.

I got up and stood behind my chair.

"You've been a terrific help, Doctor. Gold mine of information."

"I'm a medical examiner. It's not my job to be informative."

"I guess," I said.

Something must have bothered Sturz. "How come you don't ask me why I won't sign off on the report?"

"I give up," I said. "How come you won't sign off on the report?"

An evil look of amusement glinted in Sturz's eyes.

"I won't tell you that either," he said.

A cold wet fog was beginning to sweep up the avenues by the time I got to the city from Oakland. I took Fell from the earthquake-ruined shank of the freeway and cut over to the Sunset. That year an insurance agent named Mick Shaugnessy let me use the back room of his office for a couple of hundred dollars a month. I kept an answering machine there and a change of clothes. The office was bathed in fluorescent light. The golden glitter of the day had gone.

I called the dean at the university and told him about my conversation with Leland Sturz. He heard me out and then said: "I'm not surprised, Asherfeld. University's a target today. Everyone figures they might as well take a shot."

"You may be right."

The dean heard the skepticism in my voice.

"You think he's on to something, this Sturz? That what you're trying to tell me?"

"I don't know," I said. "His line of work he might just be grumpy."

"Sure," said the dean. He was glad that I had thought of that.

"There's something else," I said. "I'm going to need an office on campus, someplace I can meet people."

"An office?" said the dean incredulously. I might have been asking him for an introduction to the Pope.

"You can't get me an office, put a phone in the quad," I said. "I'll take calls underneath the Palms. Be terrific. You can tell the press I teach Leisure Studies."

The Dean sighed deeply. "Best I can do let you share space with someone. That be all right?"

I said it would be fine.

The Sunset was cold and damp when I left for the day. I cut over to the park on 12th and took my time walking north toward the Haight. One of my wives had hated the neighborhood. "These people are *so* filthy," she said with deep conviction. It was sometime in the sixties, after the first big anti-war demonstration. We had just seen a young couple copulating on the great meadow in Golden Gate Park. The girl had red hair and freckles and a healthy chubby body. She had gotten up from the grass with a defiant guilty expression on her pudgy face; my wife dug her fingernails into my palm.

Nothing much has changed. The neighborhood is still filthy. The stores on Haight that were selling bongs and posters of James Dean and Marilyn Monroe in the sixties are still selling bongs and posters of James Dean and Marilyn Monroe. The Red Star Rising movie theater that used to be owned by a workers' collective is still owned by a workers' collective. I thought of going in, but they were playing a film about sorghum. The poster outside the theater showed a Chinese girl lifting a scythe aloft.

At the corner of Haight and Ashbury, an enterprising black shaking a collection can approached me: "Say man, make a donation, keep the kids drug free?" The label on his can said PARTNERSHIP FOR A DRUG FREE COMMUNITY.

I shook my head. He looked at me closely, with that cold stare some people think expresses psychological penetration.

"You a cop?"

I shook my head again.

He lowered his can. "How 'bout some weed then, all buds?"

"Too late," I said.

"Ain't never too late."

"You're wrong," I said.

I lay in bed later that evening, listening to the wind from the open ocean move against the concrete surface of the support wall for my building. It's an old, lonely sound. I thought of the great meadow in Golden Gate park and how it had looked, flooded with light. I thought of the way getting high felt in the days when I felt like getting high. I thought of Leland Sturz slowly spooning his corn chowder. When I awoke the night had come and gone, leaving only the grey dawn behind.

UB Goode

THE FOG HAD BEGUN TO LIFT by the time I got to the university the next morning, the stuff shredding over the green hills of the coast range. The air was so bright it might have caught fire. It was the kind of day that made you remember why you lived in California and why you could never live any place else anymore.

I parked behind the engineering building and felt the morning light gather all around me.

I had called the dean earlier: I wanted the name of Montague's graduate student—the one who had threatened to cut his heart out and eat it.

The dean said: "You bet, Asherfeld, hold on a sec."

I could hear him rummaging among his papers.

"Here it is. Kid's name is UB Goode. He's dorm counselor or something over at Ujaama House."

I didn't know exactly where Ujaama House was, but a girl at the Union pointed me in the right direction. "You can't miss it, sir," she said politely.

She was right. It was the only dormitory whose walls were covered with graffiti. The stuff occupied every square inch of the chalky white concrete facing of the building and stretched upward as far as the second floor. Someone had even managed to scribble something on the wall beneath the top floor window.

I pushed open the streaked glass doors and walked into a little lobby.

The long corridor that led off the lobby had been given over to a display about Afro-American history.

The first panel showed a sullen looking black with a large Afro piloting a hang glider in front of the Pyramids. The text said that long before Europe had even been *invented,* people of color had mastered the principles of flight. Flight had given them less trouble than perspective. Someone had gotten the proportions in the picture wrong. The black's Afro looked larger than the glider and almost as large as the pyramid.

The next panel had a picture of Beethoven; he was looking out at the Ujaama House corridor with a tense unhappy expression on his face. The caption beneath the picture said FACT! BEETHOVEN WAS AN AFRO–AMERICAN!

I paused to look at the picture. A tall goofy looking kid wearing high top sneakers and a silk baseball jacket came clattering into the corridor from the stairwell; he was wearing earphones and banging a baseball bat on the ground. He saw me and stopped.

"You off limits," he said. "Ujaama House for people of color."

"I'm a people of color," I said.

The kid looked at me blankly for a moment.

"You putting me on. You don't look like you colored. What color you at?"

"Me? I'm black."

The kid leaned forward a little and almost squinted his eyes.

"You black?" he said incredulously.

I pointed to the picture of Beethoven.

"He's black, I'm black."

The kid leaned back.

"You dissing me?" he asked.

"Absolutely."

The kid tried to figure it all out. He had a sad open sweet face with a lot of white teeth showing.

"Hey," he finally said.

"Hey yourself. Know where I can find UB?"

"You mean the tall guy, dreadlocks, Spike Lee beard?"

"I guess."

"No idea. Haven't see him around since before Kwanzaa. You a cop?"

"Absolutely. Library's got word UB's late returning two books, sent me right over. You can't do the time, don't do the crime."

"You putting me on, right?"

"Would I kid a person of color? Me, a black man?"

That was too much for the kid; he rocked back on his heels and said: "You crazy, man. You know that?"

"It's the racism that did it to me. It affected my inner ear. Anyone around tell me something about UB?"

The kid thought for a moment, all the while tapping the tip of his bat on the ground. Finally he said: "You not black. You just some white dude wants to nail UB's ass."

"That's right," I said.

"So why should I tell you anything then?"

"Think of it this way. I don't nail UB's ass, I can always nail yours."

"Hey," said the kid, "I didn't do nothing."

"Makes it all the sweeter."

The kid took this all in; then he said: "Check out Carol-Lee. Second floor."

"That his girlfriend?"

The kid shrugged his shoulders; he was pretty goofy looking.

"What he do? UB, I mean?"

"I don't know that he did anything. I just want to talk to him."

The kid nodded and smiled his sweet bright smile. "That's cool," he said.

Then he banged his bat on the ground, spun on his heel, and walked off.

I trudged up the stairs to the second floor; Carol-Lee had a room right by the stairwell. There was a picture of Malcolm X on her door. It showed Malcolm stabbing his finger into space. The caption said By Any Means Necessary.

But Carol-Lee wasn't in her room and I didn't have the patience to wait for her.

*   *   *

I left the Ujaama House at a little past eleven and walk-dawdled my way back toward the center of the campus. A demonstration was in progress outside the bookstore. A group of women wearing black hoods and black robes were marching in a circle around the fountain. They each carried a sign that said Stop Rape.

Two girls were manning a table directly behind the masked women; I recognized them right away—Tiny Face and Miss Piggy. The table had a large hand-lettered sign that said Women's Coalition for Change. A large white sheet of paper had been mounted to a billboard behind the two girls. It contained a list of names.

I waited until the chanting women had marched to the other side of the fountain and walked over to the table. I asked Miss Piggy: "What's it all about?"

She nodded her glabrous head toward the billboard.

"It's like these men have the potential to be rapists."

"All of them?" I said.

Tiny Face said: "It's to personalize the issue of rape and to make individual women aware that they and all women are at risk."

An older woman came over to stand behind Tiny Face and Miss Piggy; she was tall and ungainly, with large feet, and prominent collar bone, and a long sad stupid face.

I said: "Lot of people are going to be furious to find their names here."

"That's okay," said the large sad stupid woman. "It's intended to open up dialogue. Sometimes dialogue can be painful."

"That's true of root canal, too," I said. "It's no great recommendation."

"I hear your anger," said the large woman. "That's okay. It's okay for people to be mad."

The hooded women began to chant "Dead men don't rape" over and over again.

I left the women and wandered back toward the Union. A fraternity had set up a chrome and steel espresso machine on the concrete terrace that looked over the campus; the thing stood gleaming in the warm sunlight. I sauntered over. The large toothy boy operating the machine said: "What'll it be for you, sir?"

"Just an espresso."

He poured the coffee into a tiny paper cup and handed it to me with one of those smiles that only large toothy boys have. "Cookie go with your espresso?" he asked confidently.

"Sure, why not."

The boy gave me another smile and slipped an enormous chocolate chip cookie into a paper bag.

He was pretty sure that his life was going to work out swell. I could tell.

I sipped my espresso and munched my cookie sitting at a green iron table on the terrace and watched the sun fill up the air with light.

After a while, I got up and headed down the walkway toward the philosophy department. Tiny Face and Miss Piggy and the hooded women had given up protesting rape; the fountain was placid, with only a few toddlers wandering about.

Violet was sitting placidly at her desk.

"You're that person who was here the other day."

"That's me," I said. "That person."

"You're doing things about Richard? I mean looking and all?"

"Tying up some odds and ends."

Violet nodded, moving her pretty fat head softly. "It's so strange," she said. "Someone keeps calling, asking for Richard. He keeps calling him Richie. I mean, no one in this university ever called Richard Montague Richie."

She smiled her mysterious smile: "I have cream cheese brownies in the coffee room?"

"Actually, what I need is a key to Mike Dottenberry's office. The dean said I could use it for a couple of days."

Violet looked up at me. The smile on her pulpy red lips faded. "The key?" she said vaguely. "No one said anything to me about that."

She turned her head toward the office and in a raised voice asked: "Donald, am I supposed to give a key to anyone?"

"Hold on," said whoever it was that was in the inner office.

A trim man with an aristocratic face opened the door and stood leaning with his hand on the door knob. He nodded curtly toward me.

"This is Donald Dindle," said Violet timidly. "He's the chairperson of the department?"

Dindle cut Violet off with a hard glance.

"You're this Asherfeld?" he said directly to me.

"Yup."

"I understand from the dean that you are to have use of an office?"

I nodded.

"I want it known that I regard your presence in this department as an abridgement of academic freedom."

"All right," I said.

"All right what?"

"You want it known. Now I know it."

Dindle looked at me without saying anything. He had arctic blue eyes, a finely shaped nose, and thin austere lips. He seemed to be thinking things over.

"Violet will let you in," he finally said. Then he turned abruptly and disappeared into his office, closing the door behind him.

I glanced down at Violet. She was sitting at her desk with her hands folded primly in front of her. Her lower lip was quivering.

"Hard man to work for?"

Violet shook her head carefully. "It's just that I can't stand scenes," she said.

"No one likes them."

Violet sat there, her lower lip continuing to quiver. I let my eyes roam across her desk and over to the old-fashioned glass enclosed oak bookcase by the window. There was a handsome silver photograph frame on the top shelf. The photograph showed a youngish looking man straddling a powerful Harley Davidson motorcycle. It was a big cycle, the kind that you need a lot of experience to ride. The youngish looking man was dressed in a motorcycle jacket, jeans, and heavy leather boots. He was wearing colors. Whoever had taken the photograph had allowed the sun to throw a shadow across his face. It didn't matter. I was pretty sure it was Montague.

I walked over to the bookcase and lifted the silver frame for a closer look. The inscription on the photograph said LOVE CONQUERS DEATH. I could feel Violet tracking me with her eyes. I held the frame by its backing and wiped my fingerprint from the silver with my sleeve.

"I didn't know he was a friend of yours."

"He was very kind to me," said Violet. "He was very kind to me when no one else was." Her pretty blue eyes were downcast.

I put the elegant silver frame back on the bookcase.

Violet made a special effort to give me a small smile. She swung her secretary's chair back and got to her feet by pushing herself from her desk. "I'll let you into the office now," she said. "I mean, if you want?"

In the hallway she stopped me by placing her finger in the crook of my arm; she rested heavily on her feet and looked straight ahead. I could feel her soft bulk swaying slightly.

"Love doesn't conquer death, Mr. Asherfeld," she said.

Mike Dottenberry liked to leave a lot of himself in his office. There was a little red rug on the linoleum floor, and an easy chair with an ottoman in the corner of the room, and an ornate coat rack by one side of the door, and an elephant's foot umbrella stand by the other side of the door. A poster on the cinderblock wall depicted a hardfaced Indian woman with a kerchief over her head. She was carrying a banner that read SUPPORT THE SHINING PATH. She didn't look much as if she'd enjoy drinks after dinner. The other three walls all carried the legend SAY NO TO PATRIARCHY in foot-high red letters.

I sat down in the easy chair and put my feet on the ottoman.

At a little past eleven, Dottenberry himself showed up at his office. He stood at the door, shabby briefcase in hand, and looked at me sitting in his chair with my feet on his ottoman.

"Hope you don't mind," I said. "I'm Aaron Asherfeld."

Dottenberry closed the door and gave me a shapeless smile.

"No, not at all," he said, crossing the room to his desk. "Dindle told me you needed a place. It'll give us a chance to dialogue."

He was a pleasant looking man, with a narrow face and nar

row shoulders. He was wearing a polo shirt that said NOMAS on the front.

Dottenberry caught my look.

"National Organization of Men Against Sexism," he said.

"National organization of men against sexism? Sounds like a fun group of guys."

"It's a start," said Dottenberry.

"So is lung cancer."

Dottenberry snickered just slightly; he opened his briefcase and extracted a framed picture of a golden retriever and placed it on his desk. He turned to face me and placed his hand gently over his heart.

"I used to think the world had to change, Asherfeld, but now I know the change has to come from here," he said solemnly, vibrating his middle finger on his breastbone as if he were playing a cello.

"Sure," I said, "that just what my wives always told me. *They* were beating up on me, *I* had to do the changing."

"That's your woundedness talking," said Dottenberry. "You've got to process through some of the anger that's threatening your relationships. When you don't have to run around dominating people, life gets a lot easier."

I figured Dottenberry should know: he didn't look as if he could dominate a housefly.

"I'm working on it," I said. "Only thing is every time I cut back on my primal rage one of my wives puts the arm on me."

Dottenberry nodded. "Sometimes it's hard," he said. "The thing you have to understand is that the women in our lives are *victims.*"

That was too much.

"Dottenberry," I said, "the women in *my* life are victims the way sushi is a food. Hell, one of my wives even used my fraternity bat for kindling. She called me right up and said: 'Asher, you hear that crackling? That's your precious fraternity bat going up in flames.' I let down my guard with these women, next thing you know I'll be shuffling up Market Street in San Francisco selling *Street Sheet* and asking for spare change."

Dottenberry looked at me with a milky expression. "I honor

that," he said, "I really do. But I think you need to clear a space for your grieving."

I got to my feet and said: "You're probably right."

Dottenberry sat himself down at his desk and began fussing with a few papers.

"What is it you're trying to find out about Richard Montague?" he finally asked in a calm neutral voice.

I walked over to the narrow window and looked out at the quad; it was empty in the high morning light.

"You've got a lot of rumors flying around. The dean asked me to sort through some of it. That's all."

"Don't you think this is something the university should handle by itself?"

"Man is dead, Dottenberry, and as far as I can tell the only thing the university is worried about is keeping the story out of the papers."

Dottenberry nodded carefully. "The university's a pretty special place," he said. It was the second time someone had said that to me.

"I know, I know. It has its own rules. The dean told me."

"It's true."

I walked back to Dottenberry's desk and hung over it, splaying my hands on the top.

"Dottenberry, that's what they say about prisons. They have their own rules. It's just the sort of thing that people claim when they want to cover up something. It doesn't mean anything."

I straightened up and walked back to the door to get my windbreaker from Dottenberry's ornate coatrack.

"You going to the meeting?" I asked.

"What meeting?"

"Meeting about Montague. Violet mentioned it to me."

A sly smile spread over Dottenberry's face. "Asherfeld," he said. "That's a GLA meeting."

"GLA?"

"Gay and Lesbian Alliance."

"So? I'm not fussy."

Dottenberry looked at me for a moment with the sly smile

still playing on his lips. Then he said: "You go ahead. I've got too much work to do."

"Stay sensitive," I said as I slipped out the door.

There were a few thin-armed girls scurrying along the quadrangle's walkways as I left Dottenberry's office, but the space still held its large empty feeling. I walked back up toward the clock tower and over to the campus chapel, which was opposite the bookstore. The GLA meeting was being held in the basement of the chemistry building, just behind the chapel.

I hustled myself up the building's smooth sandstone steps and into the cool marble-floored foyer. The pneumatic glass doors closed behind me with a little puff of air. A large colored mural ran across one interior wall: it depicted various white-smocked chemists pouring things into beakers and warming test tubes over Bunsen burners. From far away I could hear a car alarm going off spastically.

I walked down the broad steps that led to the basement. Someone had put a lot of money into those curved marble steps and a lot of money into the smooth mahogany banisters by the wall. The chemists had a taste for the good life; they didn't want to go hustling down a lot of cheap concrete stairs. The stairwell gave way directly onto double doors leading into a large lecture room. The sign by the doors said MEETING RESERVED FOR MEMBERS OF THE GLA. I didn't think the members of the GLA would mind if I attended; and I didn't much care if they did. The double doors were wide open; I slipped right in.

There was a stage in the front of the amphitheater and red plush seats rising toward the back in tiers. Spotlights above the podium. Recessed lighting along the seams where the walls met the ceiling. An enormous chart of the periodic table hung from the ceiling at the rear of the stage.

I wandered down from the entrance to the front of the stage. A graduate student was tapping at the stage microphone with his fingertips. "Testing, one two three four," he said over and over again. I stood there for a moment, with my hands in my pockets; there were a good many people milling about.

"You there," someone said in a sharp peremptory tone.

I turned to look at the someone doing the saying. She had short-cropped silver hair. She wore absolutely no make-up. She was dressed in leather pants and a leather jacket. The name "Hectorbrand" had been stitched onto the chest of her jacket. I nodded agreeably.

"You're not like a member of the GLA?" she asked, without waiting for me to introduce myself. "Rimbaud wants to know."

"Rimbaud?"

A much larger woman shuffled toward us with a heavy menacing tread. She had the same short hair; she wore the same leather jacket. She bent over to whisper in Hectorbrand's ear.

"Rimbaud says that if you're not a member of the GLA you'll have to leave. She's head of security."

Hectorbrand nodded her silver head toward the door.

"I'm covering the meeting for Donahue," I said. "He wants to do a special on weak women who love strong men, figured the GLA'd be a good place to start."

Rimbaud bent over to whisper again in Hectorbrand's ear.

"Rimbaud says she means it," said Hectorbrand.

"Sure," I said. "That's why she needs you to tell me."

"Rimbaud doesn't speak to men," said Hectorbrand.

Rimbaud bent over to impart another message into Hectorbrand's ear.

"Any more than a Jew would speak to a Nazi," she added.

I looked at the giantess in her leather jacket for a moment and turned toward Hectorbrand.

"Say, move her up from cruiserweight and I figure I can get her an exhibition with George Foreman."

Rimbaud shuffled on her feet and took a step toward me. I knew what she was going to do but I wasn't fast enough to get out of her way. She moved a step closer to me, stuck a foot behind my leg, and pushed me over her foot by shoving me in the chest.

I landed heavily on my hands and haunches. Rimbaud looked at me for a moment. I didn't think it was a look of respect. A few people stopped gossiping to look at what was happening. Some of the seated women hissed and rustled their feet.

Rimbaud turned toward Hectorbrand for the last time.

"Get out," Hectorbrand said, "Rimbaud wants you to get out now."

I got to my feet and dusted off my pants.

"Maybe you're just too much woman for George," I said.

But Rimbaud had already lost interest in me; she hitched up her leather pants, lowered her shoulders, and shuffled to the back of the amphitheater.

I decided that I didn't really need to hear whatever it was that the GLA was going to say about Richard Montague.

When I got back to the office, Dottenberry was sitting with his hands splayed over his knees. He looked like he might be concentrating on a difficult problem, like mastering the square knot.

"I thought you were going to the meeting," he said peevishly.

"I did. I got jumped by the Amityville Horror."

Dottenberry nodded knowingly. "You're talking about Rimbaud, right? I tried to warn you."

"What is this, you keep this bull dyke in the closet, spring the trap when a stranger comes along? I could have been killed."

"Come on Asherfeld, Rimbaud is just Rimbaud."

Dottenberry chuckled. He had a pleasant musical baritone.

"It's what happens," he added.

"What happens when?"

"It's what happens when you hold on to that anger."

I edged into the room and sat back down on the easy chair and lifted my feet onto the ottoman.

"Sure," I said. "I knew that."

Roach Motel

THE NEXT AFTERNOON, a federal civil servant named Hubert Dreyfus left a message on my machine in Mick Shaugnessy's office.

"Hey," Dreyfus had said, "it's like old times. Call me."

I had worked with Dreyfus before. He was honest and energetic; he wasn't stupid, but he wasn't gifted either. It was a little before five, but I thought he might still be at work. I got him right away.

"The Wise Guy," he said, "how you doin'?"

I told him I was doing fine.

Dreyfus chuckled his fast nervous chuckle and said: "Listen, reason I called is division's moved me into contract compliance. Me, Manny, the team. We're going through the university books, things make about as much sense as Chinese, the dean tells me you're looking at things for them over there, I thought maybe we'd get together, compare notes."

"Sounds good to me," I said.

"So you wanna get a bite to eat? My kid's busy kung fu'ing up a storm, won't be home until nine."

I said: "I'll meet you over at Tommy's Joynt on Van Ness. You can walk there."

"This some place you pay thirty dollars get midget carrots and a pile of polenta on your plate?"

"Trust me," I said.

Tommy's Joynt has a steam table and a bar and a lot of tables with red and white checkered table cloths. Years ago, the place managed to get a franchise from some federal bureau to serve buffalo meat. There are pictures on the wall of sad-eyed buffalo staring at the camera. They know something's wrong; they can't figure out what. The next thing they know *Bang!* some tourist from Grain Ball City is saying *I think I'll try the buffalo stew.*

Dreyfus was standing in front of the steam table when I got there. He had a toothpick in his mouth; he was playing with a rubber band, stretching the rubber aimlessly.

"Hey," he said.

We ordered pastrami sandwiches at the steam table and sat down with them at the back of the restaurant and asked the rumpy waitress to bring us two steins of dark Austrian beer.

I said: "Still miss New York?"

"Hard to say," Dreyfus said. "Weekend before last my kid he sleeps over some other kid's house, I figure maybe it's time I start looking, you know what I mean, it's been six months since the divorce? I go down to this bar guy at division tells me about, I

34

see this not-too-bad looking little number, maybe a little over the hill but not compost heap either, I say hello, and first thing she wants to know is what club I work out in. I say no club and she says in this ice-cube voice what *do* you do stay in shape? I say Hey, I shower regular, use deodorant and she looks at me like she's spotting cockroach and says I'm not interested in men who don't care enough about themselves to stay in shape. I get so discouraged I go right home drink two beers go to sleep."

He resumed eating his sandwich.

"So what are you doing over the cuckoo farm?"

"Not much," I said. "The dean wants to know why one of his professors died suddenly."

"This this Montague?"

I nodded.

"You know why?"

"No idea. Neither does anyone else. It wasn't from hunger."

Dreyfus nodded vigorously.

"I heard your boy was living just a little bit better than the Sultan of Brunei. Not surprised, though."

"Why's that, Dreyfus?"

"Come on back to my office. Manny'll be there. He'll lay it out for you."

Dreyfus finished the rest of his beer and looked up toward the counter.

"Think the cheesecake is worth eating," he asked, "or we talking glue?"

"Glue," I said.

Dreyfus pushed himself up from the table and sighed theatrically.

"Even when it's like New York, New York it's not," he said. "At the Carnegie Hall Deli they got a cheesecake to die for."

We walked from Van Ness toward the Federal Building. The air had grown cold. The transvestite hookers were already standing on the street corners, stamping their large feet and shrieking to one another in their uneven falsettos. The winos and junkies were nodding off on the marble building stoops. A few Vietnamese children were playing on the sidewalk. It's not exactly like walking down the Champs-Elysées.

Manny Edelweiss was waiting for us in Dreyfus's office on the tenth floor of the Federal Building. He was sitting at Dreyfus's desk sipping coffee from a polyurethane cup. He looked friendly and cheerful and fat.

"Hey," said Dreyfus enthusiastically, bustling into the room. "Manny you know."

I said sure and Manny said sure and Dreyfus said it was like old times.

Then Dreyfus said: "The university's got Asherfeld here running around like a gerbil on a treadmill. We want to put him in the picture. Tell him what we got, Manny."

"What we got," said Manny Edelweiss, "is bookkeeping make your hair stand on end."

Dreyfus braced himself against his own desk with his hip. He was playing with a rubber band again, stretching it between his thumb and forefinger. I sat down on the black admiral's chair that Dreyfus kept in the corner of his office, pressing my back against the great seal of the United States.

"We're doing contract compliance," said Dreyfus, "on account of it's Uncle's money coming into the university. What is it, Manny? Over three hundred mil?"

"More than likely four hundred time we factor in overhead," said Manny.

"What we see is pretty much what we figure we're going to see," said Dreyfus. "Far as the university's concerned contract compliance is a joke. We ask how come they don't know where the money is, they look at us like we're pissing into champagne. Over in Fort Lee, Manny and me we made the Saltambacca family cutting medicinal morphine with cayenne pepper, selling it discount to hospitals. Saltambaccas didn't have anything on the guys running the university. Wouldn't you say that's true, Manny, comes to cutting corners these guys are right up there with the five families?"

Manny nodded his round fat head; he was remembering the great days in New Jersey.

"Your boy Montague, too," said Dreyfus. "I'm telling you, you want they should hold up his Nobel Prize until we do an audit."

I arranged my hands into a pyramid, the fingertips just touching, and tapped at my upper lip with my index fingers.

Manny became professorial. He stiffened his spine and began to arrange the papers and books on the table top. "You wanna come over take a look?"

I shook my head. "I don't want to disturb my *wa,* Manny. Just tell me about it."

Manny relaxed himself in his chair. He held up a file folder with a red border. "See, what we got here is a record of Uncle's money going to Montague, fiscal year past and the year past that. Seven hundred fifty thousand dollars. Man's got the golden touch, got money coming out of the federal wazoo."

Dreyfus walked over to the narrow window and stood there facing the street and the dying light.

"Wouldn't surprise us the man was able to get federal sewage reclamation money," he said.

Manny chortled and nodded.

"University's supposed to take eighty percent of the money again in overhead, administer the grants, so Montague takes in seven hundred fifty thousand, we're talking more than three, three and one half million in Uncle's money."

I nodded.

"But it's like roach motel," Dreyfus said, moving abruptly away from the desk and over to the window. "Money goes in, it don't come out."

He stood by the window, his back toward the room.

"Show him what's happening, Manny," said Dreyfus, without turning from the window.

Manny tapped the second set of books on the table with the eraser of his yellow pencil.

"We follow the money, it goes straight from general accounting to the bursar's office over at the university to some outfit called Commercial Scientific Research—CSR."

"So?"

"So," said Dreyfus decisively, "so we're talking violation of contract compliance. Pass thru of federal funds is a major no-no. Hell, that's why Uncle pays the university overhead. We go to audit CSR, nothing. Nada, zip. Place doesn't exist. No phone, no fax. We look up the original charter of incorporation, the thing is privately held. Wha'd I tell you? Roach motel."

"Who did the paperwork?" I asked.

"Some slope we talk to him already, me and Manny. He doesn't remember anything, hardly speaks a word of English. Go to contract compliance over the university, two days later we get a fax from the Department of Labor, this is an affirmative action matter. What you know you should forget."

"Affirmative action?" I said. "It doesn't make sense, Dreyfus. Montague was a white male. Probably thought Europe was the center of a more important culture than Namibia. Wrong race, wrong sex, wrong class. His kind of guy is lucky not to be hung up by his heels at an affirmative action office."

"Go figure," said Dreyfus. "Anyway our hands are tied. Thought maybe you could ask a few questions. What we really need is the other names on the charter of incorporation. It's got to be yo-yos on the faculty, Montague's buddies. We have that, we go after them one by one. You do something for us, we do something for you."

Dreyfus turned from the window to face the room again. He was still playing with a rubber band. He pulled the rubber between his thumb and forefinger and let fly an imaginary projectile.

"What's the something you're going to do for me?"

"We talk to the DA's office, see what's holding up the autopsy report on your boy."

I thought for a moment of what I had to lose and what I had to gain.

Then I said: "Deal."

Pure and Simple

I WOKE THE NEXT MORNING after dreaming about one of my wives. She had become a beggar and was standing in the shelter of an ATM station on the corner of Green and Columbus. I tried to slink past her. She recognized me at once. "You," she sneered bitterly, "I should have known." As she spoke her features merged mysteriously with the tragic face of an elderly Bosnian woman clutching a ruined doll.

I awoke again at nine, just as the women in my dreams were explaining in exhausting detail why they needed money.

I called the dean without getting out of bed. I told him I needed to speak with the university's contract compliance officer. He said: "Sure, sure thing, Asherfeld. Get right to it. Only thing is, right now I'm up to my ass in alligators. Can this wait?"

"Absolutely," I said. "Any day I get paid without working is a good day for me. I'll take in a few kung fu movies, check back with you tomorrow, maybe the day after that."

The dean required a moment for meditation.

"All right, Asherfeld," he said alertly after the meditation had come and gone. "Here's what you do. You call up Pat Pudwinkle over in legal, tell her *I* said to call, tell her it's about contract compliance. Here, hold on a sec, I'll get you the number."

I could hear the dean rummaging about on his desk. After a while, he gave up. "Just ask for legal, Asherfeld, Pudwinkle'll be there."

I got up and took a hot shower and then a cold shower; I took a Sinu-Tab for my sinus, and an aspirin for my headache, and a Tums for my tummy. I had coffee and ate a donut and watched the local news on my little television. A delegation of blacks had been to see the Mayor. Their spokesman was the Reverend Leotis from Oakland. He was pretty angry about something; he was demanding reparations for whatever it was that had gotten him angry. "Japanese, they get money from the government, Jews, they still getting money from them Germans, how come we the onliest people we get a working over we don't get nothing?" The Mayor stood smiling with his hands folded across his narrow chest. He was pretty apologetic about things. "I wish it were in my power Reverend," he said. "How come it not in your power?" the Reverend asked. The Mayor looked wistful. "I wish I knew," he said sadly.

I turned off the television and called the university; the operator put me through to legal affairs. Pat Pudwinkle answered the telephone herself. I must have gotten her the moment she entered her own office.

"This is Pudwinkle," she said in that soft well-modulated voice a good many aggressive women adopt.

39

I told her that I was working for the dean; I told her I was hoping she could see me for a few minutes.

"What's this in reference to, Mr.—" there was a pause,— "what did you say your name was?"

"Asherfeld. And it's in reference to contract compliance."

"Mr. Asherfeld, could you put this in writing? I'm afraid my schedule is just impossible."

"Sure," I said. "Only thing is, I'm likely to send the letter to the *San Francisco Chronicle*."

"I beg your pardon?"

"No need to. You can talk to me today, say around eleven o'clock, or talk to the newspapers tomorrow."

"I see," said Pudwinkle. "Are you going to tell me what this is about?"

"Sure. I'd like to know why the university allowed one of its professors to set up a dummy corporation, take federal money as a pass-along."

"Which professor are you talking about, Mr. Asherfeld?"

She got my name right in a big hurry.

"Richard Montague."

Pat Pudwinkle said nothing for a long moment.

Then she said: "Eleven o'clock will be fine."

I thought it might have been.

It was raining when I left the house, one of those sneaky rainstorms that come at you sideways even though the sky is showing patches of blue. By the time I reached the university the rain had stopped, but the sky held on to its irregular clouds and the air was damp and cold.

Pat Pudwinkle's office was in the administration building in the center of campus, right behind the quadrangle.

Pudwinkle herself was at the door when I came in. She was a tall woman, dressed severely in a black and grey suit; her blondgrey hair was piled on her head in the sort of chignon that looked unlikely to make it through the day. She was talking with her secretary, a young woman who kept nodding her head vigorously as Pudwinkle issued instructions. "Yes, yes, I understand," she kept saying.

"I'm Aaron Asherfeld."

Pudwinkle straightened up from her secretary's desk and said:

"Oh yes," in a vague way. She shook hands with me; her palms were warm and damp. Then she said to her secretary: "Send him in as soon as he arrives."

Pudwinkle's inner office had a thin rug on the floor with a Navajo design. There were bookcases on both walls; in between the bookcases, Pudwinkle had pictures of her children. The room's only window gave out on the back of the quandrangle. The whole thing had the feel of something that is expensive without being valuable.

Pudwinkle sat down primly at her desk.

"I think we should wait for Kweisi Mfune."

I raised my eyebrows; there was a knock as they were lowering. A short black man came into the room. Pat Pudwinkle stood up and walked around the desk and said, "Kweisi," with enough warmth to kindle plywood. She turned up her cheek ostentatiously to be kissed.

"Mr. Asherfeld," she said in a thin voice, "this is Kweisi Mfune."

Kweisi Mfune shuffled off his raincoat, the better to reveal the glory of his outfit. He was wearing an expensive double-breasted grey suit with a white on red shirt and a silk tie. His burgundy shoes were fabulously polished. He wore enough gold jewelry on his wrists and fingers to outfit a middle-eastern bazaar.

He nodded to me and said: "How you doin', Asherman?"

I said I was doing fine. I didn't bother to correct my name.

Pat Pudwinkle retreated to her armchair behind the desk; and Kweisi Mfune sat at the very edge of the leather sofa. He stretched his neck so that he could straighten his tie and fussed with his sparkling white cuffs so that they were evenly exposed.

"Understand you got a problem, Asherman," he said abruptly.

"Mr. Asherfeld feels there might perhaps be some compliance irregularity in one of our university contracts," said Pudwinkle delicately.

"What contract that be?"

"NSF award to Richard Montague," I said. "This fiscal year, the one before that."

Mfune placed his hands on his wide-apart knees.

"No irregularity there," he said defiantly. "Contract's just the way it's supposed to be."

"Federal regulations prohibit pass-alongs to private corporations. Montague's money went to some outfit called Commercial Scientific Research. Sounds pretty irregular to me. I'm guessing that that's the way it's going to sound to the newspapers," too."

Mfune scowled. Pat Pudwinkle pulled back in her chair.

"Asherman, I don't know who you are, what your game is. You full of that goddam Eurocentric logic crap. You think you can just come in here, bulldoze your way around the university?"

"That's pretty much what I think."

"Do I look stupid to you?" Mfune asked explosively.

"Yes," I said.

Mfune rocketed out of his seat.

"You stereotyping me as black, that's what you doing. You wouldn't say that to a white man."

"Sure I would, Queasy. Only thing is, you happen to be black."

"You're a racist Asherman, pure and simple. This is bullshit, Pudwinkle. I don't have to stand for it. You got some white honky cracker come in here give me this racist jive."

Mfune started toward the coat rack where his raincoat was hanging. Then he said: "An another thing, my name is *Kweisi.*"

"That's terrific. Mine's Asherfeld. You get my name right, I'll work on yours."

"Now Kweisi," said Pudwinkle tentatively.

"Forget it," I said loudly.

"Forget what?"

"Forget the dog and pony show, Queasy. I'm not on the faculty. I don't want a job. I don't have a kid applying to the university and I don't care if you think I'm Simon Legree's stepson once removed."

"Now what's that suppose to mean."

"It means I can do you a lot of harm and there's nothing you can do to me. It's got nothing to do with racism. It's just the way things are."

Mfune stood where he was; he was still fuming, but he wasn't about to leave anymore.

"What kind of harm you talking about, Asherman? Montague contract was strictly on the up and up."

"Couldn't be, Queasy," I said. "The university didn't administer the money and the money is lost."

Pat Pudwinkle said: "What you may not realize, Mr. Asherfeld, is that under Title 7 the university does have certain discretionary resources when it comes to affirmative action grants."

"You mean you get a black or a woman on the arm, the university doesn't have to do contract compliance?"

"That is not how I would characterize our affirmative action program," Mr. Asherfeld, "but essentially, yes, we do have a certain latitude in administering Reach Out funds."

"That a problem for you, Asherman," asked Mfune, "or you going to tell me something's wrong with people of color getting their share of research funds."

"Women, too," said Pat Pudwinkle softly. "Let's not forget that women are empowered by these programs as well."

"Sure," said Mfune unenthusiastically.

I turned in my chair to face Mfune.

"Hey, as far as I'm concerned, people of color, women, they can have *all* the money. Only one problem, though."

"You full of problems. You know that, Asherman? You one smart white-ass that's full of problems. What is it this time?"

"Richard Montague wasn't a woman."

"I know that. Tell me something I don't know."

"He wasn't black either. How's that for something you don't know? He was white as the driven snow. Whiter maybe. I hear he had his teeth bleached."

"Sheeyit," said Mfune broadly. "Can't be. I interviewed the dude myself. He's black as me."

"There must be some mistake, Mr. Asherfeld," said Pat Pudwinkle. I have Professor Montague's grant file right here. I mean, you can see for yourself, this application is flagged as an affirmative action grant. Professor Montague listed himself as an Afro-American."

She pushed the research file toward me. I could see that Montague had ticked off Afro-American on the list of acceptable affirmative action minorities.

"Did you ever meet Richard Montague?" I asked the question of Pat Pudwinkle.

"Mr. Asherfeld, there are over two thousand faculty members at this university. I can't know them all."

I nodded.

"That's why he listed himself as an Afro-American."

"I'm telling you, Asherman, *I* met the man. He was in my office, plain as day."

"Someone was in your office, Queasy. It just wasn't Montague. You were so happy to give away the government's money to a person of color you didn't bother checking. See what I mean about causing you trouble?"

I stood up. Pat Pudwinkle got up from her chair; she stood there indecisively. From far away I could hear the campus bells chime the hour. They had finally started working.

Night of the Living Dead

A FEW MILES PAST Palo Alto the Peninsula becomes hot and flat. Whoever planted the great flowing elms and oaks in Atherton and Portola Valley figured there was no reason to plant them in Santa Clara or Mountain View. The light is grainy and bright and hurts your eyes. The streets are named by numbers. There are warehouses and body shops and metal stamping presses by the freeway and banks and loan offices and rental car agencies on El Camino Real. The place is filled with Koreans, who think they've discovered paradise, and a lot of single women who let you know when you look into their eyes that the eighties are finally over.

I got off 101 at Sunnyvale and drove slowly through the treeless side streets until I got to El Camino; then I drove south for half a mile with the light bouncing off my windshield. I parked in front of Biker's World.

There was no one at the front desk of the wooden shack that

served as the main office, but outside one of the house mechanics was heading toward the body shop behind the office, a greasy chain wrapped around his forearm.

"Know where I can find Wanker?" I asked.

"Inna back," he said. "Takin' a whizz."

I walked to the back of the office just in time to hear a toilet flush with a roar. Wanker emerged a moment later, ceremoniously adjusting his overalls.

He had always been heavy; now he was mountainous.

"Asherfeld, my man," he boomed, thrusting out his gigantic hand.

"How you doing, Wanker?" I said, looking up toward his face.

"Never better," he wheezed. Among his other afflictions, Wanker suffered from angina and emphysema. "Hold on a sec."

From somewhere in the vast depth of his overall pocket he withdrew a bottle of small white pills and with an experienced hand twisted off the top. He popped three pills in his mouth and replaced the bottle in his overalls. Then he withdrew the unfiltered cigarette that had been resting on his ear and lit it with a silver zippo that he fished from another pocket. He inhaled deeply. I could hear the rales rattling in his lungs. The nitroglycerine and the nicotine must have hit simultaneously. He smiled beatifically, first tapping the pill box in his pocket and then exhibiting his cigarette.

"One to light the fire," he said, "one to damp the furnace."

He was of the opinion that in nicotine and nitroglycerine he had hit upon a medically sound treatment for what ailed him. I wasn't about to tell him anything else.

"Come on over here," he said. "Show you something."

I followed his enormous bulk to the middle of his back lot. Sitting amidst a lot of low-slung Harleys was a gleaming police Kawasaki 1000—the kind they don't make anymore. It's a cult item.

"Beauty," said Wanker, running his hand over the dull metal of the gas tank. "Some queer over in East Oakland couldn't make payment. I had JoJo pick it up yesterday. Be yours for two, two and a quarter. Say what, Asher. Make a man of you."

"Just what I need, Wanker."

Wanker looked at me with his shrewd small eyes, the smoke from his cigarette curling around the side of his face.

"What you need and what you want, two different things," he said. "Keep worrying about what you need, you'll never get what you want."

Wanker's philosophy made as much sense as whatever the university was offering, and it came free.

"Wanker, let me ask you something. Someone on a big Harley, wears colors, rides weekends, maybe a few days a week, who'd he likely be riding with?"

"This someone righteous, we're talking about," asked Wanker thoughtfully, "or just someone likes cycles?"

"I don't know. Semi-righteous."

"You're talking about a white man?"

I nodded.

"White man, rides a big Harley, wears colors," said Wanker, rehearsing the items in his mind. "There used to be kind of a club over Vallejo, guys riding weekends, figured they were very righteous. Got busted up by the Angels. You might try them."

Wanker dropped his cigarette to the ground and crushed it beneath his boot. He withdrew his pill bottle and popped another couple of tablets in his mouth. His eyes held a cloudy look that dissipated when the pills took effect.

I nodded toward the pills.

"You living on those things now, Wanker?"

"I'm living because I don't feel like dying," Wanker boomed, "and that's the truth, my man."

He lit another of his unfiltered cigarettes and drew the smoke into his lungs with a wet rattle.

"You ever think of cutting down?" I asked tentatively.

"What for? I cut down on smokes, next thing you know someone'll be after my ass to lose weight. These days, you dip your wick and the thing's more'n likely to fall right off. And if I can't smoke and I can't eat and I can't get my wick dipped, no point in living anyway."

It was a pretty good argument.

"You're right, Wanker," I said. "Know where I can get in touch with anyone this club you're talking about?"

"They've got a house over in Vallejo, big old place, registered

46

inna name of Ingelfinger. I know on account of he did a little collection work for me some years back. You might try there. Don't go lookin' for Ingelfinger himself, though. Waste of time. He's doing hard time at Folsom."

Wanker took another long drag on his cigarette.

"You lose your boy?" he asked. "That why you're out looking for him?"

I shook my head. "Man's dead, Wanker. I'm sort of cleaning up after him."

Wanker looked at me shrewdly for a long moment.

"Night of the living dead, Asher," he finally said.

The Dindles

DONALD DINDLE lived in a house midway up Old La Honda Road, on the eastern flank of the Santa Cruz mountains.

I drove up the narrow winding road at dusk on the evening of his party, the window open and my arm dangling comfortably outside. It was a great road for a motorcycle and a great road for a red Porsche; it might even have been a great road for a bicycle if you were twenty years old and had thighs like pistons.

I could see above the smog in my rear-view mirror; the last of the light still held in the valley below, throwing pinks and purples into the air. Up ahead, night had already fallen, turning the dark green woods black; the air grew chill and heavy and quiet.

I remembered taking a motorcycle up over Old La Honda Road to San Gregorio beach in the sixties, when this part of the world was something shared by crusty professors of metallurgy and vegetarians living in redwood cabins way back in the hills and surfers who house-sat country ranches so they could spend every day on the cold water.

The county had protected a lot of space up here, but the old empty haunted feeling was gone, and so were the old mad professors, and the artichoke farmers, and the surfers. Whatever land was left had been bought up by embarrassingly wealthy computer nerds from Silicon Valley who thought nothing of putting five thousand feet of housing on lots designed for cabins.

Dindle's house was in a narrow dirt cul de sac; it sat on a little lot with a million dollar view of the Bay, but the house itself was one of those dreary jobs that people put up in the fifties—strictly prefab, with a lot of grey planking and narrow windows.

The cul de sac was already full of cars, so I backed up slowly and drove a quarter mile further on Old La Honda and parked at the far end of a turnaround. Then I trudged back down the hill, kicking up pebbles.

A tall, stooped kid with a very prominent Adam's apple greeted me at the door of *Chez* Dindle. He was wearing a sweatshirt that said Silence Equals Death and swaying just slightly to the loud thudding beat of a stereo playing an old Beatles song.

"Jeremy Dindle," he said mechanically, giving me a fish-limp hand. "Donald's in there," he said, jerking his shaggy head. "My mom's on her side of the house."

Coming into the Dindle living room after the cool quiet of Old La Honda Road was like entering an evening of red after a twilight of green.

There were at least twenty-five people in the living room itself, which looked over the valley from a narrow picture window; half of them were dancing spastically by the stereo and the other half were standing with their elbows tucked into their sides as they sipped drinks. A slight sweet smell of marijuana was in the air.

Dindle himself was standing at a serving table trying without much success to chip away at a huge lump of ice with an ice pick.

Dindle saw me coming and straightened up.

"Asherfeld," he said, "glad you could make it." Dindle had invited me to his party the day before. "Be a few people over at the house," he had said when he saw me outside Dottenberry's office. "You might come by." I didn't think he wanted to be friends. There was something he wanted to show me. But now the anger was gone from his eyes; he seemed lost in his own house. "Make yourself at home, Asherfeld," he said.

I walked over to the serving table that had been set up by the picture window; there were a couple of platters laid out—meatballs stabbed by toothpicks, vegetables with a dip, some sort of weird looking concoction with a pastry crust. None of it looked very good.

Jeremy Dindle slouched into the living room and slouched on over to me.

"You want a drink?" he asked morosely. "My dad's got the cheap scotch out, but I can get you vodka with some ice."

I shook my head. Then Dindle Junior said: "My mom wants to talk with you. She's over on the other side of the wall."

"You keep the house divided, do you?" I asked. "Wall comes down in Berlin, you put one up here?"

"Court order," said Dindle Junior sullenly. "Donald tried to torch my mom's paintings then Mom deleted three chapters of Donald's book from the hard disk. He about had a hemorrhage. *I* figured she did the world a favor. Donald, he wanted to strangle her and all. So the court ordered the house divided until the divorce is final. Which will be in ten thousand years."

"Pretty rough."

"It's relatively nil," he said shrugging his thin shoulders, which rose and fell inside his sweatshirt. "One more year and I'm out of here."

I mingled for a few more minutes. Two heavyset motherly women were sitting on the couch, showing one another pictures of children. The people who were dancing when I came in were still dancing. The Rolling Stones were singing *Paint It Black*.

I wandered out from the living room and into the open hall that served as a foyer. There were a few oils on the wall—mostly California country scenes, with a lot of golds and blues in them.

Jeremy Dindle swam silently to my side. "My mom's down there," he said.

I eased myself down the polished grey birch stairway that led to the basement. I could see that someone had actually painted a red line in the wall above the stairwell; I figured this part of the house belonged to La Dindle.

The basement had been converted into an artist's studio. There were canvases propped up on easels, and open tubes of paint lying around, and a pleasant oily smell in the air. The studio had a northern exposure. I stood for a moment looking at an unfinished canvas of a river running through a stand of pine trees.

Someone said: "My husband is *such* a jerk."

The fleshy blackhaired woman doing the saying sat herself down on one of the stools in the room, ran her tongue over her lower lip, leaned over to reveal her cleavage, and crossed her legs with a stirring sound of nylon on nylon.

"Don't you think so?" she asked.

I smiled and said: "You didn't ask me down here to tell me that, Mrs. Dindle."

"No, I didn't, but it's something I'm willing to tell *anyone,* even perfect strangers. I want the world to know. And my name is Zoe."

"Zoe," I said mechanically.

"I asked you down here because Donald said there was this very arrogant, positively *rude* person who was asking all sorts of questions about Richard's death. I was so excited I almost forgot to put in my diaphragm."

She paused to survey the effect that her speech had had on me.

She was a big handsome woman, with a wide flat face, and voluptuous lips; but there was something slightly sour about her, some suggestion of decay.

"I must say I was hoping to see someone a bit more masterful," she said. "You look like the pouty type to me."

"That's what my wives always said."

"Wives?" she sniffed archly. She looked up and levelled her dark brown eyes. "Oh, that's just wonderful. After the first one you just sort of bunch them, like asparagus?"

"Something like that. It's hard to keep track."

Zoe Dindle chuckled a large warm throaty chuckle.

Then she said: "Do you know what happened to Richard? I mean *really* know?"

I shook my head.

"At least you're honest. Donald would have explained it all to me in exhausting detail."

I smiled; it wasn't hard liking Zoe Dindle.

"What do *you* think happened?"

"Me? I think Donald killed him. He's probably *gloating* about the whole thing."

"You think?"

"For heaven's sake," she said dramatically, "I've given you a clue. Aren't you supposed to do something. I mean, you're just standing there like a Saint Bernard."

"Mrs. Dindle, it's not any of my business, but if you're angry enough at your husband to accuse him of murder, why don't you just leave him? It's a free country. You don't need half the house."

"A lot you know," said Zoe Dindle with sudden bitterness.

I stood there for a moment, the mood between us changing faster than I could register the changes.

"Why do you want to know?" I finally asked. "About Richard Montague, I mean."

Zoe Dindle turned her face up.

"He was my lover," she said. She allowed me to see the tears well and then fall from her eyes, leaving sooty marks underneath the lashes. "Do you know that kind of mad intoxicating passion that comes over you like a firestorm?"

"No," I said.

"I didn't think so."

She didn't mean it meanly, but it sounded like an accusation.

"Well, that's what it was."

Then she said: "Will you do something for me? I can be very nice to people who do things for me."

I held up my hand.

"Oh, that's wonderful," she sniffed. "Above it all, are we?"

"Mrs. Dindle," I said, edging toward the door, "I'll be going now."

"No, wait," said Zoe Dindle dramatically.

I waited by the door.

"There were these terribly steamy letters I wrote to Richard. I used to leave them in his mailbox in the department. Richard kept them in a brown pigskin attache case. If you find them I want you to promise me that you'll give them back to me. Please?"

"Not the sort of thing you want your husband to see?"

For the first time, Zoe Dindle became absolutely serious.

"Mr. Asherfeld," she said, "if Donald saw those letters he would absolutely kill me."

Back on the upstairs landing, Dindle Junior glided up to me in his spooky silent way.

"Talk to my Mom?" he asked.

I nodded and edged back into the living room. I decided to give the cold cuts and limp vegetables a second chance.

The stereo was playing Pink Floyd. Two heavy-hipped women were dancing together in the center of the room, throwing their arms up into the air and waggling their ample behinds. Jean-Christofe had moved to the window; he stood with his back to the room. I could see his jaw moving solemnly: he was busy keeping posterity up to date on his every thought.

Donald Dindle came up to me. His pale skin had acquired a reddish sheen and his eyes had a blurry look.

"Talking to my wife, I see," he said. He meant to sound tough but he only sounded uncertain.

He stood there with his hands in the pockets of his grey slacks, a slim compact man with a phocine head and a fierce lost look.

I steered him away from the living room and up toward the landing; I wanted to get him alone before he made his scene.

"Need a little air," I said, opening the front door.

"Half hour with my wife, *everyone* needs a little air," said Dindle, chuckling glumly at his own joke.

We walked slowly up the path that led from the Dindles' house to Old La Honda Road, the pebbles beneath our feet crunching pleasantly. Night had almost fallen and the thin air had lost its heat. The lights from the valley glittered and twinkled below the somber redwoods that stood between the house and the road. There was no moon, but Venus had risen in the southern part of the sky.

"My wife is a slut. Did you know that?"

I kept on walking; I wasn't sure I wanted to hear what Dindle wanted to tell me but I knew there was no way of stopping him.

"That's a pretty harsh thing to say."

"Harsh?" Dindle cackled. "You think it's harsh to call a slut a slut? Let me put it another way. My wife is a woman of universal hospitality. The inn is always open. The welcome mat is always out. Coffee is always on the stove."

Abruptly, Dindle began to cry. The tears streamed from his eyes. I didn't know what to do. It's not easy to see a grown man cry.

"It's been very hard," he said.

Then his elegant face twisted on itself. He began to weep in earnest, drawing in great ragged breaths. It was terrible to hear. He dropped his hands to his knees and leaned over. I was afraid he would howl. For a moment, he stood like that, shuddering and weeping.

I patted him awkwardly on the shoulder.

"They were having an affair, the two of them," Dindle finally said between sobs.

"You can't know that, Dindle."

"She would wait for him outside the department, Asherfeld. He would pick her up on that motorcycle of his. She would rest her head on his shoulders and put her arms around his waist. Everyone could see them ride off together."

Dindle straightened himself up; his face was streaked with tears, but he had stopped crying and his jaw had tightened.

"I can't imagine what you must think of us."

"It doesn't matter," I said. "I'm not here to judge you."

Miss Virginia Woolf

THE LONG SHANK OF THE DAY had started to taper down toward evening. I thought I might take in a movie; I thought I might take a nap. I didn't do anything but sit at my desk with my feet up and look out at the waters of the Bay.

The telephone rang.

"This is Allison Hectorbrand."

For a moment I didn't know who she was and then I did.

"Terrific," I said, "Rimbaud decided she needed a little road-work before she meets Big George, figures on using my spine as a track?"

"Rimbaud says that she's sorry she pushed you. She didn't know you were working for the dean."

"That's sweet," I said. "Tell her I knew she wasn't really cruiserweight material after all."

"Rimbaud says that she would like you to meet her for a drink. There's something she needs to discuss."

"Sure," I said, "so long as it's someplace public. Don't want to get into too many tight quarters with Rimbaud. No telling what those raging hormones might do."

"No telling," said Allison Hectorbrand curtly. "Rimbaud says to meet her at Virginia Woolf's at ten."

Virginia Woolf's was San Francisco's most elegant lesbian bar. Everyone called it Woolfies.

"I'm supposed to come in drag?"

"That's up to you," said Allison Hectorbrand. "In any case, someone will have your name at the door."

She hung up without saying goodbye.

I spent the next hour soaking in the tub and I spent the hour after that reading a book that an attorney named Blivermayne had sent me. He had given up the law to open a vineyard in Oregon. He thought it was pretty terrific to be working the earth. His book said so. The dust jacket of the book showed Blivermayne standing in a vat of purple grapes. He looked like an imbecile.

I got dressed in a quiet blue sports coat that someone at Wilkes Bashford told me spoke worlds about my taste. When I brought it home one of my wives said: "It's too short. It makes your fanny stick out." I put it on anyway. I figured the world could use a good tight shot of my fanny.

It had stopped raining when I left my apartment, but blackish clouds still hung low in the sky and when I looked up I could see them scudding by Coit Tower.

I walked down Columbus toward Broadway and got into a cab that had been obligingly inching its way down the street.

"Where to, fella?" asked the driver, who was making his rounds accompanied by a German shepherd on the front seat.

"Woolfies, Fifth south of Market."

The driver swivelled around to look at me directly.

"You sure?" he asked. "I mean, we're talking UFO's now."

"I'm sure." I said. "It's business. I'm just letting them see the competition."

"Takes all kinds," said the driver philosophically.

There wasn't much of a line outside Woolfies, but a woman the size of an Abrams tank was making a show of dropping the red rope in front of the door each time someone went into the place, and then hitching it up dramatically before she would let anyone else in. By the time I got there no one else was left on line.

I walked to the rope and said: "I'm expected."

"Here?" said the Tank. "Cupcakes, I kind of doubt it."

"Doubt it all you want, it's still true. Go ask Rimbaud. She's supposed to be inside."

"Rimbaud," said the Tank, marvelling at the unnaturalness of it all. *"She's* expecting you?"

"She's going hetero. Wants the world to know. Go on in. Mention my name. It's Asherfeld. You'll hit moisture."

The Tank backed up and lumbered off into the club; after just a minute she returned and without a word dropped the red rope.

"See," I said as I walked past the Tank, "and all this time she was only waiting for Mr. Right."

The Tank snorted.

Inside, Woolfies was low-key, soft, and soothing. A very sophisticated sound system was playing Mozart on what sounded like a marimba. The walls were earth colored and faux finished in a kind of marble glaze; the lighting was chrome neon tubing, the sort of stuff that spreads a muzzy glow everywhere. There was a long horseshoe bar in the center of the room and booths on each side of the horseshoe. The place wasn't terribly crowded yet; there were a handful of women at the bar and a few couples in the booths. Some of the women were dressed in leather. Conversation didn't exactly stop when I walked in; but no one stood up and applauded either.

I walked over to the bar. The bartender had short black hair and a finely made squared face. The wind or the sun had chapped her cheeks.

"Meet your party over there," she said without being asked, pointing with a stubby finger toward the back booth by the open end of the horseshoe.

Rimbaud and Allison Hectorbrand were sitting side by side at the banquette.

Rimbaud nodded severely to the open air. Hectorbrand said: "Rimbaud says no hard feelings."

I slid into the banquette and looked at both women.

"No hard feelings," I said. "It's a tough world."

The bartender came over and placed a flute of champagne in front of me. "Compliments of the house," she said.

Rimbaud and Allison were both drinking sweet looking red drinks; I lifted the flute and said: "Ladies."

We sat there like that for a moment and then Rimbaud inclined her massive head toward Allison.

"Rimbaud says that things aren't always what they seem."

"You're telling me." I said. "People confuse me with Charlton Heston all the time."

Rimbaud leaned over again to whisper in Allison's ear.

"Rimbaud says cut it out."

"The *young* Charlton Heston, of course."

"Rimbaud says you'd *better* cut it out," said Allison Hectorbrand. Something in her tone of voice must have sent out sympathetic vibrations; in just a moment the Tank drifted in from the front door and ground her treads casually by our table, nodding severely to Rimbaud and Allison as she passed.

I took another sip of the awful champagne and leaned back in my chair.

"I guess we aren't going to let our hair down and just be girls after all," I said.

Rimbaud leaned over to Allison.

"The world is full of blatant homophobia."

"Man is born in Sin, no doubt about it."

There was a pause as Allison listened.

"She's afraid that heterosexist forces on campus are going to use Montague's death to compromise gay and lesbian rights."

"That's just awful," I said.

For a moment, Rimbaud sat stock still, staring straight ahead. Then she leaned over again to whisper in Allison's ear. Allison lifted her head up and spoke directly to me.

"Richard was a very naughty boy."

"I'll bet. Probably ate cookies before dinner."

Rimbaud had stiffened in her seat and a rosy flush had spread over the cheeks of her fat face. I realized that she was rigid with embarrassment.

Allison Hectorbrand began to speak. "Rimbaud says—," she began, but I cut her off.

"I don't have time for simultaneous translation. Tell me yourself."

Rimbaud relaxed by a fraction and Allison Hectorbrand nodded. "I don't know how much you know about the gay and lesbian lifestyle," she said tentatively.

"Lesbians like to pretend they're truck drivers, gays like Judy Garland. That's about it."

"There are these aspects to the gay lifestyle," said Hectorbrand delicately, "like when gays try to *enhance* their pleasure during intimacy?"

Like Rimbaud, Hectorbrand was finding the conversation an agony.

"You're talking about poppers," I said helpfully.

"No, no," said Hectorbrand, "not drugs. This is more like *natural.*"

She stopped, flushed.

Rimbaud leaned over to complete her thought.

"Rimbaud says," Hectorbrand said, grateful that she was not speaking for herself, "that a lot of gays like to have themselves strangled during, you know, lovemaking."

"What could be more natural?"

"Rimbaud says that's probably what happened to Richard. Something went wrong in the end."

"So?"

"There are supposed to be these videos," said Hectorbrand miserably.

"Not the sort of thing you want to send to alumni," I said.

Rimbaud shook her fat head.

I sighed and took a sip of the awful champagne.

"And you were just wondering whether I could get my hands on those videos before someone else does."

"Rimbaud says a scandal is absolutely the last thing progressive forces on this campus need."

"I'm not in the recovery business," I said, pushing the flute from me. A sheen had covered Rimbaud's eyes; she was about to cry. "But if I run across them, I'll be discreet."

"Rimbaud says that's all we ask," said Allison Hectorbrand.

I got up and said: "Ladies," and walked past the bar and out into the street.

The Tank was still patrolling the red rope in front of Woolfies and there was still no one lined up to get in.

"Make her go all trembly, Cupcakes?" she asked.

"It was nothing special," I said. "Any man could have done it."

Rainy Day

THE RAIN started sometime after two in the morning. The papers had said a late Pacific storm was moving into the city, and the papers were right. I could hear the drops hit the living room windows from my bedroom and I could smell the dense close smell of the weather coming into the apartment. I got up and walked into the living room in my underwear and watched the rain fall slowly over the scraggly little garden in the back of my building, the blackberry vines glistening, black and wet. After a while I went back to bed.

It was still raining when I got up, and it was still raining when I had breakfast and watched Max lumber through his exercise routine, and it was still raining when I got on the oil-stained freeway and drove across the Bay Bridge toward Vallejo. I drove slowly and listened to the sound that the windshield wipers made.

A little past Terminal Island, traffic slowed to a crawl. A low cut pick-up painted in day-glo colors edged next to me; I could hear the car stereo and feel the thudding of its bass. The driver was a young black with a kerchief on his head and a lot of razor bumps on his neck. He was rocking his head forward, keeping time to the music. He didn't much look like he'd appreciate a request to turn the volume down. After a while, I could see what had slowed traffic: There was a car stopped on the left lane with a flat tire. The driver was a tense looking woman; she sat clutching the steering wheel, staring straight ahead. She probably figured that if she even got out of the car to look at her tire, someone would rape her. I cut in front, pulled my car close to the bridge railing, and walked back to her car. She kept staring straight ahead. I bent over and rapped on her window. She rolled down her window a quarter of an inch and said: "You get away from me, you."

Vallejo is the sort of sour little city that generally fills up space on the map between where you are and where you want to go. There's a refinery by the Bay. The place smells vaguely of oil and even when the weather is fine in San Francisco, a kind of inky smog blows in over Vallejo from the waterfront. Truckdrivers live out here, and men who run stamp presses, and women with hard flat eyes who dress in pressed jeans and high heels on Saturday night and listen to country music at bars with names like The Oasis. Ingelfinger had no telephone that I could trace; but a reporter at the *Examiner* named Leo Rubble used a reverse directory to get me his address. I drove down Parkside toward the waterfront and then followed a rabbit warren of back streets until I came to Wamus. It's a scraggly one-way street that dead-ends on a vacant lot. I got out of my car and counted down the houses until I came to Ingelfinger's. It wasn't hard to spot. In a neighborhood of shabby wooden houses, it was the shabbiest. Someone must have loved the thing once. Now you couldn't even tell that it had ever been painted.

The neighborhood was empty. No women in curlers. No kids on the street riding tricycles. Far away a dog was barking to himself. It was still raining a cold hard mean rain.

The front of the house was pretty much boarded up. I edged down a concrete walkway that led to the back of the house. I couldn't see anyone and the only thing I could hear was that dog, barking mournfully into the wet air. An old-fashioned Dutch door, its top half open, let into the kitchen. I stood listening for a moment on the stoop, then reached over to unlatch the bottom half of the door.

The place was filthy and stank of garbage. Someone had left a terrific pile of dishes in the iron sink. A cockroach slithered out from the pile and stood on top of one of the dishes, waving its antennae.

I walked as quietly as I could to the threshold of the kitchen. An enormous Harley was parked in the middle of the room beyond the kitchen. A small puddle of oil had collected on the floor under the engine block. I couldn't imagine how anyone had managed to get the thing through the door. I noticed that someone was sleeping on the ratty sofa, whose back faced the boarded-up front window. He was about fifty or so, almost completely bald, small, from what I could tell, with a flamboyant red potato nose. He was clutching an empty Jack Daniels bottle in one hand. I didn't think there was much danger that he'd wake up.

I took the wooden stairs behind the living room quietly anyway. Anyone prepared to drive a Harley into his living room might have certain old-fashioned scruples about breaking and entering.

The second floor landing was as filthy as the kitchen: chicken bones on the floor, a couple of pizza carton boxes that someone had tried hopelessly to fold, and a stack of wet rotting newspapers in the corner. It was a terrific place.

Three doors led off the second floor landing; all of them were closed. I opened the nearest one by a crack and peeked in. The air inside was stale and unmoving. A king-sized mattress with a lot of cigarette burns took up almost the whole of the room. A poster of Tracy Lords was on the far wall.

The second door was locked and I didn't much want to force it open; the third door opened noiselessly when I tried it. The room inside wasn't clean but it wasn't a pigsty either. There was a single mattress on the floor, covered with an expensive red North Face sleeping bag. Someone had taken the trouble to arrange it neatly over the mattress. Along one wall, two plywood planks propped up on cinder blocks served as a makeshift bookcase. A stack of old *Playboys* from the nineteen sixties had been arranged neatly on the bottom shelf. I spent a few minutes leafing through them. The sad pneumatic women with names like Cindi and Candi and Kimberly stared out at me from the glossy pages.

I stepped over the mattress on the floor and over to the streaked and filthy window that overlooked the back yard. It was still raining outside, the kind of steady rain that isn't romantic anymore. The dog that had been barking was still barking. I didn't know what I was hoping to see out there and after a little while I decided I wasn't going to see it.

The only thing left to check in the room was a closet opposite the bookcase; its door had an elegant old-fashioned glass handle. The closet released a smell of cedar and redwood into the room when I opened it. Someone *had* loved this house once. I thought of the Italian ironworkers up from San Francisco who had probably settled here at the turn of the century; I thought of their wives, women with beefy no-nonsense forearms and determined black hair on their upper lips, standing before closets like this, folding laundry and singing Italian songs. When I first came to San Francisco they were still singing in all the backyards of the city.

The only thing in the closet was one of those pigskin attache cases that cost a fortune and look like they plan on travelling to Europe on the Concorde. It felt heavy when I swung it down from the narrow closet shelf. The initials on the side said RM. I squatted down and pressed the latch above the combination lock. The lock had been set.

There was nothing left in the room to see and nothing left in the house for me to do.

I sidled out of the room with the briefcase under my arm and walked past the chicken bones on the landing and softly down the wooden stairs. I thought I might just slip out the back of the house, the way I came in, but the drunk who had been sleeping so peacefully on the living room sofa was now sitting up.

He looked at me with surprised red eyes.

"Hey, you don't belong here," he said thickly.

"You're absolutely right," I said. "It's not my kind of place at all. Probably doesn't even have room service."

He took this in for a moment and then said: "If it's not your kind of place, how come you're here then? Answer me that."

"I'm on assignment," I said, "for *European Travel and Life*. There's been a terrible mistake."

A new thought occurred to him. "Say," he said, "did Buddy

61

sent you over here? That's it, isn't it? Buddy sent you over here spy on me. See if I was drinking on the job or something."

"You? Drink on the job? Buddy knows better."

I started to edge down the last step.

"Darn tootin'," he said. "See, I'm a drinking man, I admit that, but I don't drink while I'm working, if you get my drift. You tell Buddy that. Tell him that I don't drink while I'm working."

"Or work while you're drinking," I added helpfully.

The drunk peered at me intently. I could see that he had one of those noses that sprouted stray hairs along its stalk.

"Right," he finally said.

I nodded; I was about to say something. For a fraction of a second, I thought I saw his eyes widen momentarily, and then I heard a crashing roar. The wooden floor came up to meet my face.

When I awoke, my tongue thick in my mouth and the back of my head throbbing, the elegant pigskin attache case was gone and the man who didn't drink while working or work while drinking lay sprawled against the sofa back, his arms at his sides, a single wet red hole drilled in his forehead, just above the bridge of his hairy nose.

THE PAKISTANI NEUROSURGICAL resident ran a thin finger around the outlines of the egg-shaped lump on my head; he said: "That is quite a bruise you have there, sir. How did you acquire it?"

Heebleman, the heavier of the two cops who had brought me to the emergency room at Vallejo General, shifted his great bullocky haunches and said: "She crossed her legs, Doc. Let's get on with it." Dreisch, the second cop, snorted explosively. The smell of their leather belts and boots filled the little room.

I sat at the edge of a stainless steel gurney. My head was still throbbing wetly. Every time my heart beat it felt like a cannon going off underwater. The doctor continued to probe my skull, paying no attention to the cops.

"Anything broken?" I asked woodenly.

"You have a mild concussion," said the resident. "Possibly

there is a hairline fracture that we are unable to see. A CAT scan would tell us more." He held up his hands apologetically.

"Not gonna happen," said Heebleman authoritatively. "Boy's goin' inna tank. Day or two he'll be muff divin' again. That right, Asherman?"

"Asherfeld," I said mechanically.

"Whatever," said Heebleman.

The Pakistani looked at Heebleman somberly. "It is within my rights to order this man to sick bed," he said.

Heebleman rocked forward on his heels; he had been leaning against the wall.

"Lot of things within your rights still be a bad idea doin'," he said evenly.

"You are being impertinent," said the resident. "I am a physician."

"Don't matter what you are," said Heebleman imperturbably. "Fact is the captain still wants the man inna tank."

The resident looked for a moment as if he might continue his little protest, and then all at once the air leaked out of him. He nodded and said: "Very well, I see. I am taking no responsibilities."

"That's fine, Doc," said Dreisch, standing up decisively from the stool on which he had been sitting.

Together the two of them frogmarched me out of the emergency room, through the large empty sounding hall of the hospital, and over to the police cruiser that they had used to bring me to the hospital.

I sat next to Dreisch in the back of the car, his shaggy warm smell filling the air. Heebleman slid into the driver's seat and turned on the blinking overhead light. He eased away from the hospital ramp, guiding the car by his wrist, his hand draped indolently over the steering wheel.

"You doin' okay, Asherman?" he asked.

"Me? Never better."

"That's good," said Heebleman, driving thoughtfully through the dark streets. "No sense spending a lot of time hanging around an emergency ward."

"Sure," I said. "Especially when I've got a concussion."

Dreisch shifted on the leatherette seat of the cruiser and looked deliberately out the window.

"You're right," said Heebleman, chuckling.

At Vallejo Central, Heebleman and Dreisch fingerprinted me carefully, making sure to take imprints of my index finger as well as my thumb; and then the two of them maneuvered me from the Hall of Records over to Heebleman's cubicle in the police duty station.

Dreisch stood behind me as Heebleman settled himself into his chair and began the business of writing up things in triplicate. He had an illiterate's knack of approaching paperwork with a good many flourishes of his wrist and hand.

I yawned as he was fussing and felt around the margins of the lump in the back of my head.

I had already given one statement to Heebleman and Dreisch when they met me at the house on Wamus. I wasn't much in the mood to give them another; but Heebleman was actually filling in a personnel action report and not a preliminary statement. It was designed to show the world that he and Dreisch had taken terrific care of me. It took Heebleman about ten minutes to go through the questions, which he answered with a great display of concentration. When he finished, he pushed the triplicates toward me and said: "Look it over, everything in order, just sign at the bottom."

I signed the form without reading it.

Heebleman placed the thing officiously in his out basket and stood up heavily.

"Get you squared away with the duty room, we'll be all set."

With Heebleman in back of me, I followed Dreisch's rolling haunches down one long corridor and over to the duty room. The place looked like a high school locker room, except that the lockers were all behind a wire mesh fence.

Dreisch walked over to the chipped and pitted wooden table that occupied a hole cut in the fence and got a basket from the sergeant who was sitting at the table.

"Watch, wallet, ring, personal effects," said Heebleman. "You'll get a receipt, you want one."

Heebleman placed my belongings in a plastic bag, which he

sealed with tape. He put the bag in the basket. Then he said: "Belt and shoelaces, too."

I looked at him quizzically.

"Captain doesn't like to cut dead meat down from the cell," he said. "Makes him feel out of sorts."

I untied by shoelaces and pulled them from their grommets; then I slid off my belt.

Heebleman paused to survey me as he placed my shoelaces and belt in another plastic bag.

"Club Med," he said. "Think of it that way."

There were a few disgruntled characters in the tank when I got there: they had been involved in a barroom brawl and were concerned to retell their experiences to one another. "See where I hit him with the stick, Vinnie?" one of them said. "Hit him upside of the head with the stick, bust his head wide open."

"I seen it," said his companion sourly; his left cheek was blue-black and shiny with a wicked looking bruise. "Only thing is how come you didn't figure on hitting him upside of the head before he smacks a Bud light into my face?"

"I hear you," said Vinnie, "except you got to let your man make his move before you make yours, you know what I mean?"

After a while, the two of them were marched out of the tank and led off somewhere; they were still talking about the fight.

A little later, a very thin black was brought into the tank in handcuffs by Heebleman and Dreisch. Heebleman stood him against the cell door and cuffed his cuffs to the iron bars. He couldn't sit and he couldn't move his hands.

"Hey, Asherpeckerfeld," Heebleman shouted. "Good thing I got this boy chained up. He bad and that's a fact." He withdrew his ebony nightstick and poked it at the midsection of the chained man. "Ain't you bad, boy?" he said.

After Heebleman left, I asked the black companionably what he was in for.

"Smoked the bitch," he said somberly. "Smoked her bitch kid, too." He began to weep silently by the door of the tank. Tears fell from his eyes and dropped to the concrete floor. "I don't expect Jesus he love me anymore," he said.

Heebleman and Dreisch took the black away around ten; he was still weeping. A few minutes later they brought in a sober looking middle-aged man in a natty grey pinstriped suit.

"Be no more than an hour, sir," Heebleman said. "Paperwork's got to come down from the sixth floor."

The well-dressed man nodded courteously. He was reeking of alcohol.

"DUI?" I asked from my side of the cell.

"Lawyers," he said bitterly. "You'd think with what I pay him the son of a bitch wouldn't give me grief when I call."

"It's what every lawyer wants," I said.

"What's that?"

"Be woken up in the middle of the night by some moron thinks six scotches improves his coordination."

The man glared at me from his side of the cell.

"You a wise guy or what?"

"I'm a wise guy. When we bust out of here, you do the driving, I'll do the talking."

The man looked as if he were about to say something very sharp; he shrugged instead. Heebleman came back for him twenty minutes later. After that the tank was quiet. I rolled up my jacket to form a pillow and stretched out on the floor. I was tired. I felt I couldn't sleep beneath the harsh indoor light, but I must have dozed off anyway. When Heebleman jabbed his nightstick against my shoulder, saying "Captain'll see you now," I had that gummy feeling you only get when you've been asleep.

The captain's interrogation room had the harsh unpleasant feel of any public room in the middle of the night. There was nothing on the walls; no windows. A long green metal table stood in the center of the room. Heebleman pointed to a chair with his nightstick and said: "Make yourself real comfortable." I sat down and stretched my legs in front of me.

I rubbed my eyes deeply with the heel of my hand, noticing how filthy my hands had become. I hadn't eaten anything since breakfast, and I hadn't had much to drink, and someone had knocked me unconscious.

Heebleman sat himself beside the door, his chair tipped backward.

We waited like that for a few minutes, neither of us speaking.

There was a clatter of heels outside in the corridor; the door opened and two men entered the room. One was dressed in a captain's uniform; the other, in a rumpled brown suit. He carried a clipboard and a sheaf of papers under his arm. Heebleman got to his feet with a show of alacrity. Brown Suit nodded affably to me and said: "Name's Sniderman," and then, pointing to his companion, added: "This here's Captain Brockmeister."

Sniderman sat down easily at the head of the table and hooked his leg over the chair arm.

Brockmeister sat himself down with a great show of hitching his pants neatly and arranging his plump posterior carefully in his chair. He smelled of harness leather and toilet water.

"Man's a disgrace," he said abruptly. "Man's an absolute disgrace. Man's not washed, he's not shaved. He's not clean. Comes in here smelling like a sewer. Expects us to extend him every courtesy. Expects us to treat him with respect."

The captain shook his fat head theatrically.

"Not going to happen, mister," he added.

"Say, Captain?" I said.

"I'll ask the questions here, mister."

"Okeydokey."

It took no more than a few seconds for Brockmeister's curiosity to get the better of him.

"What?"

"Weren't you the guy used to date Oprah Winfrey? Made her stick on her diet and all? I read a feature about it in the *Enquirer.*"

Sniderman snorted from the head of the table.

"Years ago I would've torn a man's head off talking to me like that," said Brockmeister.

"Years ago you could have got away with it. Now you can't."

"What makes you so sure?"

"I'm not poor. I'm not black. I've read more than ten books. How'm I doing?"

Brockmeister nodded to himself as if he had figured things out.

"Man's got a pretty cocky attitude for someone facing some very serious criminal charges, wouldn't you say, Mr. Sniderman?"

Sniderman laughed from the head of the table. "All right, all right," he said. "Look, Asherfeld, don't have a cow. No one's roughed you up, no one's leaned on you. You spent what? Couple of hours in the tank? You aren't even close to habeus corpus. State of California says to me I can hold you seventy-two hours suspicion only, so don't get yourself in an uproar. Not good for you, not good for me, not good for the captain."

"Why don't we leave the captain out of this. He's got enough trouble dating celebrities."

"You're not going to score points with me being smart, Asherfeld," said Sniderman evenly. "Captain here is a man of outstanding courage. Deserves better from you."

I rubbed my eyes and stretched the skin of my forehead with my thumb and index finger.

"Sniderman, you want me to think better of the captain, have him stop leaning on me like a gorilla."

"Leaning on you?" said Brockmeister in disbelief. "Man spends two hours in the tank, the way he goes on you figure we've got him on a rack."

"That's logic for you," I said. "You don't give me the third degree, you figure the second degree is just swell?"

"Asherfeld," said Sniderman softly, "I were you I'd worry more about the future than the past."

"Meaning what?"

"Meaning how come a fella from San Francisco like you is in the living room of a house in Vallejo during commission of a felony?"

"Beats me," I said.

"That's what you're going to tell the district attorney?" asked Brockmeister.

I said: "If it's good enough for you, it's good enough for him. I'm not going to play favorites."

"Man was killed today, Asherfeld. Don't you think you owe this investigation the courtesy of an honest answer?"

"No."

"Why's that?"

"I didn't kill him and it's not my job to find out who did."

Brockmeister snorted deeply from his chair and said: "Waste of time, interrogating this man."

Sniderman looked at me contemplatively; he seemed to be deliberating. Then he said: "Asherfeld, you got an attorney you can call, this'd be the time to call him. You can use the phone in the hall. Heebleman'll take you out, give you ten minutes."

I called Shmul Wasserstrom in San Francisco. It was the middle of the night; I was still pretty sure he'd answer the telephone.

I explained the situation to him; he was incredulous.

"You, you're so smart you wind yourself up in jail someplace in Vallejo?"

"Pride goeth before a fall," I said. "Here's the thing. All you have to do is drive up here, demand that I be ROR or charged."

"I drive up to Vallejo, it costs extra," said Shmul.

"I'll make it up to you in business."

Shmul Wasserstrom got to Vallejo within the hour. I met him in the conference room next to the interrogation room.

He looked at me and said: "Good you don't look."

"I'm fine," I said. "Just get me out of here."

Shmul got up and rattled the door of the conference room; Heebleman brought us back to interrogation. Sniderman was there, but not the captain. The two of us stood by the green metal table.

Sniderman said: "So Counsellor, you going to tell me what your guy's doing out on Wamus during the commission of a felony?"

"Selling encyclopedias," said Shmul Wasserstrom. "He goes door to door." He looked theatrically at his watch. "One hour I file for habeus corpus. You know he's not a shooter. We'll all be better off you just release him on his own recognizance. We have to post bond, I file for false arrest."

"How do I know he's not the shooter?" asked Sniderman.

"Some shooter. First he knocks himself out, then he pulls the trigger and throws away the gun. You didn't do a paraffin test, you know beforehand he isn't the shooter."

Sniderman released the tension in his body by dropping his feet from the table abruptly; he laughed wolfishly. "I know he's not the shooter," he said, "just tell your boy to give me something I can go on."

Shmul Wasserstrom turned to me and said: "You have some-thing you can give this man?"

I said: "What was the name of the guy who was shot?"

"Epinall," said Sniderman, "George Epinall. You know him?"

I shook my head: "All I can tell you, he wasn't too interested in encyclopedias," I said. "And I offered him the free World Book, too."

I lay on the couch in my living room after I got back to the city, too tired to take off my clothes, too tired to move to the bed. The grey greasy dawn had come and gone; the fog had rolled over the little garden outside my window and then disappeared. I had been bopped on the head and I had spent a night in the tank up in Vallejo and I had seen a man die.

After a while, I called the dean; I told him what had hap-pened. He listened alertly.

"Anyone tie this thing to the university?" he asked.

"Montague had a lot of secrets," I said carefully.

"Not what I asked, Asherfeld."

"I know," I said. "The place in Vallejo? I left the telephone number on my answering machine. Anyone could have fol-lowed me there."

"Who's this anyone we're talking about?"

"A lot of people might have been interested in things I might have found."

"You think someone from the university's capable of a thing like this?"

"I think someone from the university could have followed me and lost their head. It's the way most murders happen."

Then the dean said: "I hear what you're saying. I'm sorry you're upset, Asherfeld."

I fell asleep after a long while. George Epinall wandered in and out of my dreams, a wet red hole in his forehead. He was curiously uninterested in the encyclopedias in which I was try-ing to interest him, pushing away the handsome, leather bound books with a weak and trembling hand.

Country Life

I took Sand Hill Road west from the freeway and followed the looping two-lane road for a few miles. Violet had asked me to come out to her house; she said that Richard Montague had left some papers with her. She wanted to show me how much she cared. There were hunched bicyclists in stretched day-glo tights on the side of the road, pedalling furiously; you could tell they had been exercising seriously for a long time. They had that whipped look men get in northern California. Overhead the sky was clear, with only the faintest hint of white at the edge of the horizon. The woods on both sides of the road held the deep green of trees that have finally gotten enough rain.

I drove past a little Episcopalian church, and past a stable with a lot of women riding their sleek horses in a ring, and past an orchard selling cherry cider and almonds.

The turnoff for Violet's house was just beyond the orchard. "You can't miss it," Violet had said optimistically. "It's a dirt road and there's a sign marked 'Omo' and a call box."

I almost missed the road anyway. The sign marked "Omo" was actually a little copper plate mounted on a tree trunk. A much larger sign above it said Unauthorized Access Forbidden. A swinging metal gate stretched across the dirt road. The call box was built into the right stanchion of the gate itself. I pressed O. After a while, someone answered, "Yes," in a tight tense voice.

"The name is Asherfeld."

There was a whirring in the branches above my head; a video camera was panning slowly from left to right, taking in my car, taking in me.

I said: "You want I should drop my trousers, show you a birthmark?"

There was no answer. The camera panned back from right to left and the metal gate swung open.

71

I drove for a quarter of a mile along the well-maintained dirt road, past scrub oak, glistening in the afternoon sun, and California cypress, bent over by the wind, and past an open meadow with a pond on its far side.

I opened the car window wide and smelt the strong tangy smells of the dirt and the young leaves.

The coach house was on the crest of a small hill; it was painted red, with white trim along the windows.

Violet was standing by the door, cradling a fat cat in her arms. I parked beside her VW, got out of my car, and looked at the coach house and the surrounding land, hot, dry and glowing in the noonday sun.

"Isn't it beautiful?" Violet said.

"Just beautiful."

"I'm so lucky. Mike Dottenberry arranged it all for me."

"Pretty nice," I said.

"Every so often I have to leave the house for a night, but that's such a small price to pay for all this."

"Leave the house? Why?"

"I don't know," said Violet. "That's just the arrangement."

I let my arms sweep over the hill beyond the house. "Who owns all this? It must go on for hundreds of acres."

"Oh, more. I think it's the largest piece of private property on the Peninsula. I mean, the property line only *starts* at Skyline Boulevard and it goes almost down to Los Gatos."

The cat wriggled from Violet's arms and landed heavily on its paws.

"You didn't say hello to Mister Cat," said Violet with a note of injured dignity.

I looked down at the poor fat thing. "How you doing?" I said without much enthusiasm.

"You've got to say *Mister* Cat," said Violet. "Otherwise he gets offended."

Inside, the coach house was dark and cool. It had once been a real coach house but someone had remodelled it in the way that only people with a great deal of money ever remodel anything. The old floor had been scraped and polished and bleached. The wooden walls and beamed ceiling had been sanded and painted a harsh clean white. Old-fashioned carpenter's tools were mounted on the walls for decoration.

There was a big white rattan chair with a white cushion in the middle of the room, and a white Parsons table by one wall, and a white bookcase by the other wall. There were lot of colorful Navajo rugs scattered on the floor.

I walked over to the side of the room to look at Violet's bookcase. Her books were about feminism and losing weight. I picked up one called *Feeling Our Fire*. The author identified herself as a Shakti Woman; her picture showed her as a blonde with large teeth from Berkeley.

"Feeling our fire?"

"It's about shamanism," said Violet in a small voice, "and healing the planet."

I nodded and placed the book back on the shelf.

"I'd offer you something," said Violet, still standing in the center of the room, "but I'm only eating Jennie's cuisine now."

I shook my head. "I'm fine."

Violet stood indecisively in the center of the room and then said: "I'll get Richard's papers. I mean, if you want?"

"That'd be fine, Violet," I said.

She was a fat pretty lost woman; she trudged off to the bedroom and trudged back carrying a red cardboard file folder. She settled herself on the footstool of the large rattan chair, tucking her large legs underneath herself. There was a long heavy pause. I knew she wanted something from me before she'd give me Montague's papers.

"Can I ask you something, Mr. Asherfeld?" she said softly. "Do you think something happened to Richard?"

"You're a lot closer to things than I am, Violet," I said. "What do you think?"

"I don't know," she said. "I don't even know who to trust. Can I trust you, Mr. Asherfeld?"

I shook my head. "I didn't love Richard, Violet. I didn't even know him. All I can do is try and sort things out."

Violet turned her heavy head from me and let her gaze travel from the living room to the fields beyond the window.

"I suppose I'll have to settle for that," she said, sniffling heavily.

I walked over to the Parsons table and braced against it with my hip; I thought it might be easier for Violet to talk if she couldn't see me directly.

"It's so wrapped up and ugly and complicated," she said. "I mean, when he was alive everyone was *so* interested in being Richard's friend and being close to him and all and now everyone's gossiping and spreading these rumors. People are so false. I can't stand it how false people are."

"You'll find it easier if you don't expect so much from people," I said. "That way they can surprise you."

Violet nodded and said: "I know that, Mr. Asherfeld."

"Let me ask you a question, Violet," I said. "Can you tell me who Richard's friends on the faculty were, people he was close to?"

Violet nodded her head.

"He was close to Mike Dottenberry," she said. "And he was close to Bulton Limbish. Not close close. Just close. They all had these enormous motorcycles and used to ride them on weekends and things."

"Bulton Limbish?"

"He's sort of a research associate and all? He's very militant."

"What about Donald Dindle?"

Violet looked up in surprise. "Donald? No, Donald *never* liked Richard. They had this macho thing between them, you know, like which of them was the bigger star in the department. Donald couldn't *stand* it that Richard was more successful than he was."

"That the only thing between them? Academic success?"

Violet turned her shoulders to look at me; I thought her face might have reddened slightly.

"There were these rumors. You'd think people had better things to do with their time than spread rumors."

"You'd think," I said. "What kind of rumors?"

"Oh, that Richard and Zoe Dindle were having an affair."

"Not true?"

Violet hesitated before speaking.

"I don't know, Mr. Asherfeld," she finally said.

"That's a good answer, Violet," I said. "You're probably the only person on campus honest enough to give it."

I straightened up from the Parsons table and walked over to the rattan chair. "I'll be going now," I said softly. "I'll take care of these."

Violet reached down and handed the file folder up to me. "The week after Richard died I slept with these under my bed."

"You did the right thing," I said.

The sun outside caught me the way the high California sun always does; I blinked and squinted until I got my sunglasses on.

I drove slowly down the dirt road, with the windows open to let out the stale hot air. As soon as I was out of sight of the coach house, I pulled over and walked back up the dirt road, walking carefully around the meadow in front of the coach house and over the little hill that folded the meadow upward like a green bow. The dirt road picked up on the other side of the meadow. I followed it for a hundred feet or so. A red-tailed hawk swung lazy circles in the sky above my head.

After a few hundred feet or so, the road emptied into a flat clearing. Wooden benches were set in a semicircle around the clearing, with a lean-to over by the side. Someone had built a small campfire by one of the benches. The whole place had a thick strange smell. I noticed a folded sheet of paper by the burnt out campfire. I picked it up and smoothed it open. It was obviously a sheet from a newspaper that had been carefully cut with a knife. The thing was entirely in Chinese.

I folded the newspaper back up and put it in my jacket breast pocket.

It hadn't taken me more than ten minutes to walk up to the clearing from my car, and ten minutes to walk back, but when I drove down to the security gate, someone was standing by the white concrete stanchion. He was wearing a khaki security guard's uniform and opaque metalled shades; he was also carrying a shotgun.

I rolled to a stop and opened the window halfway.

"Mind telling me where you've been, sir?" he asked.

"Sure I mind."

"Tell me anyway," he said, dropping the "sir" in a big hurry.

"I'm a curious sort of guy." He lowered his shotgun just slightly so that the barrel was pointing at the hood of my car.

I said: "You're curious, read a book."

"You're on private property, fella. You got an awful big mouth for someone on someone else's property."

I pointed to the fence and to the camera above it in the tree.

"Someone let me in," I said, "and someone took a picture of that gate swinging open. That makes *me* a guest."

The security guard looked me over through his metal shades for a very long while.

Finally he said: "Have a good day."

The gate swung open. I inched the car onto Sand Hill Road.

I had planned to drive straight back to the city, but instead I drove to the university and hustled over to Dottenberry's office. I knocked on the door and Dottenberry shouted "Yo. It's open."

He was right where I'd left him, sitting at his desk, staring into space.

I stood leaning my shoulder against the door frame.

"Asherfeld," he said in that irritating gentle way he had.

"How's it going, Dottenberry?" I said. "Got time for a few questions? Just take a second."

Dottenberry compressed his face by narrowing his eyes; it was his way of expressing suspicion.

"I don't know," he said. "I don't know if I approve of what you're doing."

"I can relate to that," I said. "University's a pretty special place. It has its own rules."

"Right," said Dottenberry vigorously, moving his head up and down like a pigeon.

"On the other hand, you're better off me asking the questions than other people, if you catch my drift."

Dottenberry stared at me.

"I'm not sure I do, Asherfeld," he said.

I let my voice drop down. "I'll make it simple for you, Dottenberry. The questions I'm asking are going to get answered, one way or the other. I'm still on your side. Bring in the police, they're on the other side. They're *always* on the other side."

Dottenberry nodded glumly. "What do you want to know, Asherfeld?"

"I want to know how come Violet gets to stay at a swell coach house."

"Why don't you ask her?" said Dottenberry with a sulky note in his voice.

"I did. She said you arranged it. Pretty nice favor, seeing how the house and the land around it are private property. I'm just curious how you managed it."

"That's just it, Asherfeld," said Dottenberry, brightening. "When you let go of your anger, all sorts of things happen."

"Tell me," I said. "I've let go."

"Actually, it's this workshop. NOMAS runs a men's workshop. Odo Omo asked to join, suggested we use the ranch."

"Odo? There really is an Odo?"

"Odo Omo," said Dottenberry.

"Sure," I said. "Odo Omo. It's a name anyone would recognize."

"He owns the ranch." said Dottenberry. "One of the heirs to the Omo fortune."

"So one thing led to another."

"It always does, Asherfeld. That's what I've been trying to tell you."

"You help him deal with his anger, he tosses in a coach house for Violet?"

"Something like that."

"So how come you asked him for a favor like that? Sounds like a pretty big deal to me."

Dottenberry waited a long time before answering. Then he said: "Richard asked me to set it up."

"Why?"

"I can't tell you that, Asherfeld," said Dottenberry; he said it in the matter-of-fact way weak men have of saying things when they make up their mind. "I've told you everything I can."

I got back to my apartment at a little after four. I was hot and I was tired and I was sweaty.

One of my wives had written me a long letter from a women's commune in Oregon. She said she had known much sadness and suffering; she said she was working through her grief; she said she wanted to become a holistic massage health practitioner. She said she needed five thousand dollars.

The air in my apartment had the stale unmoving feel that stale unmoving air gets after a long day; I dumped the file folder and the mail on my desk and opened the living room window and stood for a while, looking at the garden and letting the cool, moist air wash over me. A dove, busy feeding for the last time before night fell, flew from one end of the garden to the telephone wires at the other end, its wings whirring.

The foghorns had just begun to sound, low over the Bay; and a long elegant white cruise ship was making sedately for the Golden Gate and points beyond.

Later I looked over the folder Violet had given me. There wasn't a whole lot in it that I could use. Montague hadn't figured on dying and he hadn't spent much time organizing his affairs. There was a list of his insurance companies in the folder and a very detailed guide to his own publications and finally, a list of names. Most of the names meant nothing to me, but I knew his attorney, Seybold Knesterman. I made a note to call him.

I lay on the couch after that and watched some kung fu guy take on the world; and after *that* I watched a soft-porn movie on channel 8. It was the sort of movie in which two knockout women discover that the thing they want to do most in the world is dress up in garters and push-up brassieres and sort of coo over one another while some guy watches appreciatively from an easy chair.

I remembered mentioning lingerie to one of my wives once. "Oh, please Asher," she had said, "the only thing I want from underwear is that it shouldn't ride up my crotch."

Honoring That

MIKE DOTTENBERRY looked dubious when I told him that I wanted to meet Odo Omo.

He was sitting at his desk, staring into space.

"I don't know, Asherfeld," he said, running his tense thumb and forefinger down the sides of his cheek to the point of his chin. "I honor and respect Odo Omo. He might feel that I was abusing our relationship if I set things up like that."

"I understand that, Mike," I said with as much sympathy as I could put into my voice, "but on the other hand he might just feel that you were abusing your relationship if you didn't set things up."

It was an argument that wouldn't have worked on a schoolgirl; I thought Dottenberry would go for it.

A few days later he said: "I spoke to Omo, Asherfeld. Told him all about you. He said he'd meet you after the NOMAS meeting, Saturday morning."

"That's swell, Mike," I said. "Give me a chance to start letting go of my anger."

Dottenberry looked up at me with a hopeful expression; he didn't say anything.

On Saturday morning I had breakfast at Gino's and then took the long way over to the freeway, cutting through Golden Gate Park. The great meadows were already full of yelping children and frolicking dogs chasing ducks and sturdy women pushing fat little babies in their strollers and gangs of exuberant teenagers eyeing one another.

Out on the avenues, a wedding was about to commence: a puffed up patrolman was routing traffic around the limousines bunched at the curb of the Church of the Immaculate Conception. I caught a glimpse of the Filipina bridesmaids in their stiff taffeta and silk dresses.

I drove up to Portola Valley, following the wide curves of 280 through the green hills, the car window open.

The security gate at Omo's ranch was down; there was a uniformed security guard with a clipboard in hand standing before the gate.

"Your name, sir?"

"Asherfeld," I said, "with an A."

He ticked off my name and gave me a number to put in my windshield.

"Park anywhere along the road, but not past the coach house," he said.

I drove up the dirt road and parked in the shade of a beech tree, a few hundred yards from Violet's coach house. I thought she might be out, but when I walked past, I saw her VW was still there, Mister Cat himself snoozing on the warm hood.

The NOMAS meeting was being held in the natural amphitheater that I had stumbled on the week before. I must have been the last to show; there were a dozen or so men sitting on the benches when I trudged up.

Dottenberry spotted me right away. "Glad you could come, Asherfeld," he said, shaking my hand stiffly so that the other men could see the gesture. I nodded to the men on the benches and they nodded to me.

Dottenberry withdrew to the lean-to and emerged carrying a large Japanese drum; he proceeded to bang it slowly. The sound boomed and reverberated through the hot hollow hills.

The men got themselves into a semicircle; they were seated shoulder to shoulder, squatting in the clearing. I tried to squat along with them, but after just a minute or two, my thighs began to ache, so I surreptitiously dropped from a squat to a seated position. The man next to me put a warm hand on my shoulder and said: "No poses here, brother. Sit the way you want."

The sun was nearly at its zenith, and the warm air was motionless.

Mike Dottenberry stood in front of the semicircle and continued to bang his drum mournfully. After a time, the men began to clap rhythmically and roll their heads from left to right. Some of the men moaned softly.

Dottenberry wound up with an especially vigorous spasm, his hand thrashing, and then abruptly stopped beating his drum.

He said: "I'd like for us to welcome Aaron Asherfeld here today. I want to honor Aaron for making himself vulnerable by coming here."

There was a murmur from the group.

"I want to celebrate that," said Mike Dottenberry.

The men murmured again.

"Aaron," said Dottenberry, explaining things to me, "We do work in areas of co-creativity and the development of an integrated, spiritually centered brotherhood of men in planetary stewardship."

80

I nodded; I had no idea what else to do.

"We've been working our asses off to process through some of this stuff that has been threatening our relationships. We've still got a lot of work to do."

The men rumbled appreciatively again.

Mike Dottenberry turned to one of the men and said: "Last week you mentioned your gayness, Odo. I want to thank you for that."

The tall spare entirely bald man whom Dottenberry was addressing bowed slightly from the waist and flushed with pleasure.

"Well, thank *you*," he said. "It's liberating to have that honored."

"You're welcome," said Dottenberry. "But really, thank you, I do honor it."

"Thank *you*."

"And I think for us as men, it's important to celebrate it, even. So thanks for that."

"Thank you."

"No, no, Odo, thank *you*."

"Well, thank you," said Odo.

It went on like that for almost two hours. Two men asked that their gayness be acknowledged; and Dottenberry honored and celebrated their gayness. One man talked for almost twenty minutes about his father, moving ever closer to tears and wound up banging his fist impotently against his thigh. The man next to him turned to embrace him and the two of them began blubbering together. Another man confessed to difficulty in processing through his anger.

"It comes over me," he said, mystified that such a thing could happen, "and then I just let go and haul off."

"Sometimes you gotta do what you gotta do," said one of the men, still squatting at the edge of the semicircle. "She pushes you too hard, you gotta push back."

Dottenberry honored that, too.

When the NOMAS meeting was over, Dottenberry introduced me to Odo Omo. He looked at me with sharp glittering eyes.

"I'm gay," he said abruptly.

I nodded. "I heard."

"I can't dialogue with anyone who's homophobic," he said. "I want to know whether you honor my gayness."

"It's wonderful. There's only seroconversion and taxes standing between you and paradise."

"Taxes don't count," he said. "I don't pay them."

Omo wiped his glistening bald head with the towel that he had looped around his belt.

"Go up to the house," he said, motioning toward the hill.

He turned awkwardly to embrace Mike Dottenberry, who patted him on the shoulder. Then Dottenberry and the rest of the men in the NOMAS group trudged back down toward their cars; Omo and I took the scuffed dirt road in the other direction. Omo walked with a tall man's loping stride; I was panting to keep up.

The road ascended through the hot open meadow, the tall grass green but already drying in the bright sun, and then entered a stand of California oaks which gave way after a few hundred yards to redwoods. It must have been ten degrees cooler with the trees shading us.

Omo kept walking steadily. After another quarter mile or so, the grove gave way to an open field, this one with a view backward over all the Bay and the golden hills on the far side of the water. Omo's house was on top of a rise.

It was a modest weathered two-story structure which had been allowed to fade in the sunlight so that it had taken on a dun color; it looked somber and elegant and lonely on the rise in the meadow. It was a house, I realized, that could be reached only on foot. Not even a jeep could have followed the twisting footpath up the hill.

Omo banged on the door with his fist and shouted. "I'm home," and opened the door.

Inside, the house was dark and cool; it took a moment for my eyes to adjust. The place had the look of any place lived in by men without women. It was neat enough. A sectional sofa covered in some brown fabric ran against two walls, bending itself in a ninety degree angle. A couple of canvas-backed chairs faced the windows. But the house had an odd and temporary feeling, a kind of distress. I recognized it right away; it was the feeling I always got in my own apartment.

A blond young man of about twenty-five entered the room from the patio in the back. He was dressed in cowboy boots, tight black leather pants, and one of those corny fringed buckskin tops that lace up in the front with rawhide thongs, leaving the chest exposed. He had an ornate pistol belt and holster draped around his narrow hips; there was a pearl handled revolver in the holster.

Omo walked directly up to him and kissed him ostentatiously on the lips.

"Aaron," he said, "this is Skipper. Handles security for me."

"That's not all I handle," said Skipper, smirking.

Omo reddened slightly. He walked stiffly back toward the stairs and said: "I'm going to wash up. Lunch in five minutes. Skipper'll get you a drink, if you want."

Skipper walked around me. "Why am I getting *such* bad vibes?" he said.

I sat myself down on the brown sectional sofa and looked out over the Peninsula, brown in the hazy air below the house.

"Could be because I don't like you," I said.

Skipper stood in the center of the Navajo rug, his hands resting casually on his hips.

"Aren't we being bitchy today," he said. "Must be PMS."

Omo clattered down the stairs; he had changed to shorts that revealed his knobby knees and hairless legs, and a running shirt inscribed with the legend Year of the Queer.

"Let's eat," he said with satisfaction.

The table on the flagstone patio had already been set with rustic copper colored stoneware and pitchers of water, milk and something that looked like sangria.

Omo sat himself down and promptly tore off a hunk of bread.

"Sit," he said. "No invitation."

Another young man emerged from the side door to the house carrying a stainless steel platter. There was fried chicken on the platter, corn on the cob, and a plate of green beans.

The young man put the platter down on the serving cart by the table. He was dressed entirely in cut-off shorts; his belt buckle said Boy Toy. He had the same wiry muscular physique as Skipper.

"Aaron Asherfeld," said Omo, his mouth full, "Ralph here does cooking, helps Skipper with security."

I half-stood up to shake hands.

Ralph said: "We're here, we're queer, get used to it."

"How long it take to train him to say that?" I asked. "Week or so?"

"You'd be surprised," said Omo.

"Don't make me angry," said Skipper petulantly. "I have a very unreliable temper."

"What do you do when you get angry, Skip? Run your fist through a glory hole?"

"All right," said Omo authoritatively, "knock it off."

I sat down again. Omo heaped his plate up with enough food to stun an ox. I noticed for the first time that he had a large tattoo covering the back of his hand. It showed a Chinese dragon with two heads, both breathing fire. The thing was constructed so that the tongues of flame flicked over Omo's knuckles. Skipper took no food. I took a couple of pieces of fried chicken; I figured the boiling oil would have been enough to kill any bugs.

We ate in silence.

After lunch, Omo leaned back. He said to Skip and Ralph: "You two boys run along now."

Skip and Ralph obligingly rose from the table and retreated to the house.

Omo lit a cigarette, took a deep wheezing drag, coughed wetly, and then said: "Alright, Asherfeld, why're you sticking your nose into my business?"

The change that had overcome him was remarkable; he seemed lean and focussed and tough.

"My wife send you?"

"Your wife?" I was flabbergasted.

"I love and honor Marianne," he said, "but I'm not going to let that bitch tell me how to live."

I chuckled in the warm sunlight and shook my head.

"I'll honor that," I said, lifting my glass.

"I'll tell you something else I'm not going to allow."

"What's that?"

"I'm not going to allow any prune faced son of a bitch come up here and screw me over. My security people tell me you're wandering around my property. Nature Conservancy ask you to stick your head up my butt, that it? Want to know if I'm planning to put up condos on my own property?"

"You got it wrong, Omo. I think condos be a tremendous improvement. All this open land's an eyesore. On the other hand, it's kind of curious that you'd be letting other people use your property."

"Meaning what?"

"Meaning how come Violet gets to live in a swell coach house? Meaning how come you've got people shacked out on the hillside reading newspapers that sell only in Hong Kong?"

"I don't have to answer those questions, Asherfeld."

"You don't have to give *me* the answers, Omo. You're going to have to answer the questions sooner or later. You know that."

Omo looked levelly at me, staring through the curled smoke of his cigarette.

"Asherfeld, you see this house? No road goes up here. Means that I had to have every piece of timber in the goddamn place hauled in on someone's back. Cost me big bucks. More than you're likely to see in a lifetime. You really think anyone's going to make me answer any questions I don't feel like answering?"

I waited before saying anything.

Finally I said: "Probably not." It was what Omo wanted to hear; and it was the truth.

After a while I got up to leave. The heat on the hillside had become intense. Violet's VW was still parked in front of her house. There was no one at the security gate.

Tuna Fish

IT WAS A TERRIFIC DAY for a lot of things. It was a terrific day to get a refund check from the IRS and it was a terrific day to have a big lunch with a bottle of wine and then sleep it off in a hammock in a garden and it was a terrific day to meet a blonde with large lavender eyes who would say things like *you are so cute when you crinkle up your nose like that.*

I thought of going over to my office in the Sunset, but the more I thought about it the more it just seemed like some place to go. I didn't much want to go down to the university; and I didn't much want to sit at my desk and do any of the work that I might have done.

So instead of doing anything useful, I dug out an old pair of shoes from my closet, dumped them in a paper bag, and headed off for the Italian shoemaker on Columbus.

Outside, the air was bright and the light hard-edged and glinting, the young mothers wheeling their babies down to St. Mary's park, the old neighborhood codgers shuffling down the street, or just sitting on their stoops, running their fingers over their leathery chins.

I walked up to Columbus with that fantastic high morning light falling from the air all around me, looking at the little gardens on the way, and the vacant lots overgrown with dwarf trees and dark green ferns, and the strange little alleyways that straggle off from the street, back beyond two-story wooden houses with flower boxes on their sills and pentatonic wind chimes. I could smell the deep roasted smell of coffee on the street and the dark chewy smell of fresh bread from the Italian bakeries. There may be better places to be alive than San Francisco on a spring morning. I didn't know about them and wasn't about to learn.

The Italian shoemaker on Columbus turned my shoes over dolefully in his hand. He palpated the upper leather of one shoe professionally and tapped at its heel; then he poked his finger through the thin leather of the sole.

"Gonna cos you forty dollars fix these shoes," he said. "Fifty, I put on a full uppers."

"Fifty dollars! For heels and soles?"

The shoemaker shrugged.

"Is up to you," he said, turning back to his lathe; the cupboard above his head was filled with shoes.

I walked down Columbus toward Broadway with my shoes under my arm. At the Wells Fargo ATM, a tense looking beggar dressed in a windbreaker and a stocking cap was peddling the newspaper that the homeless peddle. He wasn't saying anything, just leaning into the passersby with his bundle of newspapers.

"Say, man," I said. "Use a pair of shoes?" I withdrew my scuffed brogues from the paper bag.

The beggar looked at the shoes briefly and said: "Do I look like a beggar to you?"

"Sure you do."

"That's your hang-up," said the beggar decisively, turning himself to thrust his pile of papers into the pedestrian stream.

I figured me and the shoes were meant for one another.

I cut over to Montgomery and sat myself down at one of the outside tables at the Café Maudit. The food isn't much at the Maudit and neither is the coffee, but they put real chairs outside, not the plastic ones that feel as if they are going to collapse when you sit on them, and the street faces the park. On warm days, it's pleasant just to sit there and watch the young girls throw frisbees to their panting golden dogs.

I ordered coffee and a tuna sandwich on a croissant from the pretty young waitress. The owner of the café, a morose Lebanese, had a reputation in the city for hiring good-looking young women without asking too many questions about their green cards. The pretty young woman stayed just long enough to hook up with a rock guitarist or a drug dealer or a yuppie lawyer; just as you got used to someone with a Danish accent, her replacement asked for your order in Portuguese accented English, a film of moisture on her barely moustachioed upper lip.

I sat there in the yellow sunshine and watched someone maneuver a large Cadillac from a small space by the curb; the instant the Cadillac had cleared the car in front of it, a fire red Porsche slipped into the spot.

Two men got out of the car. They had the heavy solid dense look of men who had been power lifting for a long time; you wouldn't expect to see them on a Stairmaster. Both had bunched shoulders and massive pectoral muscles and narrow waists. They both wore earrings.

They walked directly to my table, pulled two chairs from the table next to mine, and sat down.

"Aaron," said the first man, speaking as if he knew me. "I'm Paul."

The other man said: "Bruce."

I said: "So?"

Paul reached over to take my table knife from its setting and began ostentatiously to clean his nails with its tip.

"You know what, Aaron?" he said, "I peg you as a very hostile person. I'm telling you this for your own good. You've got to let go of that anger."

"Why should I?"

"You don't want to know, Aaron. You're better off."

"Much better," said Bruce.

"That's what one of my wives used to say, she came home late."

"See, there you go."

"I got rid of her, along with the house."

"No reason to be defensive, Aaron," said Paul. "Did you know that research shows that hostility is one of the co-factors in the development of heart disease?"

"That's what they said about cigarettes."

Bruce inclined his head fractionally toward me and said: "It's true about cigarettes. Everyone knows that."

I nodded *my* head toward Paul: "This guy able to tie his own shoelaces or do you have to do that thing with the train?"

I stabbed at the air with my fingers.

"The choo-choo train goes through the tunnel and over the hill?"

Bruce flushed deeply; he knew I was making fun of him. He had at least that much on the ball.

"Aaron," said Paul, "you know the book, *When Bad Things Happen To Good People?*"

One of my clients had given it to me on the occasion of a drop in the market.

Paul didn't wait for an answer.

"You're in danger of being one of those good people to whom bad things happen, Aaron," he said.

"You're telling me. I've got three ex-wives keep asking me for money, I get sinus headaches in the morning, I've got a pair of shoes here I can't give away, and now I got you two guys sitting here and breathing the same air I'm breathing."

I sighed a deep heavy sigh.

Just then, the pretty young waitress came back; I could tell that she found the presence of two more people disorganizing. She frowned and started flipping through her order pad.

"Are you going to have lunch, too?" she said to Bruce and Paul; she seemed dismayed by the prospect.

"Just a Calistoga with a twist of lime," said Bruce.

"The same," said Paul, continuing to pick at his nails.

"Separate checks," I said.

"There you go, again, Aaron," said Bruce, when the waitress left. "That's the anger in you taking over."

"It could just be the sight of you picking your nails with my breadknife that does it."

Bruce turned to look at Paul and frowned fastidiously.

Paul put the breadknife down and said: "I know what you're thinking, Aaron."

"He's psychic that way," said Bruce.

"You're thinking where there's smoke, there's fire. You're absolutely right. The person we work for, he *does* have something to hide. He wants to hide it from you and from everybody else. So I'll make it real simple for you, Aaron. Stay away from other people's private property."

"Or what?"

"See, that's your anger talking again, not your head. Let me ask you something. Do you know what we do for a living, Aaron?"

"Frosting? Am I right? The minute you walked over I said to myself, these guys are into frosting."

"We hurt people, Aaron," said Paul. "We generally start with their fingers. Isn't that right, Bruce?"

"Absolutely right."

"We break someone's fingers, they look like chicken bones sticking out from their hands. People scream when we do that."

"Sure," I said. "Ruins their nail polish."

A wave of rosiness flushed over Paul's massive neck and face; he was getting tired of the pose.

Our waitress came over with two Calistogas and set them down.

"Tuna be right up," she said.

"Asherfeld," said Paul softly, "there's going to come a time when being clever isn't going to do you any good."

"No good at all," said Bruce loyally.

"It stopped doing me any good a long time ago," I said. "Now why don't you go away? I got the message. Guy you work for likes his privacy."

The waitress came over and deposited my tuna sandwich in front of me; it was one of those overstuffed numbers, with the tuna leaking from the croissant.

"We'll be going in a minute, Aaron," said Paul.

He stood up heavily from the table, his huge chest rippling. Bruce clambered to his feet directly. Paul reached over and then deliberately poured his Calistoga over my tuna sandwich, the water fizzing on the croissant.

"Shame about the croissant," said Paul. "But look on the bright side, Aaron. You get to pick up the tab for our Calistogas. That way you can start dealing with your anger right away."

I sat myself down at my desk later that afternoon and tried to make a sketch of the tattoo on Odo Omo's hand. The thing was harder than it looked. I could get the two heads down on paper all right, but I had no idea how to impart that peculiar Chinesey look to the dragons and the proportions came out all wrong so that the tongue of flame on Omo's hand looked curiously like a bent pencil. Still, I figured that someone who knew tattoos would know what I had in mind.

I didn't know where to go to get a tattoo and the San Francisco yellow pages didn't tell me a whole lot more. There was a place on Broadway that called itself The Stencil and another place on Mission near Fifth called Hard Marks.

I had the afternoon to fill and nothing to fill it with, so I pulled on my blue windbreaker and clattered downstairs, the double-headed dragon in the pocket of my khaki shirt. I thought I'd hike over the side of Telegraph Hill and down to Broadway.

There are some things that absolutely nothing can ruin, and the walk up to Coit Tower is one of them. The neighborhood used to be almost entirely Italian; in the last ten years or so, the Chinese have moved in, hanging their laundry from lines strung between the little alleys, their small neat dark-eyed children playing solemnly in the street. They give the neighborhood an austere distant feeling, a sense of possession.

I walked uphill, the wind at my back, past the only apartment building on the upper slope of Telegraph Hill, an elegant white job, with balconies and a lot of fancy art deco plaster work, and a beautiful old-fashioned green glass door. It's a terrific apartment building; it was built in the days when everyone knew how to build terrific things. It's the kind of building you'd want to park your dark-eyed mistress in if you had a dark-eyed mistress. Me, I just liked walking past it.

I climbed over the top of Telegraph Hill and down the worn steps that meandered around its eastern flank; I could smell the star jasmine climbing up the garden walls and the rosebushes releasing all that perfume into the windy air. Telegraph Hill was still the sort of place that reminded you of what things were like before they got bad.

The Stencil was on the corner of Broadway and Montgomery, next to a rock club catering to sullen kids from Concord or Lafayette. The Stencil's window was full of exotic tattoos, mounted on translucent paper for display. There were fantastic sunbursts, and women with outrageous bosoms, and knives that looked like scorpions. A sign said We do Whole Body Work.

I walked in and jangled a doorbell; the place was dark, with dark curtains on the windows and a mirrored table against one wall. In a moment someone slipped through the black bead curtains that separated the store from whatever was in the back. He was a thin man of about forty, with dark slicked back hair. He was wearing a white shirt, open at the throat, with the sleeves cuffed back. Almost every inch of his torso was covered with blue ink. He nodded severely at me; he was carrying a tattoo needle in his hand.

"What can I do you for?" he asked in the pleasant neutral voice of a busy man.

"I'm interested in a tattoo."

The thin man motioned to his store with his tattoo needle.

"This look like a fish market?" he asked.

I smiled. "No, it doesn't. The thing is, I was wondering if you do custom work?"

"All my work's custom."

I took out the sketch I had made and smoothed it on the table top by the mirror.

"You tell me anything about this design?"

The thin man took a perfunctory look at the sketch.

"You mean aside from the fact that whoever drew this can't draw?"

"Aside from that."

"Strictly Mickey Mouse."

"Aside from that, too."

"Where were you fixing to put it?"

I pointed to the space between my knuckles.

"Nice spot. You'd be better off with a tiger, though," said the thin man. "I can do you two colors, have just the head and paws coming through your knuckles. A lot of class. This kind of stuff, be an embarrassment to you, embarrassment to me."

"You're probably right," I said. "I was just wondering if you've ever seen anything like it before."

From the back someone shouted: "Lennie, can we *please* get on with it, *please?*"

Lennie shrugged and shouted right back: "Coming, coming."

He looked at the dragon again and shook his head decisively.

"Like I say, I do only custom work. This isn't mine."

I walked back out onto Broadway and folded my sketch back up. Fifth and Mission was a hike from Broadway; I decided it was a hiking sort of day.

I took Montgomery down into the financial district, the tall massive skyscrapers blocking the view and the light at every turn. Everyone said that putting up skyscrapers in downtown San Francisco would ruin the place and everyone was right. Then I walked down Market and over to Fifth. The city had spent millions trying to make Market Street look like a Parisian boulevard. The place still looked like a third-world slum, winos sleeping it off in the vestibules of banks and homeless nuts pushing shopping carts in the street itself, shouting to the wind.

Hard Marks was the sort of place you went to if you were blind drunk at three in the afternoon and thought it might be a great idea to nail a picture of Rita Hayworth to your biceps. The sign above the door said TATTOOS, but the store did double duty as a pawn shop: there was an assortment of small pistols in the window, with price tags affixed to their triggers, a couple of handcuffs, and a few musical instruments—an electric guitar, a pair of bugles keeping one another company, a melancholy clarinet, its fish pads scaling in the sunlight, and a harmonica with an elaborate headset meant for morons who want to play the harmonica and keep their hands free for strumming a guitar.

The proprietor was taking his leisure in front of a portable television set. He was an evil looking man of more than sixty, with enormous hairs curling out of his nose and ears, and an air of indescribable filth.

He was watching a soap opera on the little television; he held up his hand to shush me and said: "Be over in a second."

I waited patiently for whatever was happening on "All My Children" to finish happening.

"See," he said at the fade-out, "there was this colored fella gonna make a play for Allison."

I nodded and said: "Terrible thing."

"Used to think so, used to hate the Jews, before that the Italians, then I got to hating the colored, now it's mainly the queers. Had one of them come in here other day, ask if I could put a tattoo name of some other queer right where the sun don't shine. Said he wanted it to be a surprise. Don't that beat all!"

"You do it?"

"Course not. Tattoos for men."

"You're right," I said. "I forgot."

He turned his large tubby torso away from the television and leaned his elbows congenially on the counter top.

"Now you, you're a fella needs something with a little snap on his biceps, am I right? I can put Rita Hayworth on your arm in about an hour. Cost you two and a quarter in blue, three in blue and black. Do three colors you want, but first I gotta mix the ink up."

I put my picture on the table.

"What about this?" I asked. "Back of my hand, between the knuckles?"

The man looked at the dragons closely; I thought his eyes might have widened.

Finally he said: "Can't help you."

"Why not?"

"You know what them there dragons is?" he asked with a sly note in his voice.

"No. I don't. That's why I'm here."

"Didn't figure you did," he said. "Didn't figure you knew squat about what you was talking about, you pardon my French. That there's a tong mark. One of them chop suey gangs puts it on. It's not even a tattoo. Goes on with a heated stencil, like in that television series about the kung fu guy he has to lift some big bowl?"

He was talking about David Carradine.

"Tong mark? In 1994?" I was incredulous.

"Sure," said the fat man. "You got your basic chop suey gangs right here in the city, you got your gangs coming over from Hong Gong. You got your slope gangs from Saigon. Like I say, this here's strictly chop suey. San Francisco and Hong Gong. Them Hong Gongers they figure better the US of A than them communists. You know what I mean? So they come over here, same old same old."

I nodded slowly and then said: "You're sure about this?"

"Sure I'm sure. I couldn't put that on even if I wanted to. Word gets out on the street I'm doing tong marks, next thing you know them slopes be serving me as sweet and sour pork some restaurant out in the Mission. That's why I never eat Chinese. Can't tell what's in it. Cook doesn't like his brother-in-law, *whap!* next thing you know brother-in-law's on the menu. Am I right? You want to eat, eat American. Now you gonna go with Rita or what? Reason I ask, I got "The Young And The Restless" coming on in a couple of minutes."

I said I'd pass.

The Furies Gather

THE DEAN was on the telephone to me at seven fifteen the next morning.

"Asherfeld," he said, "glad I got you."

I sat up and rubbed my eyes and looked at my bedside clock.

"Not much chance you'd miss me at seven in the morning."

"That's why I called early," he said. "Can you make a ten o'clock?"

I said sure thing and hung up the telephone and rolled over and tried to get back into the dream I had just left. It didn't do any good; it never does. I got out of bed and padded into the bathroom. My face felt puffy and my fingers were stiff. I took a long hot shower and then a short cold shower.

I had coffee and a donut sitting at the kitchen counter; I watched Max for a few minutes. He was doing pushups with his blonde assistant sitting on his back. It seemed a waste of a good blonde, but then again, there weren't *any* blondes willing to sit on *my* back while I did pushups, so who was I to criticize?

After a while I took my coffee over to the living room window and looked out over the bay. When I first came to California I had met a tax assessor named Alanbogen at a party on Potrero Hill. He pointed out toward the bay with his drink and said: "Sometimes I can feel the water calling my name."

His wife left him for another man later that year. Alanbogen called me from a pay phone in Golden Gate Park. "I'm going to jump," he said defiantly.

"It's the right thing," I said.

Alanbogen hung up, walked from the park to the bridge, and jumped. One man out of a hundred survived the drop; Alanbogen not only survived the drop in robust good health—he was able to swim to the shore by himself. The newspapers ran pictures of him clambering sheepishly up the little beach by the base of the bridge. From time to time I see him around. He never talks about jumping anymore. I don't know if the water is still calling his name.

I got to the dean's office at a little after ten. The dean himself bounded out of his office when I knocked. He had his jacket on; he was clutching a leather briefcase. He looked ample and rumpled and sweaty.

"Come on, Asherfeld," he said. "Meeting's in the president's office."

The dean turned me at the elbow and propelled me back out

of the office. He pointed across the quadrangle, just filling up with sunlight and students. "We'll cut over."

He began walking very briskly, breathing with the peculiar jerkiness of men who never take exercise.

"Thing with Montague's totally out of control," he said. "President's livid."

He didn't say anything else until we reached the other side of the quadrangle.

The meeting was actually scheduled for the president's conference room and not his personal office. The dean opened the heavy walnut door to the president's suite slowly and let me walk ahead of him; he elbow-guided me down a darkened carpeted hallway and across another hallway. The conference room was at the end of the second hallway.

The dean punched an access code into the computer lock by the door and the door swung open silently, turning on the recessed overhead lights inside automatically.

It was one of those rooms that are designed to wow whoever is sitting in it; the Joint Chiefs of Staff would have been impressed. The great elliptical conference table, a gigantic vase of elaborate artificial flowers at its center, had been polished with enough elbow grease to light up a small city. The chairs around the table were reclining jobs with chrome arms and deep red plush pads. There was a kind of kit on the table in front of each chair, with a pad of expensive looking paper, a nifty German fountain pen, and an exotic Hewlett-Packard calculator. Just beneath the lip of the table was a slide-out ledge with a portable computer lodged on it—one for every chair.

It was a terrific room for anything but work.

The dean bustled around the table and sat himself down at the far end in front of a control panel that looked like it might have come from a Boeing 747. He spread his papers on the polished wood in front of him; I sat at the other end of the table and played with the German fountain pen.

After a little while, the door swung open again and a small man rolled into the room in a wheelchair. He had a thin pained face and a wasted torso with a little pot belly.

The dean stood up and walked over to the door and shook hands with him gratefully. "Molé," he said. "Hell of a thing."

The man in the wheelchair said: "Now, now, let's not cross our bridges before we come to them," in a calm, authoritative voice.

The dean nodded, standing awkwardly by the wheelchair.

"Aaron Asherfeld," he said, "Molé Anbisol, special counsel to the president."

Molé Anbisol nodded precisely toward me; there was something spiderish about his movements and his manner. He rolled himself to the far side of the elliptical table and cocked his head; the dean returned to his seat.

One of the three lights above the door glowed red.

"The president is on his way," said Anbisol.

The conference door again opened noiselessly and the president of the university poked his head into the room. I recognized him from television news shows that had shown him sweating before various congressional committees. He had a trim, absolutely uninflected face. He was wearing gold aviator glasses.

"Mr. President," said Anbisol reverently.

"Molé," said the president.

He nodded quickly toward the dean and then toward me.

"Nice to see you again," he said to me with a sudden toothy smile.

Then he said: "I want to be deniable on this, Molé." He was still standing half in and half out of the conference room.

"Of course, sir," said Anbisol.

"Don't leave me standing out there my dick in the wind."

"No, sir," said Anbisol. "I won't let that happen."

The president said: "Good, good," and nodded again to the three of us; then he withdrew his head from the room, the door closing silently behind him.

The dean let out a great wheeze; I realized that he had been holding his breath.

"Asherfeld," he said, "you coming up with anything on your end?"

"Can you get the board down?" I asked the dean.

"Sure thing," he said, fumbling with the panels at his desk. A gleaming green chalkboard descended quietly from the ceiling.

I got up from my chair and stood before the board, feeling professorial.

"Montague discovered a wonderful scheme," I said. "He used federal research money to set up a dummy corporation.

I wrote CSR on the board, using the fat yellow chalk from the chalkboard's metal tray.

"And he used affirmative action to make the thing disappear."

I wiped the letters CSR from the board with the back of my hand.

"How did he accomplish this?" asked Molé Anbisol.

"It wasn't hard. I'm guessing he had his graduate student, kid named UB Goode, go over to contract compliance and swear he was Montague."

"Go on," said the dean grimly.

"There's not much more," I said.

I told Molé Anbisol and the dean about Violet and the coach house and Dottenberry and my visit to Odo Omo's ranch; I didn't mention his friends. I figured that that was his business.

"This Odo Omo is a man who likes his privacy," I said.

"Not a crime, Asherfeld," said the dean.

"No," I said. "It's not a crime."

And I told them about the thugs who had tracked me down in the city.

The dean waved his hand impatiently when I finished.

"Doesn't mean a thing," he said.

"You're probably right," I said. Then I added: "I'm pretty sure that Montague wasn't in on CSR alone."

"Why is that, Asherfeld?" asked Molé Anbisol.

"I don't think he had the nerve," I said carefully. "I don't think he had the nerve to do something like that alone."

"Any idea who else'd be involved in this?" asked the dean.

I stood there, holding the fat yellow chalk between my fingers; someone had swaddled the thing with a soft chamois cap, so that no one's precious fingers would be contaminated by chalk dust.

"Not yet," I said. "Montague, Dottenberry and Bulton Limbish used to ride together, kind of a club, playing at being tough."

The dean nodded indifferently. "What about the other stuff, Asherfeld?" he asked, his face reddening.

I spread my hands apart at the board.

"Lots of rumors on campus," I said delicately.

Molé Anbisol said: "I'm concerned to keep the president deniable, gentlemen. So far, I've heard nothing that worries me excessively."

"Molé, you haven't heard the latest," said the dean.

"Now, now," said Anbisol. "It couldn't be as bad as all that."

"We're being blackmailed," said the dean explosively. "There are these guys out there want more than half a million dollars from us."

"Probably a parent," I said. "Just got his tuition bill."

Molé Anbisol snickered gently. "How did you come by this demand?" he asked.

The dean bent over to withdraw a miniature tape deck from the tattered leather briefcase he had placed between his feet; he fussed with the thing for a moment so that it was evenly aligned with the edges of the desk.

"Listen to this," he said. "Came yesterday morning."

The cheap tape deck hissed momentarily and then an odd metallic voice began speaking: "Pay attention," the bizarre voice said, "this is not a joke."

The tape hissed; the voice continued: "If we do not receive five hundred thousand dollars, videotapes of Richard Montague's final moments will be made available to selected news media. Do not do anything foolish. Otherwise . . ."

The voice became unintelligible. The dean switched off the tape deck.

"That could mean anything," Anbisol observed.

"What I thought too, Molé," said the dean. "Today I get a telephone call, I'm telling you these guys are serious."

I said: "Same strange voice?"

"What's it mean?"

"Whoever's talking to you used a security scrambler. Makes the voice untraceable. It doesn't matter. Wha'd they say?"

"They said they have a video of Montague's death. They said it's not the sort of thing the university would be proud of."

"Meaning precisely what?" asked Anbisol.

"They're probably suggesting," I said, "that Montague died in some sort of S&M ritual went a little too far."

"Looks that way to me, Molé," said the dean. "Sort of thing gets out we're going to see the Fund Drive dry up so fast your head will spin."

"Look on the bright side," I said. "You can make the video the centerpiece of this new gay and lesbian studies program."

The dean frowned deeply and was about to say something censorious when Molé Anbisol snickered again. Then he said: "What do *you* think, Mr. Asherfeld?"

I thought things over for a moment; then I said: "I don't think someone's putting the arm on the university, Anbisol."

The dean sputtered: "What're you talking about, Asherfeld? I'm telling you, these guys are threatening to blow us out of the water with this thing."

"You're probably right about that part of it," I said. "On the other hand, CSR could have run up some real debts that Montague didn't cover. I think someone's out there trying to collect. They're using whatever leverage they've got. I don't think they've got much."

"Why is that, Mr. Asherfeld?" said Molé Anbisol in his seductive soft way.

"They're asking you to take too much on faith. If they had an embarrassing video, why didn't they send a copy? I think you ignore them, they'll go away."

"I'm inclined to agree with you," said Molé Anbisol.

The dean looked tense and fretful, but he didn't say anything more.

The Worker's Fist

I HAD LUNCH at the student cafeteria that afternoon. The thing was housed inside the Union. I remembered student cafeterias as the sort of place where a woman who looked like Godzilla would heap a pile of fries on your plate along with a grey slab of something called Salisbury steak. If you were still hungry after that you got to order a slice of rubbery angel food cake with yellow frosting and sprinkles. *This* place was divided into ethnic counters. You could get tacos or rice and beans at one counter, and Chinese food at another. There was a stand selling soul food and a stand selling Vegen Only! One last stand identified itself as serving European cuisine—hamburgers, mostly, from what I could tell of the menu.

I got a burger and some fries and a coke. The radiant young woman at the cash register said: "I *knew* you'd be ordering European."

"Why's that?"

"You *look* European, you know, white and sort of middle-aged and all."

I took my European chow out to the terrace and ate about half of it; whoever had been busy in the kitchen hadn't quite gotten the hang of European cooking.

I wanted to catch up with Bulton Limbish; Violet had said that he could generally be found outside the bookstore.

It was just twelve o'clock when I left the cafeteria. The campus chimes began to chime. They stopped at six. I paused for a moment, waiting for the other six chimes. The tower stayed silent. No one seemed to notice.

Limbish was in front of the bookstore; he was manning a table covered with a white cloth. There was a large framed picture of a stout looking Stalin on the table and a pile of newspapers called *The Official International Journal of the Maoist International Movement*. The graphic legend on the upper-right corner of the paper showed a worker in black profile, a cloth cap on his head, his fist in the air. Next to the newspapers was a pile of books. The fattest book was called *Theories of Ideology*. It looked like must reading. The little book next to it was called *Always Historicise!* I figured it was kind of an after-dinner chaser. You knock back the fat book, you take the thin book to even out the flow. Limbish had a copy of the newspaper in his hand; every so often he would shout "Official Journal of the Maoist International Movement" to the empty space beyond his table. The walkway beyond his stand was thronged with students; no one paid him the slightest attention.

101

I took one of the newspapers and looked over the front page and looked sideways at Limbish. He was a compact, tense looking man, dressed in a work shirt, jeans, and heavy work boots. He had thick black hair and an enormous walrus moustache; his face had the kind of skin that suggests a layer of epidermal muscle running just beneath its surface.

The lead article in the newspaper was a complicated defense of Stalin and Mao; the only criticism it had to offer of Stalin's policies was that he hadn't killed enough people. Limbish gave me an irritated glance.

I nodded at the large framed picture of Stalin.

"Still a big man on campus?" I asked.

Limbish said: "Lot of bourgeois misconceptions about Stalin." He didn't seem too interested in getting into a discussion with me.

"Sure," I said tapping the newspaper, "it says so right here."

Limbish glared at me in a fierce short-sighted way. Finally he said: "What would you have done, fascists and Hitlerites on every side, class enemies at home?"

"Me? I'd have killed sixty million people, too. No question about it. Hell, I'm generally in favor of killing sixty million people even *without* fascists and Hitlerites on every side. Especially here in California. Think what 101 be like without sixty million class enemies. No lines Sunday morning for dim sum. Be great."

Limbish regarded me scornfully for a moment. Then he turned his head toward the campus and resumed his monotonous chant. I read a few more paragraphs of the article about Stalin and Mao. It seemed Mao had *also* made this terrific mistake in not knocking off a few hundred million more people. For a couple of shrewd operators, it turned out that Stalin and Mao were awfully tender-hearted guys.

After a while, I said: "Violet tells me that you and Richard Montague were pretty close, shared a lot of class interests and all."

That got his attention. Limbish lowered his arm and put his newspaper on the table and looked me full in the face. I could see that he was weighing his options; I could see that deliberating was not what Limbish did best.

"Who are you?" he finally asked.

"Aaron Asherfeld."

"You're the guy Donald Dindle said we didn't have to talk to."

"That must be me."

"I don't have to talk to you," said Limbish triumphantly.

"You're right. You don't have to say a word."

We stood there like that, two grown men glaring at each other in the brilliant spring sun.

I took a card from my wallet. "You get to feeling otherwise," I said, "give me a call."

"Why should I?" said Limbish truculently.

"Confession is good for the soul."

I tapped the pile of newspapers again.

"It says so right here," I said.

I left Limbish at the bookstore, still waving his newspaper in the air, still hawking to no one in particular, and walked back up toward the Union.

Ami Goode

I FINALLY CAUGHT UP WITH Carol-Lee on the telephone. I heard her come clattering down the stairs; she picked up the receiver breathlessly. She didn't seem terribly excited when I told her who I was and what I wanted.

"Mr. Asherfeld?" she said querulously. "Do I know you?"

"Probably. I'm on all the talk shows," I said.

"Oh, sure," she said vaguely. "Aren't you on David Letterman a lot?"

"We went to school together."

"You're putting me on."

"No really. City of Hope Community College. It's in Winnemucca."

"Is he really that cute in person? I think he's so cute."

"He's much cuter, Carol-Lee. I'd love to talk more. The thing is I really do need to track down UB. It's something I'm doing for NBC."

"Can you tell me about it? Please."

"I'm sorry, sweetheart, but no can do. It's all pretty hush-hush. I'll give you a hint though. David thinks he needs to build bridges to the Afro-American community. He's interested in talking with people I'm talking to. And I'd like to talk to UB."

"Oh, I'm so excited. He's probably either with his aunt or somewhere in the city and I know he's going to do a rave tonight in the Mission."

"His aunt?"

"She's over in the Marcus Garvey projects."

I said that that was terrific, and she said that that was so exciting, and I said I'll be in touch, and she said oh please tell me more and I said no can do sweetheart again.

It was like taking candy from a baby. I felt the way you generally do when you take candy from a baby.

I hung up the telephone and stared at my shoes for a while. Then I put on my blue windbreaker; I walked over to my living room window and looked down at the little garden below. No one ever planted anything there and no one ever looked after what was growing by itself. The garden was full of flowers anyway, and strange blooming vines, and tangled blackberry bushes, and pale green ferns that might have been at home in the Jurassic era.

I don't know what I expected to see down there; I kept looking anyway until I snapped out of it and hustled on out of my apartment.

I caught a taxi at the Columbus Avenue stand. My driver was a tough looking middle-aged woman with hard features and small determined eyes. She would have looked all right with a cigar.

I told her where I wanted to go. I wasn't any more worried about going into the Marcus Garvey projects than I would have been about spending the weekend sunbathing in Somalia. She turned the flag on the meter down slowly and eased into the stream of traffic.

"Taking a hell of chance going where you're going," she said forthrightly.

"What can I say?" I said. "He who dares wins."

She shifted her powerful torso in her seat and rotated her head to take a sharp look at me.

"Hey what?"

"He who dares wins. It's the motto of the Legion."

"What Legion you talking about?"

"Canadian Foreign Legion," I said. "I'm going over see my buddies. We fought together against the French in Quebec. Great group of monolinguals. Never forget them."

"*Canadian* Foreign Legion? You're shitting me, right? I mean I heard of the *French* Foreign Legion. I never heard of no *Canadian* Foreign Legion. You're going to Swaziland to score, am I right?"

I had gotten tired of the joke. I said: "You're right."

"Figured," she said dispiritedly. "I'll put you down at 16th and Guerrero, you get to the projects yourself." Then she muttered: "No such thing as *Canadian* Foreign Legion." The whole idea offended her beyond measure.

At 16th and Guerrero, Miss Charm accepted her tip without a word, but as I was getting out of the taxi she leaned over and said: "Take care of yourself now." When I slammed the door shut, she peeled off from the curb with a tremendous squeal of rubber.

I stood at the curb for a moment and tried to ease the stiffness in my lower back. Then I headed slowly down 16th, past the bookstores selling tantric literature, and past the coffee shops featuring cranberry muffins and herb teas, and past the check-cashing place at the corner of 16th and Valencia, with its angry scrawl of graffiti on the wall.

The girls in the street wore their hair in corkscrews or in cornrows; they had double nose rings through their nostrils and double or triple rings through their ears; they looked vaguely unclean, but they still looked young and their skin had that lustrous oiled shine that only young girls have; when it's gone it's gone forever.

The Marcus Garvey project is toward the end of Valencia, just before it meets Market. It comprises four concrete apartment blocks with concrete walkways connecting them. UB's aunt lived in the second block of the project. I had gotten her address from information.

I walked quickly across the concrete square.

The glass door leading to Block B was shattered, the door itself swinging on its broken hinges. It led onto a small mail vestibule. The corridor beyond was lit by a single bulb hanging from an electrical cord. I pushed the broken door open and walked into the vestibule. The place smelled of urine and onions. The mailboxes looked as if they were made of titanium and designed to withstand a nuclear blast. I checked the names on the boxes. They had all been scratched out.

I was almost ready to give up and look for a telephone when two large black men entered the vestibule. One stood leaning against the door; he looked like a Fire Plug. The other positioned himself at the entrance of the stairwell; he looked like a Tree Trunk. They looked as tough as an SS squad and a lot meaner. I didn't think they were there selling encyclopedias.

"Yo," said Fire Plug. "What you want?"

"I'm looking for Mrs. Ami Goode?"

"What for?" said Tree Trunk.

"Spike sent me."

"Spike?"

"Spike Lee," I said impatiently. "You seen Malcolm?"

"Sure I seen Malcolm," said Fire Plug irritably. "Spike, what he want wid'choo?"

"He's doing a new movie. Story about black cross-dressers. Figured this be a good place to start."

"How come Spike he sending you over here?" asked Tree Trunk. "You a white man."

"You know what Malcolm said: 'By any means necessary.' "

Tree Trunk shifted his torso and looked at Fire Plug.

I figured I was ten seconds away from getting mugged and then beaten into jelly.

From outside the shattered glass of the door I could see a large stately woman moving down the concrete walkway toward the vestibule.

She came into the dingy vestibule like an ocean liner. She gave Fire Plug and Tree Trunk a single peremptory look.

"What you two no account hoodlums doing here?" she asked.

Fire Plug said: "Nothing. We doing nothing."

"Then do your nothing someplace else."

Fire Plug and Tree Trunk shrank simultaneously and slunk out of the vestibule without another word.

"I'll ask you the same question. What you doing here? You looking for the crack cocaine, you in the wrong place."

I smiled as broadly as I could manage.

"Actually, I'm looking for Mrs. Ami Goode."

"Well, you found her. I still want to know what you want?"

I looked more closely at the woman. She was perhaps sixty; she was more massive than stout, with fine shoulders and an enormous bosom. She had a handsome well shaped head with short-cut grey hair.

"I'd like to talk to you about your nephew, if you have a moment, Mrs. Goode."

Ami Goode gave me a fixed stare that might have cut through steel.

"Is he dead?" she finally asked.

"No, no, no," I said quickly. "Nothing like that at all."

"What's he done, then? Tell me quick so as I know the worst."

"He's not dead. He's not hurt and he hasn't done anything, Mrs. Goode."

"He's still in trouble, though."

I hesitated a moment before answering.

I said: "I think he *may* be in trouble."

"I figured. Only time a white man comes around here either he wants to buy the crack cocaine or he wants to get some of the local pussy or he's got bad news in his back pocket and wants to hand some of it out to colored folk before it's all gone. You no different. You better come upstairs with me."

She turned from me and opened the heavy steel door that led from the vestibule into the apartment building itself. I leaned over to try to hold the door open.

"Do I look like I can't open a door?" she asked.

"I guess not."

"Then don't be trying to hold doors open for me. You want to work for me, I got an oven that needs cleaning."

The tiny elevator had walls faced in corrugated steel. The light fixtures in the ceiling were protected by steel mesh. The emergency button on the elevator panel was protected by a brass cage. A sign on the far wall said: *This is your building. Keep it clean. Building residents only. No loitering. No unauthorized access. No defecation in the hallways.*

We got off at the fifth floor; Ami Goode walked down the hall with a slow, massive deliberate step. I followed behind her. I didn't have anything to say and if I had anything to say I wouldn't have said it.

Her apartment was at the intersection of two halls.

She paused at the door to open what seemed to be a dozen locks. There was even a New York style police lock that was jammed into the floor and needed to be toggled from the outside to be released.

The apartment inside was clean and full of grey light from the windows that faced south over Daly City and west toward the ocean. The floors were polished oak with a herringbone pattern. The furniture was all heavy, solid, respectable stuff, with comfortable red pillows on the sofa, and easy chairs by the window that looked as if they had been designed for big men needing after-dinner naps. A fine old chestnut sideboard stood in the corner; there was expensive looking china mounted on its shelves. The plates had yellow floral patterns.

It would have been a terrific apartment if it had been located somewhere else.

Ami Goode hung up her coat and put her purse on a small mahogany table.

"You going to stand there like a flagpole or you going to sit down?" she said.

She sat herself on one of the easy chairs, putting her feet out in front of her and resting them on an ottoman. I sat on the sofa with the red pillows.

"Now why don't you just tell me what kind of trouble UB's in? Just spit it out."

I told her pretty much what I knew, which wasn't much, but she put the pieces together right away and sighed deeply.

"I guess that boy don't have a whole lot of sense."

"I guess not."

"So what you're telling me is that sooner or later the police they going to pin this Montague thing on UB."

I nodded.

"Sooner or later."

"Black man threatens to make a volcano erupt, volcano erupts somewhere next thing you know police are at his door asking him what he knows about lava."

"You think it's like that, do you?"

"What do *you* think?" she sneered.

"I think the police are like anyone else. Sometimes they're lazy and sometimes they're tired. But tell them you're going to kill someone, naturally they're going to pay some attention when he turns up dead."

"They wouldn't pay that sort of attention to a white man."

"That's a good reason for a black man to mind who he threatens, don't you think?"

"You disrespecting me now?"

I shook my head.

"You'd know it if I were."

Ami Goode settled back in her chair.

"Bad luck always followed that boy," she said. "You know his daddy was about the first man killed in Vietnam?"

"No, I didn't."

"In 1961, it was. Stepped on a land mine no more than ten minutes after he got off the plane took him there from San Francisco."

"Awful," I said.

"An *American* land mine."

"I see what you mean about bad luck. What about his mother?"

"Died giving birth to UB. No one left to raise him but me."

"How'd he get to the university?" I asked.

"You mean how'd a black man get to be some sort of graduate student at the university?"

"Sure. That's what I mean."

"He was always a smart boy. They took him in right out of Martin Luther King. That's the high school he went to. Gave him a scholarship and all on the affirmative action. Why? You got a problem with that?"

"Me? No problem. Why would I have a problem with affirmative action, seeing how it's worked out so well for UB?"

Ami Goode regarded me with her heavy, shrewd, tired and hooded eyes.

"Four hundred years we cleaning your toilets and sweeping your floors and raising up your children and once just *once* in four hundred years someone gives a black man an even chance get ahead and white folks they couldn't find a blessed thing to say for four hundred years are out there harrumping into the backs of their hand like a chorus of bullfrogs complaining that this it isn't fair and that it be giving the black man too many breaks and the other thing it screwing over some poor white man positively ain't got no opportunities in life unless they opportunities he takes out of a black man's behind. Don't you go talkin' to me about fairness."

It was a sad bitter speech. I had nothing to say that would have changed her mind. I stood up.

"What you going to do about UB?" Ami Goode demanded from her seat.

"Warn him," I said. "It's all I can do."

"Spring break, he plays at these raves they got," she said. "He'll be at some club over the Mission tonight. You'd best warn him sooner rather than later."

"I'll do that, Mrs. Goode."

I shuffled on my raincoat and walked over to the door with its collection of locks.

Ami Goode looked at me from her chair; she hadn't moved.

"I'd walk you down, only thing is I'm tired now," she said.

I smiled and said: "I don't need to be walked, Mrs. Goode. I'll be fine."

"Sure," she said. "White man, he walks on through the valley of the shadow of death, nothing happen to him. Black man walk through the same valley, he catch ten diseases, gets himself arrested just before he's about to help himself to some of that milk and honey."

I said: "You're probably right," and let myself out.

There was no one in the hall when I left the apartment, and no one in the elevator, and no one in the vestibule either.

Frat Rats

NOTHING MUCH HAPPENED and then some more of nothing happened too. I spent one afternoon sitting in Mike Dottenberry's office and another afternoon at Mick Shaugnessy's office in the Sunset, catching up on paperwork. I took a day off to get some work done for an English firm called Body Best. They put out a line of environmentally safe perfumes and toiletries; their claim to fame was that they never tested the goop on animals. You could go blind using their stuff and they'd never know. They wanted to open a chain of stores in San Francisco; they were worried about site selection. I told them they'd be in heaven anywhere in the city.

On Wednesday, I called the student newspaper from my apartment and had them run a small ad in their personal section. It was the soul of discretion; it said only that I would be willing to speak with anyone who knew Richard Montague. I had them run my home number and Dottenberry's office number.

I got down to the university later that morning and stopped in the Union for coffee and a cruller and a copy of the student newspaper. I took the styrofoam cup and my pastry out to the deck and sat in one of the iron chairs with my feet propped up on another. I sipped my coffee and ate the sweet waxy cruller and looked out over the campus in the pale early morning light.

Later that morning, someone named Dee Dee Frobenmyer called me at Dottenberry's office; he had a smooth, round, young plummy voice.

"There are some things I might be able to tell you about RM, sir," he said carefully, using Montague's initials.

"I'm all ears."

"Actually, it'd be easier if we could talk here, sir."

"Here?"

"At the house. The Alpha Tau Alpha house? On University. We'd be more comfortable and all."

I said that'd be fine and Dee Dee Frobenmyer said that'd be super, sir, but the only thing was there's like this demonstration outside the house and all, sir, and I said not to worry, I'd make my way in, and he said that'd be super, sir, again.

I left Mike Dottenberry's office at a little after noon, just as the quadrangle flooded with students; I thought briefly of walking all the way from the university over to Palo Alto, but then I remembered what a senior partner at one of the downtown law firms once said to me: "Anytime I think of walking instead of driving, Asherfeld, I say why the hell should I?"

I drove into Palo Alto and parked down from the fraternity house on Middlebury. It was the sort of golden afternoon that made you think of childhood bicycles with fat tires and popsicles and large panting dogs. The soft southern light was all around me and the air was already perfumed with the evening smell of star jasmine.

The Alpha Tau Alpha house was about the size of the White House; from the outside, it looked like it was in better condition. It took up the northwest section of the block at the corner of Middlebury and University. Frobenmyer was right about the demonstration. A parade of young women was marching in front of the well kept lawn. They were chanting "Hey hey, Ho ho, Heteropatriarchy has got to go," over and over again.

I stood on the west side of the street and watched them for a while. Two women had set up a table at the far end of the sidewalk, just before the street—Tiny Face and Miss Piggy. They were ubiquitous. The sign mounted on their table said PISSED OFF WOMEN. Someone had illustrated the sign with a large cartoon. It showed a muscular grim-faced woman delivering a blow to the solar plexus of a pudgy oaf wearing an Alpha Tau Alpha sweatshirt. POW! was bubbled alongside the woman's fist.

"Sounds pretty serious," I said. "What's it all about?"

"It's about ending the rapist mentality in this house," said Miss Piggy.

"It's about smashing heteropatriarchy on this campus," said Tiny Face.

"It's about time," I said.

I thought Miss Piggy might have nodded her head; it was hard to tell. She didn't have much neck.

I left the two of them, standing there by their table, and headed up the walkway to the large white doors of the fraternity house.

A small black man in a butler's uniform let me in. The house itself seemed to be vibrating to the thudding bass of a very powerful stereo system; I couldn't hear the music at all.

"Mr. Frobenmyer, he be down in the billiard room," said the butler, pointing vaguely toward the back of the house. "I'd take you down only I'm suppose stay by the door in case any of them women they try and bust in."

"You stay right there," I said. "That's where you're needed."

The fraternity house must have once been a stately and imposing mansion; the interior was still stately, but only insofar as it had good bones. The dark wooden floors were scuffed, the plaster was chipping on the cove ceilings, and no one had really polished the wooden mouldings on the walls in a long time.

The vestibule by the door emptied onto two large rooms separated by a little hallway. The room on the left contained an enormous stone fireplace; the room on the right a few disorganized couches and chairs arranged in a jumble, and an empty mahogany newspaper rack.

The thudding bass continued to thud.

I walked through the hallway and down the staircase that the butler had pointed to. When I came to the bottom, the boom of the bass had disappeared.

Dee Dee Frobenmyer was standing by an expensive pool table in the basement; I recognized him right away. He was the big-toothed kid who had been selling espresso by the Union.

He gave me one of his blazing smiles and shook my hand suavely.

"I'm really glad you could come, sir," he said. "Can I get you a drink? Beer? Wine cooler?"

I shook my head and rested my hip on the pool table edge and eased the small of my back. There wasn't much in the basement room except for the pool table; the walls held a series of framed pictures of naked women on crushed velvet—the sort of thing you see in Las Vegas hotel rooms.

"Lot of angry women out there," I said.

Frobenmyer rubbed a chalk square across the top of his cue; I could see that the thing was custom made.

"Angry isn't the word."

"What's got them in an uproar?"

Frobenmyer leaned over the table to line up a shot; there were only a few balls left. He ran the pool stick through his braced fingers a few times and then deftly sank one of the opalescent balls into the side pocket.

"Some of the brothers put out a little booklet," he said delicately, straightening up. "It's caused some controversy."

"What's it called, this book?"

"A Guide to the Women's Coalition for Change," he said, smirking.

"What you do, rank the women by butt size?"

"Sort of."

"That's very interesting, Dee Dee," I said. "But that's not why you called me."

A small sly smile played across Dee Dee's face; it was one of those startling smiles that looks as if it belongs on a much older man. He bent over to line up another shot. I reached over and put my hand on his cue as he was sliding it across the bridge of his hand.

"I'm not one of the brothers, sonny. You can play pool later."

Dee Dee snapped up immediately.

"You're right, sir," he said. "I'm sorry, sir, but actually you are sort of involved in this whole thing."

I folded my hands across my chest and slid them under my arms.

"How so?"

"This business with the WCC isn't all fun and games, sir, if you get my drift. They've filed a sexual harassment complaint with Dean Climax and all, claimed that we're in violation of the speech code."

"Hard to believe."

114

"Three violations and Alpha Tau Alpha goes on automatic suspension. My dad was Alpha Tau. He's going to kill me if he finds out we're on suspension."

"Tough break."

"We've already done Sensitivity twice."

"Sensitivity?"

"That's when you get together and sort of beat up on yourself for not being sensitive to other people's needs and all."

"I can see all that training really took."

"Yeah, well," said Frobenmyer, "but you can understand why I don't want this thing with the WCC to get out of hand."

"It's all very concerning, Dee Dee," I said, "probably keep me up nights, but I'm not exactly on campus to mediate fraternity disputes."

"I appreciate that, sir," he said. "But you *are* here to like sort out things about Richard Montague?"

I nodded.

Dee Dee stood his pool cue upright and held it close to his body.

"There was this graduate assistant he had, UB Goode. Tall spade. Strictly Aft arf."

"Arf arf?"

"Affirmative action."

"So?"

"Dude was dealing, man. I want to tell you that."

"Dealing what?"

"Pot, hash, mainly LSD."

"A lot of guys deal. Give me something I can use."

"He wasn't dealing with *his* money, sir. He wasn't that smart."

"How do you know this?"

"UB told us."

I must have looked at Dee Dee skeptically.

"I told you. Arf arf. The dude wasn't that smart."

I released my hands from underneath my arms and walked slowly around the pool table; I leaned over and patted one of the shiny balls to the opposite cushion with my fingertips. The ball made a pleasant thudding sound as it hit.

"What do you think I'm going to do with this information, Dee Dee?"

"Nothing, sir. I'm volunteering it. I think it's important that the university not be embarrassed any more than it has to be. I mean, this place has been caught with its pants down so many times it isn't even funny anymore. I mean, talk about stumble city. There was the speech code and putting all those third-world types in Core, that really ticked off the alumni. News that some professor's been bankrolling a campus laboratory, that would be terrible, sir. Probably be the straw that breaks the camel's back."

The small sly smile returned to Dee Dee's face. "It's the sort of thing that I think Dean Climax should know, don't you, sir? I definitely think it should be brought to her attention. She'd be pretty worried about the story getting out to the media. She really would."

"You want to blackmail her into going easy on the fraternity?"

"I didn't say that, sir."

"You didn't have to. What makes you think she's going to know the story came from you?"

"She's a bright woman, sir. It may not seem like it, but she is. She'll figure it out."

"Why should I say anything at all to Dean Climax?"

"Well, it's something you know now, sir. You can't unknow it. Sooner or later, you'll have to mention it. I don't think you have a lot of choice."

I reached over the table and flicked one of the billiard balls toward the side pocket.

"You're a little weasel, Dee Dee," I said.

"Oh, I know it, sir. Absolutely. You're entirely right, sir."

"What are you studying here?" I asked.

"Pre-law," said Dee Dee, giving me his large radiant smile. "I'm pre-law."

I don't know why I even asked.

I got back to Greenwich Street that evening at a little past five. The grey fog had already come in across the Golden Gate, covering the Bay. It had slipped up Columbus Avenue and was ascending the flank of Telegraph Hill. In an hour or so, the city would be shrouded and dark and cold. I always liked the fog; I always liked what it did.

I trudged up the wooden steps, smelling the deep splintery wooden smell of the hallway and the light tight smell of the clove cigarettes that the two Dutch sisters smoked. I had been in their apartment once in order to fix their clogged disposal. The air was absolutely rank with tobacco smoke. Both sisters were over eighty, grim women, with faces from which the spare flesh had long since been burned. They never left their apartment and they never opened their windows.

My mail was stacked neatly in front of my door; I kept the lights off inside my apartment and looked through the stack by the last of the day's grey fogged-in light. There wasn't much—a letter informing me that *Aaron Asherfeld* had won ten million dollars or one of five other valuable prizes; someone I had known in college had died of AIDS, and someone else had died in an automobile accident. One of my wives had opened a practice as a clairvoyant trance channeller and past lives regression counsellor. She was setting up shop in Marin. The picture accompanying her flyer showed her as she looked more than ten years ago. I thought of her sitting in the Marin sunshine, telling dopey women that once they had been mistress to the King of France.

I left my suit and shirt draped over the reclining chair by my desk and with the lights still out took a long hot shower and then a long cool shower.

Then I watched the news sitting in my leather easy chair with a towel wrapped around my waist and the grey fog behind my back.

The mayor was introducing his newest appointment to the world, someone named Betty Ann Bracken. He stood there beaming, a small shabby man in an ill-fitting suit. Betty Ann Bracken took the podium. "I am proud to be a lesbian," she said. The audience applauded. The camera panned to her lover, a tall woman, with close-cropped silver hair and a repulsive purple birthmark on her neck. Then it panned back to the mayor, who was looking off-camera to the side of the stage.

I got up from my chair when "Wheel Of Fortune" came on.

I was hungry in that vague way you get when you live alone, but I didn't want to sit in a restaurant by myself and I had nothing to eat at home. I hung up my suit instead and got myself dressed in chinos and a white shirt, the fog and damp making my back stiff. Then I stood by my living room window for a while. I couldn't see the Bay anymore, the fog was too thick; but I could hear the Bay's foghorns distinctly, and I could see the tangled blackberry vines in the garden below my window glistening in the wet evening air. When I first came to San Francisco, every foggy evening seemed to open up like a midnight rose; now they were all closed on themselves, those evenings, and belonged to other people. It didn't make the fog any less beautiful. Just different.

Carol-Lee had told me that UB Goode was playing at the D-Grade in the Mission. I trudged downstairs and walked down Greenwich toward Columbus, fussing the whole way with the zipper of my windbreaker, which had inched halfway up my chest and then decided to that things were just not working out. The fog slithered up the street and the wind came up right behind it in cold fitful gusts. I thought of walking for a while; instead, I got into a taxi at Broadway and told the driver to take me to the Mission.

The stocky woman behind the wheel reluctantly turned off the miniature television mounted on the dashboard.

"Hey all right," she said. "You see Betty Ann Bracken on the tube? I'm telling you I am *so* proud to be a lesbian."

She banged her fist on the steering wheel, she was so proud.

"I can relate to that," I said. "I'm proud to be a mesomorph."

"Hey what," she said sympathetically. "I know you guys had it rough too."

I got out at Van Ness and 16th and wandered around the neighborhood for a while, just to kill time.

I like Mission. It's a place where runaways go to mooch in the streets. Motorcycle gangs hang out here; frail young women working the upscale health clubs as massage therapists rent the large open apartments in triplets and take drugs in the evenings and dance themselves into a stupor in the clubs and thrill themselves with how dangerous it all is.

The D-Grade occupied an old printer's warehouse on the

corner of 17th and Mission. I remembered the place from the old days; it used to do specialty printing. The warehouse was behind the store and had held paper and old-fashioned printing presses.

A Harley was parked on the sidewalk in front of the club. A dirty looking young woman was draped over the seat; she was wearing jeans with holes at the knees and a tube top and mittens with the fingers cut off; she was chewing gum vigorously and talking with someone who could have been her twin sister.

I looked at them both for a long moment; the one on the bike caught my look.

"So like what is it?" she asked.

"Nothing," I said.

"No, I mean like what are you looking at?"

She wasn't going to let it go.

"Whatever I want," I said.

"Asshole."

"But totally," said her twin.

There was no one at the door that led from the street to the old store. I walked in and looked at the advertisements for printing supplies that were still posted on the wall. The place was empty but I could feel the music through the floor. The entrance to the club itself was by the door that led from the store to the warehouse in the back.

An enormous sullen looking young man in jeans and a leather vest was sitting on a three-legged stool in front of the inner door. He wore a greased orange mohawk and triple rings in his ear, and a small ring through his eyebrow, and a silver nose ring. The thing was the size of a police handcuff. His upper biceps were heavily tattooed. He was swaying his enormous bulk to the music, snapping his fingers erratically.

"Yo," he said. "A little out of your element, aren't you? We got a special for seniors on Sunday, play a lot of Mantovani records."

"Yo yourself," I said. "That your bike outside?"

The bozo nodded pacifically. "What about it?"

"Looked to me like a couple of kids pouring sugar in your gas tank. Girl in a tank top, cut-off jeans."

Bozo stopped snapping his fingers and sat up in shock: "The hell you say." He got up from his stool in a big hurry and lumbered off down the hall.

I slipped into the D-Grade.

There weren't many people inside—no more than ten thousand or so. And it wasn't too noisy either—no noisier than a herd of caribou in heat.

Everyone was dancing in the kind of self-absorbed druggy way in which young people dance, not making body contact, swaying languorously, hands above their heads.

The DJ controlling the sound system stood on a raised platform at the back of the warehouse. I figured he must be UB. He was relaxed and busy all at the same time, retarding the record on the turntable with his fingertips, blending the sound on the elaborate system in front of him, keeping time sinuously with his torso.

There was an enormous picture on the far wall. It showed a man being suspended from a crossbeam by a series of fishhooks embedded in his chest and back.

A bar stretched across the back wall of the warehouse; I wandered over to wait out the set. I didn't want to disturb the Master at work.

The young woman tending bar had dark rich brown hair and large brown eyes and skin so smooth and taut that when she frowned no lines formed on her forehead. She wore no jewelry, not even a nose ring. I took it as a mark of considerable austerity. I could see she kept a book on the ledge beneath the counter.

I ordered something called A Red One. The drinks were supposed to impart mental virtues. A sign said so, listing the various drinks by their effect. Red drinks were useful in revivifying memory; I didn't much want my memory revivified, but I ordered it anyway. I watched the pretty young woman blend a variety of ingredients and then put the goop into a silver blender. She had small deft precise movements.

"What're you reading?" I asked, when she served me the awful stuff.

She withdrew the book from the ledge and showed it to me. It was entitled *A Guide to the Goddess Within*.

"It's about the goddess and all," she said.

I sipped at the red drink. "Sounds pretty spiritual."

"It's all how the goddess ruled everything once and how women were happy together."

"What happened?"

The pretty young woman shrugged her frail shoulders and smiled. She had small, even white teeth.

"These men came along," she said sadly; she had things pretty well figured out.

"It's what always happens."

"Really."

Just then, the music stopped. I pushed the drink away and said: "Best love to the goddess."

The young woman said "Whatever," and shrugged her thin shoulders again.

I crossed the dance floor, walking against the shuffling crowd, smelling the rich unfriendly smell of sweat and hormones, and climbed the few steps leading to the DJ's podium.

He looked a little young to be a graduate student and he looked tired; he had a long thin narrow face, and wore a pointed goatee. His hair was combed in dreadlocks.

"UB?" I asked.

He looked me over with a long slow lazy look and shook his head.

"Izzy," he said. "I'm his cousin. UB, he promise you something?"

"He didn't promise me anything."

Izzy Goode continued to clean up the ledge, putting CDs together on a pile.

"What you want from UB, then?"

"I don't know that I want anything from him," I said. "Warn him, maybe."

"*Warn* him? Warn him about what? About having a black skin?"

"It'd be a start," I said.

"He already know that."

"Give it a rest, Izzy," I said. "Whatever kind of trouble UB's in has nothing to do with the color of his skin."

"You sure of that? I forget how quick a white man can get himself colorblind."

"I'm not interested, Izzy," I said.

Izzy Goode looked at me skeptically.

"How come you're not interested?"

"It's a free country."

"You prejudiced against people of color," he said flatly.

"That must be it. Don't take it personally."

Izzy Goode brightened up improbably and said: "Not me." He had gotten the speech off his chest, the one all blacks want to give.

I withdrew a card from my wallet.

"Just pass this on to UB, have him call me."

Izzy took the card and studied it. Then he said: "You the second dumb white guy tonight looking for UB."

"You're moving in better circles already," I said.

Izzy Goode looked at me blankly.

"The other guy was probably a cop," I added.

"That a fact?" said Izzy.

"One other thing."

"Yo, what's that?"

"Tell UB that running isn't going to do him much good."

"Why's that?"

"He isn't fast enough, Izzy. That's why."

I walked back to the bar, but the pretty young woman had gone. I decided not to wait for the next set.

The Behemoth was back on his stool by the door.

"Hey," he said, "you're the guy was messing with my head."

"Nah," I said, slipping past him. "You got me confused with the next guy in line. *I* was admiring your nose ring. *He* was messing with your head."

Never Say Never

THE OFFICE OF MULTICULTURAL AFFAIRS was housed in a building named Diversity Hall; it wasn't bigger than the Taj Mahal, but it wasn't a whole lot smaller either.

I had called Neava Climax from Mike Dottenberry's office.

The woman who answered the telephone said "Neava, Neava?" as if I were asking that the dead be raised. "I think she's at Sensitivity now, with Gorden Wooper. You can probably reach her there."

"Who's having their sensitivity sensitized?"

"Oh, its those Sigma Chis again," she said. "They are *so* naughty."

"What they do? Call a person of color a colored person? That can be pretty hurtful."

"Oh, no," said the woman, "they sponsored a Domestics Night dance to raise money for the Afro-American Center. It was terrible. They all came dressed as domestics and carried mops."

"Sounds all right to me."

"Oh, no, Mr. Asherfeld. It was very, very insensitive to people of color. It made it seem as if domestics were *traditionally* women of color. It was very stereotipifying."

"Next thing you know someone'll be claiming a lot of railway porters were black."

"Exactly."

"When will she be back?"

"Neava? Oh, she's not coming back until next week. She's going to a conference on—let me see now—quality, creativity and renewal at Ventanas. She's giving the keynote address, you know."

I didn't know and I didn't much care; but I did know that Ventanas was a resort at Big Sur that charged you an arm and leg if you wanted just to breathe the cool ocean air.

I asked Miss Vagueness where Sensitivity was being held.

"Oh, it's right here in the basement," she said.

It figured.

"You think you could have Dean Climax wait for me? Tell her I'll be there in a minute. Tell her it's Aaron Asherfeld," I said.

"Will she know who you are?"

"Tell her I'm a friend of Maya Angelou's."

"*Really?* Neava will be so thrilled."

I got back into my suit jacket and locked up Mike Dottenberry's office and splashed some water onto my face from the fountain in the hall.

Diversity Hall was on the far side of the campus, past the Union. I walked rapidly with the golden afternoon light coming in from the hills at a slant.

The building had obviously cost a lot of money. All the other buildings on campus were tan and sandstone. This one was white and made of some shiny stuff that caught the sunlight and gleamed. There was a spacious flagstone plaza in front of the building, with bike racks on either side of the walkway, and an enormous freeform iron sculptures that looked as if it had been rescued from Hiroshima.

The main doors of the building led to a fantastic rotunda, a huge five-sided space with light streaming onto the marble floors from convex skylights set high in the ceiling.

A photographic exhibition had been mounted on the rough stone walls of the rotunda: it was entitled "Whiteness is a Signifier of Power." There were pictures of sorrowful Guatemalan peasants, and American Indians, just realizing what a bad deal they had cut in Manhattan, and Appalachian women, and squatting working-class blacks, their forearms resting on their thighs. The legend beneath the photographs read: IN A RICH MAN'S HOUSE, THE ONLY PLACE TO SPIT IS IN HIS FACE.

An enormous blob of something had been placed under glass in the center of the rotunda. From a distance, it looked like a mound of lard. I walked over for a closer look. It *was* a mound of lard. The glop was entitled "Rage." The caption said: ISHIGOSHI CRITIQUES A PATRIARCHAL COMMUNITY WHERE EATING IS TRANSGRESSIVE.

I hustled myself out of all that grandeur and down the steps to the basement.

Two maple colored doors opened onto a long, narrow amphitheater, one door close to the stairs, the other at the end of the corridor. A tall, somewhat stooped woman of about forty was standing by the far door, her arms crossed over her chest. She was looking into the theater.

I stood at the near door. There were about twenty scrubbed

looking coeds in the room. They had that pampered look that only pampered children have.

Gordon Wooper was standing behind the podium on the stage. He was a tall black, with a well cut Afro; he was wearing mirrored sunglasses and an expensively cut blazer over a silk turtleneck; he looked like a pimp.

"All right people," he said, moving dramatically away from the podium, "listen up and on your feet."

The coeds stiffened and rose.

"I want all you white bitches keep on standing, black *ladies,* you can sit."

The handful of blacks in the room sat down.

"Now, bitches," said Gordon Wooper, "do I have your attention? Good. Now listen up. I want all you bitches went to integrated public schools, sit down. Rest of you bitches remain standing."

No one moved.

Wooper paced across the stage. "Good," he said with satisfaction. "Now we cookin, now we know who needs be sensitive. You the bitches stickin' in my throat for four hundred years, all that time I be wondering what's matter with my throat, something sticking there like a piece of chewed up old meat, all that time it be *you* just sticking there in your white skin and your fancy clothes and your daddy's money and you figure you gonna just march into this university and order around people of color just the way you did at home? I got something to tell you, bitches. It is not going to happen. No. You are gonna learn that your white skin is the lowest form of filth in the universe. The time I finish makin' you sensitive you gonna look in the mirror and ask yourselves why on earth you ever wanted to be white in the first place."

I left the doorway just as Wooper seemed to be warming up, and walked down to the second door.

Neava Climax heard me coming and turned her face reluctantly from the amphitheater.

I said: "I'm Aaron Asherfeld."

She placed her hand on my forearm.

"Isn't he wonderful?" she said.

"Wonderful. What do you do when the girls do something really, really bad? Call in the dobermans?"

Neava Climax smiled in a superior sort of way and resumed looking into the amphitheater. Wooper had somehow managed to divide the group again, so that only half as many young women as before were standing.

Neava Climax turned back toward me and said: "I make it very plain to members of this faculty that the dynamic I establish has to do with the fact that I intend to counter the silencing of people of color. I want to make sure that they feel empowered to speak."

"You're not talking about Shaka Zulu in there, are you? Because to me it looks like he's already been empowered too much."

"Mr. Asherfeld, I have no idea who you are but at this university we take racist remarks very seriously." She wasn't a bad looking woman. She had a long gentle face and shapely lips.

"Sure you do," I said, "as long as they're made by white men."

I held up my hands with the palms out to stop her from saying anything more.

"I'm not here to argue with you, Dean Climax. Can we go somewhere, talk?"

Neava Climax straightened herself up from the door and motioned me to follow her. We walked in silence to the end of the hall to a classroom. The dean opened the door and switched on one set of lights.

"Sit down, Mr. Asherfeld," she said, motioning me to one of the old-fashioned oak chairs with a wooden elbow rest. She sat facing me, her long legs crossed at the knee, her poplin skirt pulled down severely over her shins. It was cool and quiet and dark.

"What is it you wish to know?"

I told her about Richard Montague and mentioned the rumors about his death; I brought up UB Goode. I didn't say anything about CSR or affirmative action.

Neava Climax brushed her hand across her face impatiently as I was speaking.

"That's all very well," she said. "Frankly, I am more concerned about UB Goode than any imbroglio concerning a dead white male."

I looked up in surprise.

"Why is that?"

"UB Goode represents the future of this institution, Mr. Asherfeld. He is what a multiracial, multicultural, multispecied institution is all about."

"Multispecied? You planning on giving degrees to dogs next? Have the pooches line up on graduation day?"

"I don't expect *you* to understand the purpose of this institution," she said.

"My white skin and all?"

"Among other things," said Neava Climax coldly. "You know your boy was overheard making threats against Richard Montague?"

"To be a person of color at this university is to be full of rage."

"Why is that, Dean Climax?"

"Mr. Asherfeld," she said icily, "as someone privileged by their white skin and gender you are obviously unaware that this is a racist society."

"No, it's not."

"I *beg* your pardon?"

"Serbia's a racist society, Dean Climax. Iran, now that's a racist society. Ditto for India. I mean, you catch those pictures on the tube of that mosque being blown up? The way I figure it, *this* place is paradise for people of color. That's why ten billion of them want to come here."

"I do not have to sit here and listen to the blatant Eurocentric fulminations of a racist."

"Sure you do."

"And why is that?"

"It's because I have something to tell you that you're going to want to know."

"I sincerely doubt that."

"How about this, then. UB Goode was dealing drugs to the fraternities. Not very multicultural if you ask me."

"I find you very judgmental, Mr. Asherfeld."

"Look, Dean Climax, a man is dead. Someone is overheard

threatening his life. I'm telling you that there's a rumor going around that the same guy has been dealing to your fraternities. Don't you think there's just a little cause for judgment here?"

"There is *never* a reason to be judgmental," said Neava Climax firmly. "I find your attitude elitist, racist and heteropatriarchal."

There was just the slightest beat in her delivery, a sly pause.

"Now I must ask you who has given you this information."

"I can't tell you that, Dean Climax. You know that."

Neava Climax sat there without saying a word; Dee Dee Frobenmyer had been right. She *was* an intelligent woman when she put her mind to it. She sat there like that, thinking things over.

Finally she said: "Mr. Asherfeld, I *cannot* believe you are a friend of Maya Angelou's."

Class Struggle

I DIDN'T HEAR ANYTHING from anyone over the weekend, and then Bulton Limbish called me bright and early Monday morning.

He got me at home. I was half asleep; the other half of me had a splitting headache, one of those terrific sinus numbers that feel like a knife behind your eyes, but I could still hear the ragged edge of anxiety in his voice; it's not a sound you can miss.

"Asherfeld?"

"Not here," I mumbled, "this is his headache talking. I've sort of taken over things at this end."

"It's me, Bulton Limbish."

I snorted and said: "I feel better already."

"You be down here today, Asherfeld? It's important."

"Limbish, Limbish," I said, rolling the words around a little. "Aren't you the guy that said he didn't have to talk to me?"

"Come on, Asherfeld," he said. "You want me to grovel?"

"Be a start, Limbish."

"All right. I'm grovelling. Can you meet me down here?"

I told him to hold his horses; I told him I'd be down at the university; I told him that I'd meet him at ten. He hung up without saying good-bye and he hung up without saying thanks.

I got to Mike Dottenberry's office at a little before ten; Limbish was waiting for me, pacing outside.

"What do you say, Limbish," I said. "Good day for the class struggle?"

Limbish lifted a heavy index finger to his lips and shook his head; he took my elbow and walked me away from Dottenberry's office and out toward the quadrangle.

"Go over to the Grove," he said tensely.

The Grove was a little concrete oval behind the row of departmental buildings. There was a terra-cotta statue in the center of the Grove, with benches around it and a few young saplings set in metal tree guides between the benches. A marble plaque said the statue was dedicated to the university's gay and lesbian community. It showed a balding man with a small moustache staring off into the distance.

I figured he was looking for a bathhouse.

Limbish squatted on the bench itself, resting himself on his thighs and haunches. I sat beside him.

"Listen," he said melodramatically.

"I'm listening."

"I got busted this weekend."

"By whom?"

"Palo Alto police. I'm out on bail."

"For what?"

"Dealing, two counts of possession."

"What a loss to the revolution."

"Asherfeld, this is serious. The police have me on *felony* possession. I could go to jail."

"Look on the bright side, Limbish. A lot of guys down in Soledad probably don't know what a swell guy Stalin was. You'll have your work cut out for you."

Limbish lowered his head so that his chin almost touched his chest.

"Is there anything you can do for me, Asherfeld?" he asked.

"Go over, speak to the police. I thought that someone your type of background might be able to put in a good word for me, sort of explain things."

"What's in it for me, Limbish?"

Limbish raised his head; his face had the doughy thick look of someone who has just been told he has a terminal illness.

"You want something?" he said incredulously.

"I'm not a professor," I said. "I can't afford to work for nothing."

Limbish eyed me, his face drawn in on itself.

"How can you look at yourself in the mirror, Asherfeld?"

"It's tough. I manage. On the other hand, I don't worry a whole lot about parole dates, prison food, stuff like that."

Limbish nodded miserably.

"How much you want, Asherfeld? I'm paying my attorney, might as well pay you, too."

"I don't want your money, Limbish. This is the real world."

"What is it you want, Asherfeld?"

"I'll let you know," I said.

I didn't think it would do much good to talk with Bulton Limbish's attorney and it didn't.

Drina Spazlosch kept an office in Palo Alto. I called her up later that afternoon and told her that Limbish had suggested I call. She sounded suspicious and sullen.

"You say Bulton asked you to call?" she said, as if the whole thing defied belief.

"Look," I said, "I'm not trying to horn in on your case. I'd just like to know what's going on."

"What is it you'd like to know, Mr. Asherfeld?"

"How did Limbish get busted?"

"It was a police setup," said Spazlosch confidently.

I was incredulous. "You've got crack dealers over in East Palo Alto armed like panzer squadrons and you're telling me the police have time to waste trapping some research associate?"

"Mr. Asherfeld," said Drina Spazlosch in a voice of ice, "I really shouldn't even indulge your racist fantasies, but the fact of the matter is that the police in this country have declared war on people of color. You should wake up and smell the coffee."

130

"That accounts for the fact that they're going to all this time and trouble to frame an innocent *white* man like Bulton Limbish."

"Bulton Limbish is a part of the progressive movement in this community."

"What's that mean?"

"It means he is anti-racist, anti-sexist, anti-classist and anti-ageist."

"So is everyone at the university. It's like a mantra. Everyone says it, makes everyone feel good. What's so special about Bulton Limbish?"

"His visibility," said Spazlosch promptly. "Bulton Limbish is willing to put himself on the line for what he believes."

"You call standing in the sunshine waving some newspaper putting yourself on the line?"

"I call running the risk of police entrapment putting yourself on the line," said Drina Spazlosch.

"You're going to plead entrapment?" I asked; I was incredulous.

"Yes. Do you have a problem with that?"

"Me? I don't have a problem with it, but I'm not the one going to be doing five to fifteen because of my attorney."

"Mr. Asherfeld, if you're not part of the solution, you're *part* of the problem. And you are definitely not part of the solution."

Drina Spazlosch hung up; talking with her had been as edifying as talking to a cat.

I returned the ebony telephone receiver to its obliging cradle and rotated myself in Mike Dottenberry's chair. I didn't much think anyone at the Palo Alto police department would talk to me about Bulton Limbish. I wasn't the attorney of record and I didn't know a soul at the department. On the other hand, I didn't much want to spend another hour sitting in Mike Dottenberry's office.

I locked things up and drove down University Avenue to Palo Alto, the afternoon sun bouncing off the hood of my car and then winking off the windshield. Long-legged girls were loping up the pedestrian path alongside the avenue, their healthy young bodies covered with a delicate sheen of sweat; they looked like antelopes; half-naked bicyclists weaved in and out of traffic, muscled legs pumping methodically.

I parked behind a store selling elegant Swedish furniture and walked the block to the squat brick building that housed the Hall of Justice and the Palo Alto police station and hustled myself up to the second floor. A sign over the duty desk said: WE ARE HERE TO SERVE YOU. The sergeant on duty was very patiently interrogating a woman about someone she had reported missing.

"You say your husband's been missing eleven years, ma'am?" he said.

"More'n likely twelve."

"Don't you think it's a little late to be filing a missing persons report?"

"No," she said. "No, I don't"

The sergeant rolled his eyes upward just slightly to let me know he was dealing with a psycho, then directed the woman to the table, a missing persons report form in her hand.

I introduced myself.

"I was wondering I could get some more information about someone your men picked up for possession? Bulton Limbish?"

The sergeant nodded affably.

"You with the university?"

I said: "Yup."

The sergeant smiled a large improbable smile.

"Go on in," he said. "You want to talk to Captain Dulpstrindle."

He pointed me down the corridor behind the duty desk.

Dulpstrindle was sitting in his office, placidly reading a copy of *The Wall Street Journal*. He put the paper down when he saw me standing at the door.

"A minute of your time?"

"Sure, sure," said the captain, folding the paper in half. "I'm long on pork bellies, short in the spot market. Need to keep an eye on things."

He tapped the *Journal*.

"What can I do for you?"

He was a solid well-set man of about fifty, with a receding hairline and a lined face; he had powerful square hands.

I introduced myself and said: "Tell me anything about the bust on Bulton Limbish? Strictly off the record. The university sent me down see if I can sort things through."

Dulpstrindle nodded.

"Wish you'd coordinate with the man's attorney. She's running off at the mouth about entrapment, this, that and the other thing."

"Not true?"

"You really think I got any interest busting some nut professor on possession. Your boy, he's got no priors, he could have walked the same day if his attorney hadn't jumped all over me, told me Palo Alto's no different than Nazi Germany."

Dulpstrindle pointed to a framed photograph mounted on the wall behind his desk. It showed a young man of perhaps twenty-two dressed in a soldier's uniform.

"My dad," he said. "Died at Anzio. He was twenty-two. I don't appreciate hearing how this country's no different than Nazi Germany."

I stood up.

"I appreciate your time, Captain."

I didn't much blame him for not wanting to get beaten up by Drina Spazlosch.

I caught up with Limbish later that afternoon. He was at his table by the bookstore, but he was sitting down and simply staring out over the fountain.

"Cheer up, Limbish," I said. "I got good news for you."

"I could use that, Asherfeld," he said. "I really could. What do you have?"

"No, no, Limbish, you first. What do *you* have?"

Limbish nodded; he understood. "How much you know?" he asked.

"I know UB Goode was running drugs over to the fraternities. I'm figuring you were acting as his broker. Where'd the money come from?"

"I floated it through CSR," Limbish said. He had the unfortunate habit of looking guilty when he felt guilty. "Look, I did it for progressive reasons." He tapped the pile of newspapers. "Money went right here. It's what Guzman did in Peru."

133

"This is Palo Alto, Limbish, not Peru, and Guzman is going to spend the rest of his life in some dark hole."

Limbish reached down to hug his knees.

Then he said: "How'd I get busted, you know?"

"Sure," I said. "Some of your friends don't love you."

Limbish looked up at me, his dark brown eyes disappointed.

"Who's your chemist?" I asked.

Limbish waved his hand forlornly in the air.

"Guy we used to ride with, hung out with the Angels."

"Montague know all about this?"

"Richie knew what he wanted to know," said Limbish. Then he said: "This thing goes deep. I'm not going to be the only one whose career is ruined."

I looked at him in astonishment.

"Give me a break," I said. "You don't have a career. You've got a sinecure from the State of California."

Limbish turned to glare at me.

"I know, I know," I said. "That's my false consciousness talking."

For a moment, Limbish looked as if wanted to argue with me. Then he gave it up.

"You talk to Mike Dottenberry yet?" he asked.

"He's the guy's up nights worrying about the patriarchy? I'm using his office."

"You want to talk to him."

"Why's that?"

"Look, don't make me do your job for you, Asherfeld. I'm telling you, you should talk to Mike Dottenberry. Dig around a little. Be amazed at what you'll find. You just lift a couple of rocks, Asherfeld, see what comes out. That's all I'm asking."

I nodded. "All right, Limbish," I said. "Now I owe you one. You're in trouble, but it's only going to be deep trouble if you act like an idiot."

Limbish looked up, his heavy muscular face curious.

"So what do you think I should do?"

"First, fire your attorney."

"Drina? Why?"

"Because she's incompetent. Second, call up a man in San Francisco name of Shmul Wasserstrom. He could care less about the revolution but he knows what to say to the police. If he tells you to plead guilty to possession, plead guilty to possession. If he tells you to give him ten thousand dollars, give him ten thousand dollars. Don't say anything that Wasserstrom doesn't tell you to say. Don't ask any questions. Don't tell anyone that Palo Alto is no different from Nazi Germany. Don't tell the cops they got a problem with false consciousness. You got all that?"

Limbish said nothing for a long while. Then he said: "Thanks."

He had to choke it out.

That evening, Shmul Wasserstrom called me at home to thank me for recommending him to Bulton Limbish.

"Work out a fee?" I asked.

"Sure," said Wasserstrom. "Everything he's got."

"Couldn't be much, Shmul," I said.

"You'd be surprised," said Wasserstrom happily. "I told him that for him the price was ten thousand dollars. He paid me in cash."

Some Like It Raw

I GOT UP THE NEXT MORNING with the television still on; I must have fallen asleep before turning it off.

I rolled off my couch and lumbered off into the bathroom; after I had eased my bowels, taken a shower, brushed and flossed my teeth, combed my hair and drunk a cup of coffee, I called Seybold Knesterman at his office.

"Knesterman, Woodger, Schutzenberger and Thom," said Knesterman's secretary. "Mr. Knesterman's office."

"Let me speak to Knesterman," I said.

"And who shall I say is calling?"

"This is the B'nai Brith," I said.

Knesterman came on the line in a moment; he said "Yes" in a rich ripe tone of voice.

"Your lucky day, Knesterman," I said. "You've won the Hadassah trip to Miami Beach. All expenses paid. Mahjong coupons for the missus, free golf for you. All you have to do is spend a weekend touring the condo, listen to an informative lecture."

Knesterman had never given up on anti-Semitism.

"It must be you, Asherfeld," he said. "No one else would conspire to ruin an entire day."

"It *is* me, Knesterman," I said. "Tell me about Richard Montague."

"Who?"

"Richard Montague. He was a client of yours."

"You know I can't do that, Asherfeld. Why do you even ask?"

"Man's dead, Knesterman. He won't mind having a few confidences divulged."

"I can't tell you anything that isn't a matter of public record."

"That's fine by me, Knesterman, tell me what you can tell me."

"Richard Montague's estate is in probate pending resolution of the autopsy. It is not a matter, I assure you, that I am handling myself."

"You have some associate doing the scut?"

"Precisely," said Knesterman.

"Can you tell me the next of kin, Knesterman?"

"I'll have someone call you, Asherfeld."

"You're wonderful as always, Knesterman," I said. "I've put you down for a subscription to *Circumcision*. It's a new journal for men thinking of making a midlife conversion."

I didn't wait to hear Knesterman's indignant snort.

A few fat white clouds hung over the Bay. The air was cold and the light had a knife-edge to it that made you want to take deep sharp breaths tasting of peppermint. It made you want to chuck a football around. It made you want to sip hot chocolate. It made you want to take long walks with your best girl. I drove across the Golden Gate Bridge with the window wide open, my arm resting on the door frame. Someone was playing a trumpet fanfare on the radio. At Mill Valley I took the Stinson Beach exit and headed for Route 1. It's the highway on all the posters and in all the commercials. I drove up one flank of Mt. Tamalpais and down the other. After coming down from the mountain, the highway climbs up the chalky cliffs again and then winds its way up the coast, the great ocean emptying itself out toward the horizon at every turn in the road. I remembered driving on this road for the first time. I had never seen the Pacific. I had never seen redwoods. I had never seen green winter hills with sheep grazing on them. I had never seen anything like the coast high-way. I still haven't.

I got to Stinson Beach a little before noon and cruised slowly past the seafood restaurants in grey weather-beaten wooden shacks and the road-front bookstores and the stores selling sturdy woolen clothing and rain gear. Nothing much has happened around here and nothing much has changed.

I parked by the post office and went in to check the town zoning map. Arroya Flats Road was on the north side of town.

It was noon when I left the post office: the sun was blazing and it was still early spring. Beefy men wearing cut-down sweat shirts and cowboy boots were sauntering down Main Street or leaning their ample stomachs over the open hoods of automo-biles. Young girls with terrific long legs were sitting on wooden porches and combing their hair in the sun and stretching those terrific long legs out in front of them.

Aptum Hilyar lived on the north side of the beach itself, an area of solid old-fashioned Victorian houses, some of them on the marshy part of the estuary and others straggling up the hill beyond.

His house had an unobstructed view of the open ocean and the Pacific headlands further south.

Hilyar opened the door himself. He was a tall tough looking man somewhere in his eighties, with leathery skin and a great jagged beak of a nose and shaggy eyebrows and enormous hands.

He looked at me suspiciously for a moment as he mulled over my name. I had called him two hours before.

"How old you think I am?" he asked abruptly.

I looked at his bald head and his large ruined face with its deep creases.

"Pass for sixty," I said. "Easy."

Hilyar cackled happily.

"Everyone says that. Eighty-four. I'm eighty-four."

"That's pretty terrific."

Hilyar gave me a fierce inquisitive look.

"Aren't you going to ask me how I do it?"

"Sure. I forgot. How do you do it?"

"Yeast," he said triumphantly and slapped himself on the chest.

He looked at me with a sly expression.

"Still get it up too."

"I can see getting old, it's really something to look forward to."

"You bet," said Hilyar. "You the fella wants to talk about the gas, that right?"

I shook my head.

"I want to talk to you about your nephew."

Hilyar's eyes lost their fierce sheen for just a moment.

"Rotten kid," he said. "Come on in."

When he escorted me back from the front door, I noticed that he limped, dragging his left leg behind him.

"Show you around the place," he said grimly, stumping off down the hall.

It was a handsome old house, the sort of thing that lumbermen put up in the last century, full of wood and heavy plaster.

"Mollie used to sit in here," Hilyar said, opening the door to a first-floor sitting room.

He stopped by the door and looked at me, the life leaving his face and then coming back into it.

"Show you the kitchen," he said. "Showpiece."

We inspected the kitchen, which really did look as if it had been laid out for a culinary magazine, with a lot of counter space, and a gunmetal grey double-doored refrigerator, and one of those black cast-iron stoves big enough to roast an ox.

"Great kitchen," I said with as much enthusiasm as I could muster.

"Yeah, well," said Hilyar, "you like cooking it's a good place to cook. Me, I never eat cooked foods. Be the death of you. You never see a wild animal cook its food, do you?"

"I guess not."

"There you have it. Want to see upstairs?"

"No."

"Good," said Hilyar. "I don't want to show it to you."

I guessed that Hilyar had been married to a much younger woman; the house didn't belong to him and he didn't belong to the house.

He took me instead to the front parlor. By the time he opened the door, he was almost holding his own leg and thrusting it forward.

"Bother you much?" I asked.

"Nothing wrong with my leg," he said irritably. "Stiff, is all. Damn fool doctor, first thing out of his mouth is cut this, cut that. I said to him: 'Doc, something's missing from my diet is all.' So I triple my yeast, vitamin C and B, take lysine three times a day."

He hobbled over to an overstuffed easy chair that faced inward from the bright windows.

"Look at me now," he said triumphantly.

I sat down in the easy chair facing the window.

Hilyar pointed to the far wall where a series of photographs depicted him dressed in bathing shorts and covered with brown swimmer's oil.

"See that one over there," Hilyar said, still pointing. "Swam from Seal Rocks out to the Farallones."

He looked around the room and seemed to shrink. "Cold swim," he added. Then he regained his focus. He seemed to breathe life in and out. "You a friend of Richie's? Lawyers send you over?"

"I never knew your nephew, Mr. Hilyar. I'm just tying up some loose ends for the university."

"Nobody tells me anything," he said.

"Your nephew's papers," I said diffidently, "are they with his attorney or do you have them?"

"Richie's attorney got copies of the will, estate's in probate. I've got most of his other papers, stuff from the bank, checkbooks, lot of personal things, letters."

"You think I could look through those papers? Be a big help in my investigatation."

"Hell, no," said Hilyar, bristling, "them things is private."

"I understand that," I said carefully. "But your nephew's reputation, that's still public."

"What's that supposed to mean?" Hilyar asked. He was getting querulous.

"It means I'd like to make sure your nephew gets to rest in peace."

I didn't much like what I said and I didn't much like myself for saying it.

Hilyar's defiance collapsed if only because he forgot why he had been defiant.

"Sure, sure," he said. "Go up the stairs, first door to your right. Richie's papers be on the desk." He waved his enormous hand aimlessly in the air. "You go on up. Look at whatever you want."

He turned his chair to face the sea.

Richard Montague's papers didn't tell me a whole lot. Montague's most recent tax statements had been prepared by a San Francisco accountant named Wah Gee. Montague had left an estate of more than one million dollars, but almost all of the money was tied up in a trust. Half of his estate went to a married sister living in Alberta; the rest was earmarked for various charities. Montague had had a modest portfolio of stocks and a number of different checking accounts. He owed money here and there. He had belonged to a number of clubs and associations. He had corresponded with a lot of people around the world. A letter from the Bank of America in Oakland had advised him that a letter of credit from Hamburg had been posted to the Bank Suisse in San Francisco. There was an address book with the usual scribbled list of names.

There was nothing else.

I made notes about Montague's banking affairs and left everything else the way I found it.

Aptum Hilyar was still sitting in his easy chair when I entered the parlor again. He was still facing the sea. He spoke to me with his back.

"You eat a lot of cooked foods?"

I stood behind a stuffed easy chair and ran a finger over its linen antimacassar.

"Sometimes," I said. I didn't much want to get into a conversation about yoghurt.

"Cooked foods be the death of you. Happened to Richie."

"You think your nephew died because he ate a few hot meals, do you?"

"You bet," said Hilyar. "He was a rotten kid."

"He visit you a lot?" I asked.

"Hardly ever," said Hilyar glumly.

"Pretty surprising," I said, "seeing how he could get so much good advice about food out here."

"I told him he had to eat right. Every time he was here, I told him, one thing I know it's that cooked food be the death of you. He didn't pay me any attention."

"And look what happened," I said sympathetically.

"It was that cooked food," said Hilyar. "He was a rotten kid."

"I wouldn't be too hard on him."

"I'm not being hard," said Hilyar, "I'm just remembering, is all."

Aptum Hilyar lifted his enormous hand from his lap and let it drop. The gesture seemed to exhaust him.

"You still get it up?" he asked abruptly.

"I don't know," I said.

"Ginseng," he said. "That's what you need."

"You're probably right," I said.

"Know what I wish?" Hilyar asked, still facing the sea.

"No, what's that?"

"I wish I were dead."

I left Stinson Beach at a little after two and drove north until I got to the Olema road, which heads inland from Route 1. There is an inn at the intersection of the two roads. It occupies a beautiful old white wooden building; it's exactly at the spot where you'd like to pull over and have something to eat. The inn is always closed and the same group of enthusiastic young people are always in the process of restoring it.

It was still warm and it was still sunny and the trees still held their sharp vivid green color in the air. I drove with my wrist resting on the steering wheel. A little past Olema a deer crossed the highway with two tiny does straggling behind it. It paused in the middle of the road to look inquisitively at my car, which had stopped obligingly, and then proceeded to step daintily to the other side.

I could think of only two things that were terrific in my life: the first were those deer, and the second was the fact that I wasn't eighty-five.

I got back to the city just as traffic was beginning to stream northward across the Golden Gate Bridge; I paid my three dollars at the tollbooth to a woman with lustrous skin and high cheekbones and ebony cat eyes; I cut across the Marina to Chestnut and then over to Greenwich. I was home by four.

Montague's accountant wasn't listed under accountants in the yellow pages, but there was a Wah Gee who had an office on the lower part of Powell. I took a chance and called. Someone speaking smooth, very precise, lightly accented English answered the telephone right away.

"This Wah Gee," he said.

I told him that I had a confidential accounting problem; I told him that he came highly recommended; I told him that he was right around the corner from me and that I could be there in a flash.

He said very well and hung up. He didn't seem to be on fire with curiosity.

I shuffled back into my windbreaker. When I got onto the street I realized that the day was over; the light had grown heavy and a cold wind was blowing in from the Bay. The foghorns had started to sound.

Powell Street cuts over the top of Nob Hill, past the swell hotels and the fancy French restaurants, and past the elegant apartment buildings with doormen in front polishing the brass mailboxes with their sleeves. Then it slithers down Russian Hill and deadends in one of those horrible housing projects that everyone thought were a good idea in the fifties; but just as it crosses Columbus it carries a little spur of Chinatown along with it for a block. The houses are all white clapboard; there is no graffiti; the street is immaculate.

Wah Gee had an office on the first floor of one of the white clapboard houses.

I rang the outside bell; someone must have been watching me. The buzzer sounded immediately.

Inside, there was a long railway corridor leading to the back of the house with two apartments on either side and a stairway rising up toward the second floor.

It was dark in the hall and the building had that smell you get in any building in which Chinese are living—ginger, incense, strange herbs, hot oil.

Wah Gee opened the first door on my left just as I closed the front door. He was a slim man of no more than forty or so, with smooth skin and black oiled hair, which he wore combed straight back from his forehead; he had a trick of holding his head at an angle, so that he appeared to be puzzled about something. He was wearing a red cardigan and chinos and slippers; there was something unaccountable about his appearance.

He shook hands with me as if shaking hands was a distasteful task, like exchanging sputum, and escorted me from the front door down a long corridor to a little parlor at the front of his apartment. The lights were off; it was almost too dark to see and the only illumination in the room came from the street.

Wah Gee seated himself at an old-fashioned roll-top desk and swivelled in his office chair. He waved his hand gently in the air.

"May I know nature of ploblem?"

I wanted to sit down, but there was no other chair in the room.

"I'm trying to make some sense of Richard Montague's affairs," I said. It was close enough to the truth to be true. "Couple of points I thought you might be in a position to help me out."

Wah Gee looked at me imperturbably.

"I am afraid you mistaken, Mr. Ashefed," he said. "I not in position to be assistance to you."

"Why is that?"

"Are you with police?"

"Me? No, I'm not."

"Then it not point I obliged to explain," he said without raising his voice.

"I appreciate that. I just figured that as Richard Montague's accountant you'd be *willing* to explain some things to me."

"You mistaken again, Mr. Ashefed."

Then he looked at his watch ostentatiously: "Is there other

matter which I may be of service? If no, you excuse me. Hour late. I expected elsewhere."

Wah Gee nodded gravely, his hands held in front of him and crossed at the wrists. He spoke bad English without effort.

"I'll see myself out," I said. "I remember the way."

Wah Gee nodded again but said nothing.

I left Wah Gee's apartment and walked to the head of the block in the cool evening air. Then on a hunch, I crossed the street and took a seat on one of those chipped little benches that the city put up inside the graffiti-streaked bus stands. Within five minutes I saw Wah Gee leave his house; he walked briskly to the head of the block and got into a taxicab at the stand on Columbus.

I made a note of the taxi's number and stood up heavily. I could feel the cool damp air in the small of my back. I walked up toward Columbus and then down to Ghirardelli Square with the wind blowing off the Bay and the light turning golden in the city streets.

Ghirardelli Square used to be a factory; sometime in the sixties someone thought it would be a sensational idea to remodel the whole thing into a shopping complex, keeping the original red brick walls and putting in escalators and a lot of fancy stores selling imported Italian olive oil. For a while, the place threw a queer magnetic influence over the city. One of my wives used to wake up bouncy on Saturday mornings and say things like: "Come on, Asher, let's go to Ghirardelli Square. *Please.*" We'd come back home lugging an exotic stainless steel pasta maker, or a marble French rolling pin, or a collection of adorable Sicilian tiles. Now the place just sits there, the fantastically expensive shops all closed.

I got myself an espresso at the stand in front of the square and took it over to the telephone booth just beside it and called the Yellow Cab company's dispatcher on O'Farrell; I asked when the day shift would be coming in.

"Be about twenty minutes," he said.

That meant that Wah Gee's cab would probably be heading back toward the terminal after dropping Wah Gee off.

I gulped the rest of my espresso, wadded up the little paper cup and flipped it into an obliging green trash can, and walked quickly over to the foot of Hyde Street; I caught a cable car on the run, just as it was about to start lumbering up the Hyde Street hill. I took it over the hill and down the other side.

I got to the dispatching office on Polk just as the day shift cabs began streaming into the garage.

Wah Gee's cab was in the middle of the bunch. The driver parked his car and got out with that every-muscle-is-stiff grimace that cab drivers get. He looked like a regular: a big, heavyset man with grey stubble on his face and grey hair. He was carrying his routing sheet on a clipboard.

"Say," I said, walking over to him, "aren't you the son of a bitch just picked up my wife—tall, good looking redhead?"

"Huh?"

"I find out where she's going, I'm going to kill her and then I'm going to rip the heart out of the guy who took her there."

"Easy man," said the driver. "Last fare I picked up some slope."

"You're not the guy headed up the hill toward the Mark Hopkins?" I said disbelievingly.

The driver held up his routing sheet and ran his finger down the addresses.

"Pier 96, pal," he said. "Right here."

He thrust the clipboard under my nose. I checked the time and place of the last pickup just to make sure.

"Hey," I said. "It was an honest mistake."

"Sure," said the driver sympathetically. "I know how it is. She's got you running around in circles."

"You don't know the half of it," I said.

Dockwork

A COLD WIND WAS BLOWING off the Bay, gusting every now and then. It was raw out and damp. I caught a cab at Columbus and told the driver to take me to Pier 96.

"You sure you got the number right?" the driver asked, turning in his seat. "Ain't nothing there this time of night."

I said I was sure.

"Your nickel," said the driver philosophically. He must have thought things over as he drove down Columbus. Crossing Broadway he reached across the seat and held up a heavy black automatic.

"Just so you know," he said. "I don't figure on becoming another of them cabbies found with a hole in their heads. Know what I mean?"

"I know what you mean," I said.

"What line of work you in?" he asked, becoming friendly all of a sudden.

"Me? I'm in insurance. Whole life, term, adjustable. This'd be a wonderful time to talk about your peace of mind needs."

I thought maybe that would keep him quiet.

"Some other time," said the cabbie. "I only do this to make ends meet. I'm really a screenwriter. I just finished up this screenplay. See, it's about this guy he's really bummed on account of the things the CIA made him do in Nam? I figure it's Arnold all the way through. Soon as we go into production, it's goodbye Frisco for this puppy."

"You're going to need disappointment insurance," I said.

"Disappointment insurance? You're putting me on, right?"

"No, really. You take out the policy, Arnold doesn't return your call, the policy pays off. You're interested, give me a call."

I had one of the dean's cards in my pocket; I slipped it to him over the front seat.

We drove through the darkened wet streets, the water squishing from the taxi's tires as we went around corners. From time to time the squawk box on the dashboard squawked harsh obscure messages into the taxicab.

I got off at Pier 96 on the Embarcadero south of the Bay Bridge. A mile or so further north, the neighborhood goes yuppie, with cute little restaurants and boutiques that come and go every six months or so and condos with names like Bay View East or Imperial Manor; down here, the Embarcadero is still a mean street.

I could smell the deep iodine smell of the Bay from the foot of the pier and the musty smell of the rotting wooden pilings and I could hear the water splashing against the pier itself and then receding. The wind had died down but it was still raining a fine thin rain and the air was cold and damp. The great foghorns had started outside the Golden Gate and on Alcatraz and Treasure Island.

There was a ship berthed at Pier 96. I could just read its name in the red light that came from the harbormaster's quarters. It was the *Marquess de Camellia*. It sat high in the water, its great iron sides shifting with the small waves that came in from the Bay. It wasn't a large ship and it had that disreputable, weather-beaten look that tramp freighters moving across the Pacific get after thirty years or so.

I stood there for a few minutes, listening to the foghorns and the sounds of the Bay.

After a while, I walked back to the Embarcadero and headed toward the little puddle of light that came from a coffee shack a few hundred yards south of Pier 96.

It was eleven o'clock but the place was still open. Years ago, the waterfront was a twenty-four-hour operation; you could get pretty good burgers at three in the morning or thin strips of fried shell steak and home fries. It was a good neighborhood to go if you couldn't sleep or you couldn't stand the woman snoring in bed next to you or you couldn't much stand what you had done the day before and needed some food to take your mind off things.

I opened the door and slipped into the little restaurant, water dribbling down my back; there was a smell of Pine Sol in the air. The large, shoulder-sloping man behind the counter was mopping the floor.

"Kitchen's closed," he said. "Let you have some coffee, is all."

I said that would be fine and heaved myself onto the red revolving counter stool. I could see that the grill had already been wiped down and the griddle scoured and cleaned. There wasn't much that looked good to eat under the plastic half-domed plates on the counter—donuts, a couple of slices of yellow pound cake, a stack of bagels.

The counterman slid a heavy porcelain mug toward me.

"By now stuff probably tastes like dog piss," he said amiably. "Best I can do."

I waved my hand. "Doesn't matter, long as it's hot."

"Not hot either," he said, moving his mop over the wooden railings on the floor behind the counter.

I sipped the awful stuff while the counterman continued methodically to mop the floor. The little shack had the sad feel of a place that once was busy and isn't busy anymore. There were posters on the wall for Coca Cola from the forties—the kind that showed a woman with fantastically long round legs holding a tray full of shapely Coca-Cola bottles. The counter held sugar and cream in little pewter pitchers; no one had ever wiped the lips of the ketchup bottles. The juke box by the door behind me was one of those ancient affairs in which a mechanical arm took a forty-five and deposited it on a spinning platter. I could see the gonadal bubbles in the translucent tubing on the juke box sides rise slowly and then disappear when they reached the top of the tube.

"Let me ask you something," I said.

The counterman straightened himself up, mop in hand.

"You looking for poontang you're twenty years too late."

I shook my head. "I wonder you knew what they've been off-loading from the *Marquess de Camellia?*"

"Rust bucket in 96?"

"That's the one."

"Haven't been off-loading anything, far as I can tell. Thing came in couple days ago, just been sitting there."

"You're sure about this?"

"Sure I'm sure. Unless they've been off-loading the thing middle of the night, which they ain't about to be doing. Years ago, you had your ships off-loading three, four in the morning. It's all gone now, ever since they containerized over in Oakland."

"There's no off-loading here at all?"

"Couple of ships come every week, got odd cargoes have to be off-loaded by hand. Got one in the other day carrying mangoes from South America, had to be off-loaded by hand."

I didn't say anything; I sat there sipping my coffee. After a while, I said: "Make me one of these to go."

"Your funeral," said the counterman. He filled up a polyurethane cup with coffee, sealed it, and handed it to me.

148

Outside, the same sad gentle rain that had been falling before was falling now.

I walked across the Embarcadero and up to the top of the grassy knoll on the other side of the street; I squatted with my back against a PGE power station block—it was the sort of thing used to house transformer cables. I could feel something humming through my back. I could see the coffee shack and the pier and the *Marquess de Camellia* and the massive concrete supports of the bridge, graceful curving lights high in the sky above them.

I didn't know what I was waiting for, but I didn't much mind waiting. When my thighs started to ache, I sat down on the grass, still keeping my back against the station.

The clock on the Ferry Building struck one o'clock. The foghorns sounded mournfully, first the little one, then the big one, then the monster out by the Golden Gate. The lights went out in the coffee shack; the counterman came lumbering out, locked the door and disappeared northward on the Embarcadero into the gloom.

At a little past one, an old yellow school bus put-putted its way slowly down the Embarcadero, passed Pier 96, and stopped a quarter of a mile further on. I could hear the gabble of voices carrying indistinctly over the night air; I couldn't make out the words. There was a distant rattle and the bus slowly rolled backward toward the pier and the *Marquess de Camellia*.

Half a dozen men or so, looking like somber insects, had materialized on the ship's upper deck. Someone said something sharp in what sounded like Chinese, the open tones sounding like gongs, and then the gangway came clattering down. Someone must have been lowering it by hand because it hit the causeway by the pier with a bang. The same gabble from the deck, and then nothing.

I waited there, squatting again, for another quarter of an hour.

Then I heard the sound of a steel door or bulkhead being opened. A group of men began filing down the gangway. They were dressed in pea coats and had dark woolen berets pulled over their heads; they were hustling. As soon as they reached the pier, they made for the school bus at a sprint.

No one said a word.

At a little past two, the gangway was raised. The old school bus coughed once or twice, shuddered, and then made off slowly down the Embarcadero; at Folsom, it stopped again, its exhaust panting.

I got up and walked briskly down the far side of the Embarcadero. My backside was wet and cold. I knew it would be. At the corner of Folsom, I caught a cab that had been idling by the corner, its driver reading a pornographic magazine.

"You want to follow that school bus for a while?" I said.

The driver folded his copy of *Jugs* and eased across the railway tracks and made a left turn on the Embarcadero; the school bus hadn't moved.

"Bus ain't going anywhere," he said reasonably, but just then the bus coughed again and began its slow stately roll down the street.

"You're doing this on account you're with the CIA," said my driver. "Am I right?"

"Could be," I said.

"See, I *know* there no school kids that bus at three in the morning."

"You got a real feeling for intelligence work," I said.

The school bus rattled down the Embarcadero, turned on Market, and turned again on Grant; it drove straight up Grant until the Chinatown gate and then stopped.

I had the driver pull over a block away on Post and turn out his lights.

"Anything going down, I'm outta here," he said. "You know what I mean."

"Me too," I said.

"Aren't you guys *supposed* to take risks, take a bullet for the Big Enchilada and all? I saw a movie about it."

"That's the secret service you're talking about," I said. "Those guys take a bullet because there's not much up here." I tapped my forehead significantly.

"I know what you mean," said my driver, leaning over the seat to explain a fine point in his understanding of global politics.

Before he could say anything, the school bus crossed into Chinatown.

We followed a block behind. The bus stopped in front of *Jimmy Joy's* restaurant on the corner of Pacific and Grant. It was the largest and fanciest restaurant in Chinatown. The place was dark; it was after three o'clock.

We waited behind the bus. The tradesmen's entrance to the restaurant opened noiselessly; after a minute or two, the bus door slid open with a slight squeal and whoever had hustled into the bus at Pier 96, their heads buried in their pea jackets, hustled out again, their heads still buried in their pea jackets, the file vanishing in no more than twenty seconds.

Faculty Members

THE WEEK PASSED SILENTLY, taking with it the Pacific storm that had been lingering over northern California; I didn't hear from anyone and no one heard from me.

The dean called me the following Monday; it was barely seven. "We need you, Asherfeld," he said urgently. Then he said: "And Asherfeld, listen."

"I'm all ears," I said. "Just like a little bunny."

"Don't speak about this with anyone."

"My lips are sealed," I said. "Be all right if I brush my teeth though?"

I got dressed in more of a hurry than I wanted to; and I had coffee in more of a hurry than I wanted to; and I drove down the freeway just as the sun was scattering the high morning fog over the green hills of the coast range.

The dean had asked that I meet him in the president's office. That meant I didn't have to bother finding a place to park. A campus security guard was at my car before I had even turned off the engine. He was carrying a clipboard and a walkie-talkie.

"Name?" he said mechanically, scanning a list on the clipboard.

"Aaron Asherfeld."

The guard found my name and ticked it off with a pencil; someone had got things done that morning.

"You be taking coffee, sir?" the guard asked. "I'll phone it in?" He tapped his walkie-talkie.

I didn't want coffee and I didn't want the croissants he offered me directly afterward.

"I can understand that, sir," he said agreeably. "Don't like to chow down that kind of low-fiber stuff myself."

The dean and Molé Anbisol were waiting for me in the president's reception room. They looked tense and tired, even though it was just after eight, Molé Anbisol especially having withdrawn in on himself, like a spider with broken legs. The dean had already sweated through his seersucker suit jacket. They were both sipping coffee from thin red and white cups.

I took a moment to look around the reception area. The place was perfectly square, with bay windows giving out to a rose garden. There was a portrait of the university's founder over the mantelpiece; he looked stout and bovine. The university itself was named for his son, who had died young. It was a sedate room full of sedate heavy furniture.

A trim blonde woman slipped into the room and said: "He'll see you now, gentlemen." She crossed the reception area and opened the black door that led directly to the president's office, leaning over Molé Anbisol's wheelchair to hold the door open as we filed in.

The president was sitting at his massive walnut desk, his feet on the polished surface. He was dressed in sweat pants and a jogging jacket; he was sipping from a can of Gatorade.

The dean and I sat ourselves around the president's desk; Molé Anbisol brought his wheelchair to the side of the desk and then angled it so that he was facing both the president and the two of us.

"How'd your run go, sir?" he asked solicitously.

"I'm off the pace, Molé," said the president irritably.

"The president is training for the Iron Man competition in Maui," said Molé.

"That's pretty special," I said.

I noticed that the president had leaned an elegant racing bike against the corner wall of his office.

"I should be doing splits mornings and afternoons," said the president. "These damn meetings I'm lucky if I can put in 10k."

Molé Anbisol leaned over his wheelchair to place his hand

discreetly on my forearm. "Perhaps we should get down to business," he said.

The president placed his left foot over his right knee at a ninety degree angle and commenced tugging at his left knee in order to loosen his hamstrings.

"Mr. President," said the dean, "the problem we were sort of hoping would go away is sort of not going away."

The president looked vexed.

"What's he talking about Molé? Speak to me."

"This Richard Montague thing, sir. These people who want money?"

The president nodded as if he knew what the dean was talking about. "Keep me deniable, Molé. That's all I ask. I want to be deniable on this."

"I understand, sir," said Molé.

"I don't want to stand before another congressional committee with just my dick in my hand."

The dean took the moment to look toward the sun and sneeze wetly; I could see the droplets spray into the air.

"They want the money," he said. "They're pretty serious."

"Everybody wants something," said the president. "Everybody's got their hands out. You think those NSF auditors don't have their hands out? Don't you believe it. If I wanted to I could make that whole business go away with one payment."

"Mr. President," said Molé, "*these* people *do* have the capacity to cause the university a great deal of embarrassment."

"Hell of a thing," said the president vaguely.

"Asherfeld," said the dean, "what do you have?"

I got up and went to the little standing chalkboard in front of the president's desk; I drew a rough sketch of Omo's property on the board, indicating the ranch with an undulating line and marking the coach house with an X.

"Violet got to live here," I tapped at the X, "on one condition. A couple of times a week she has to leave the house. The area over here,"—I tapped the circle I had drawn to indicate the amphitheater—"I find a Chinese newspaper. Omo himself has this strange tattoo on his wrist."

"So?" said the dean, mystified.

"The tattoo is a tong mark," I said, feeling somewhat ridiculous for saying it.

"Does this have anything to do with the university?" Molé asked courteously; he had leaned over in his wheelchair and was resting his thin forearm on the chrome armrest.

"I think so," I said, still standing in front of the board. "Montague's accountant was a Chinese name of Wah Gee. He was pretty closed-mouthed about Montague when I went to see him."

"Not a crime, Asherfeld," said the dean. It was the second time he had used those words.

"No," I agreed. "It's not a crime."

I wrote Wah Gee's name on the board and then I put Jimmy Joy's name next to it.

"Smuggling illegal immigrants into this country's a crime, though," I said.

The president lowered his feet and sat up in his large, high-backed chair.

I told the dean and Molé Anbisol about Pier 96 and the *Marquess de Camellia* and about *Jimmy Joy's* restaurant.

The dean heard me out with a look of pudgy perplexity on his face.

"What's the bottom line?" he said.

"Bottom line is this. Over here,"—I tapped at Omo's name,—"you have someone needs cheap labor. Omo works through Dottenberry, Dottenberry works through CSR. Over here,"—I tapped at Wah Gee's name—"you got someone involved in smuggling Chinese to the United States. My guess is that Montague and CSR were acting as the banker. Money comes in from one side, goes out the other. The bank takes its commission."

"What an extraordinary scheme." said Molé Anbisol.

"It's definitely tenure material," I said. "Only one thing wrong with it."

"What's that?" asked the president. "Looks good to me."

"Montague died before he could make payment on the last delivery. Now you've got Wah Gee and some very tough Chinese worried about their money."

"Considering the nature of the debt," said Molé Anbisol dryly, "it's not the sort of thing that might wind up in court."

I nodded. "That's why these people are trying to put the bite on the university."

The dean shifted himself in his seat; he withdrew a cassette tape from his breast pocket.

"What's it say?" I asked, pointing to the tape that the dean had placed on the table.

"Same thing," he said. "They want the debt paid off, we don't pay, video goes to the newspapers, television, congressional oversight committee, NSF, the works."

"What video is this, Molé?" asked the president. "Put me in the picture."

The president had commenced tugging on his right leg.

"These people claim to have a a video of Richard Montague's death. It is supposed to be quite lurid."

I said: "They're claiming that Montague died during a homosexual orgy. It's consistent with what the medical examiner told me."

The president said: "Bunch of Chinese, guy owns a restaurant, how'd they come up with a tape like that?"

It was a good question.

I said: "Montague was riding with some unsavory people. Dedicated biker types. I'm guessing that they introduced him to the smuggling business, set up his contact with Wah Gee and Jimmy Joy. They're also the people who'd be likely to be,"—I paused: I didn't know how to finish my sentence—"*experimentalists* when it comes to their behavior."

"Be that as it may," said Molé Anbisol smoothly, "the idea that these people have something that might damage the university is still conjectural."

The dean said: "I have reason to believe that they really do have a video."

"What's that?" asked the president.

The dean reddened deeply. "A package was hand-delivered to my office yesterday. Instructions were to send it over to the medical school for identification. At first I thought it was some

155

sort of a gag, sent it over to the medical school anyway. Got this back."

The dean withdrew a file folder from the briefcase at his feet and read aloud from the letter within it:

"I'll skip over the introduction," he said. Then he read:

Specimen was investigated visually and appeared to be a human organ approximately four centimeters in length and of a diameter of point five centimeters in advanced stage of decomposition. Obvious ligature marks on proximal shaft; evidence of crude surgical manipulation. Specimen subsequently sectioned and evaluated pathologically. No lesions or evidence of gross or microscopic disease present. Thank you for sharing this interesting specimen with the department of pathology.

"What on earth does this have to do with anything?" asked the president.

"Maybe you'd better know what the specimen was," I said.

The dean looked around at the group.

"It was a human penis, severed at the base."

"This is disgusting," said the president.

"Think of how disgusting it's going to appear to your alumni."

The president frowned. "What do you think GLA'll do, this comes out, Molé?"

"I'm afraid they'll say the whole thing is blatantly homophobic."

"And the women?"

Molé Anbisol shrugged his shoulders eloquently.

"Don't want to give them any ideas," said the president. "God, some of the women on this campus soon bite it off as look at you."

The dean and Molé Anbisol chuckled broadly.

"Is there a multicultural angle on this, Molé? I want to know where it's coming from."

"Montague was a white male," said Anbisol.

"There you go," said the president happily.

"Trouble is," said the dean, "it's going to look hegemonis-
tic."

I chimed in: "Sexist. Don't forget sexist."

"I see what you mean," said the president. "I want to be
deniable on this, Molé."

"I understand, sir."

The president looked at us over his gold aviator glasses.

"What do they want?" he said abruptly.

"They want half a million dollars," said the dean.

"Give it to them," said the president. "Take it out of my
discretionary account. Just keep me deniable on this."

Later that day, the dean explained the system he had devised for
paying off whoever needed to be paid off. Deep lines of aggrava-
tion and worry had formed in his face. We were in his office and
it didn't seem much fun being a dean.

"Money comes out of the president's discretionary account,
Asherfeld," he said. "Means the drop's got to be untraceable.
You understand what I'm saying?"

"You're saying the drop's got to be untraceable."

"Right," said the dean. Very solemnly he pushed an envelope
toward me. "Five checks in here, one hundred thousand apiece.
They're made out to cash. You take them, set up five accounts at
the B of A. That's so there's one whole layer between where this
money is going and the university. Then what you've got to do
is make fifty ten thousand dollar drops in these accounts."

The dean pushed a piece of paper toward me with a list of
account numbers.

"It's a hell of a lot of work, but this way—"

I cut the dean off.

"This way the IRS doesn't have to be notified of any deposit."

"Right," said the dean.

"It'll take at least three business days for the checks to clear."

"No choice," said the dean.

"I suppose not," I said; I pointed to the account numbers.

"Where'd these come from?"

"The tape," said the dean.

I took the checks and the paper with the account numbers and said: "Me, I'd want the money in cash."

"Why's that, Asherfeld?"

"I'm sentimental that way."

Retro Chic

THE UNIVERSITY closed itself down. The golden coeds did whatever golden coeds generally do over spring break. Leland Sturz kept sitting on his autopsy report. I didn't know what Bulton Limbish or Mike Dottenberry were doing, or Zoe Dindle, or Rimbaud. I didn't care.

After a while I got up from my desk, slapped a little Old Spice on my cheeks, and pulled on my blue windbreaker.

It was warmer than it should have been outside, with pale cirrus clouds drifting in from the ocean; but there was a hard bright light in the air that made my eyes smart.

I ambled down Greenwich and over to St. Mary's Park and then over to Columbus, just where Chinatown starts to wash up against what's left of the Italian part of North Beach. Go up Columbus, you get hole-in-the-wall Italian restaurants—a few tables, sawdust on the floor, the place actually run by Italians with absolutely no English; the Chinese restaurants are around the corner on the side streets, beside the teeming vegetable stands and the strange Chinese movie theaters.

I crossed Broadway and stopped to look at the used book stand outside City Lights bookstore. There was the usual stuff on display and a few how-to books. How to acquire fluency in Urdu. How to learn celestial navigation. How to stop loving a loser.

Underneath all the junk was a large picture book entitled *Angels on Wheels*. It was a kind of profile of the Hell's Angels, with a lot of glossy photographs of their cut-down motorcycles and the sort of dopey captions that some people figure make hoodlums look deep.

The book wasn't old; it had been put out by a San Francisco

outfit called Lorimar. I made a note of the name and then wandered up toward the heart of Chinatown.

I had lunch at a little vegetarian restaurant just where Jackson eases into Columbus. It's the sort of place that never changes. The same elderly Chinese waiter is always eating his own lunch from a bowl when you come in. The food is always the same. No one is ever glad to see you and no one is ever disappointed when you leave.

Later that afternoon I called Lorimar from my apartment. Someone named Lettitia said she was out just now. She said she'd be back; she said she'd love to hear from me. She said bye-bye and *ciao*.

I didn't leave a message and I didn't say bye-bye. Instead, I pulled my windbreaker back on and trudged downstairs. I thought of walking over to Pacific Heights and I thought of taking a bus, but I didn't feel much like walking anymore and the guys who drive the large, stained Muni buses generally figure they're practicing for the grand prix. I took my own car.

Lorimar had an office in lower Pacific Heights, just off Geary Boulevard. Years ago this used to be a sullen, dangerous neighborhood, now it's upscale and chirpy, with patisseries on every corner and places that sell exotic coffee and boutiques run by thin men in very tight pants and one of those multiplex movie theaters playing eight feature films simultaneously. The neighborhood is still sullen and dangerous, only now no one knows it anymore.

I parked in front of a wedding cake Victorian on Clay and walked down Fillmore, past a Greek restaurant and a place serving Cajun food and a singles bar that had been very hot for a month.

At Post I called Lorimar again.

"This is Lettitia," said someone who figured that that explained everything.

I told her that I had seen the book. Liked the graphics; loved the *concept*. I laid it on thick. She didn't mind. No one ever does.

"I'm *so* glad," she said.

I told her I was interested in doing something with the Angels, something now. "Just happen to be in the neighborhood," I said. "If you've got a minute?"

"But *mais oui*," she said.

She didn't ask who I was and she didn't want an introduction. I got the impression that business might not be too brisk at Lorimar.

The office was on the second floor of a little complex between Post and Sacramento. Downstairs everything was dark wood and brass fixtures, but the stairs themselves were cinderblock with a red iron railing and they gave the impression of swaying as you walked up them.

I rapped on Lorimar's door with the edge of my ring.

Lettitia Lorimar opened the door herself. She had a lot of brunette hair and a long face and she wore very aggressive red lipstick and dangly brass earrings; she was chewing gum in a way calculated to suggest she was too cool to be vulgar.

She shook my hand and sniffed the air: "Love what you're wearing."

"What? Old Spice?"

"Retro chic," she said with a shrug, "Come on in."

The office consisted of a single large room. There was a huge picture of Madonna on one wall.

"Get you something?" asked Lettitia amiably, cracking her gum as she spoke.

I shook my head and patted my stomach.

"I know," she said. "I had a garlic pizza for lunch, now I'm so gassy I could die."

She sat down and slung her leg over the arm of her chair. She wore black leggings over her ankles and heavy black lace-up boots.

"So you're like in the business?" she asked.

I nodded. "I represent Hong Fong Wong, shipping, cruise lines."

Lettitia nodded knowingly. "He's LA but no? Very big?"

"Bigger than big."

"Do a lot of work for the Angels?" I asked.

"Promos, TV, some runway work, you name it. We are absolutely exclusive in northern California. You were like processing what concept?"

"It's all still pre-pre," I said. "Needs to be brainstormed, but something like Cruise with the Hell's Angels."

160

I spread my hands out in front of my face as if I were framing a scene.

"You know what I mean? We'd put the Angels and their bikes on a cruise out of LA. Convert the jogging path into a demo track. Let people get up close and personal, autograph brunches, Captain's table with the Angels."

"I love it," said Lettitia. "It's nouveau *and* it's classic."

"You've got a publicity book, some photographs of the boys, something to go on?"

"But *mais out*," said Lettitia. She left the table and fetched a large leather covered photograph album from the bookstand along the wall. She spread the book on the table and opened it with the tip of her pointed fingernail.

The first photograph showed a moustachioed thug wearing Angel colors; I recognized him right away. I also knew he was in prison.

"Now I can't get you Sonny," she said. "He is absolutely booked until, oh, at least five years into who knows when. What about Frank?"

She pointed to the next photograph. It depicted a giant straddling a motorcycle and almost dwarfing it; he was at least seven feet tall and carried on his face an expression of prehistoric ferocity.

"He's very poised, good copy. Were you thinking of like on-board seminars?"

"Absolutely."

"Frank is a terrific motivational speaker," said Lettitia.

I looked up from the picture of the monster.

"What's he talk about?"

"Overcoming fear," she said. "Interpersonal hang-ups. Relationships."

I flipped through a few of the pages. I figured that the real low life came at the end of the book. I pointed to a ratty looking character standing on what seemed to be a dingy suburban lawn.

"That's Ratman," said Lettitia.

"Ratman?"

"He's sort of a performance artist."

I must have looked quizzical.

"Works with animals, into ecology."

I remembered that Wanker had told me once that one of the Angels liked to bite the heads off live rats.

Lettitia shrugged.

"I don't know if he's still available. I'd have to call. He spends a lot of time in the Twilight one, if you know what I mean. But he'd be terrific for promo. We can arrange for pictures and I can cover you with file copy."

"I don't know," I said, rubbing my hand across my mouth. "His kind of performance art and all on board ship?"

I rotated my hand in the air to signify doubt.

"I know what you mean," said Lettitia.

I flipped a few more pages until I came to a picture of a tense looking man leaning against a cut-down chopper.

"Dennis Bigelow," said Lettitia. "Oh, he is a sweetie. Cruise, he'd be perfect. Very with it."

I squinted at the photograph.

"What is this, Berkeley?"

"Oakland, I think."

I flipped through a few more pages and then got up heavily and closed the book.

"Looks good to me," I said. "I'll talk to Mr. Wong directly. I think he's going to love the concept. Probably want to do a cruise the next couple of months. Use a lot of the boys."

"Not a problem," said Lettitia, cracking her gum luxuriously. "Keep me faxed."

I scooted down the steps of the office complex and called information in Oakland from the payphone on the corner of Post and Fillmore and asked for Dennis Bigelow.

The number *is*, said the operator, who seemed tremendously pleased at having found something that morning. Then I called Bigelow. I had just enough change on hand. He wasn't there but the woman who answered the telephone said that he'd be back in a few minutes.

"Think he'll be around in an hour or so if I come on out?"

"Sure," she said. "He'll be in the front with his head stuck in the hood of an '82 Camaro. Amount of time he spends working on that automobile, you've got to believe there's gold somewhere in the crankcase."

I chuckled and hung up.

Bigelow lived in the Oakland flats, about a million miles from where Richard Montague had had a house. The neighborhood isn't ugly, but it isn't attractive either; the pink bungalows and stucco houses were put up after the war by people who were thrilled by all that sunshine and didn't much care for urban planning. Now everything looks vaguely disorganized without being charming.

I turned on Juarez and again on Maioranos and parked at the head of the block.

Bigelow's house was two down—a faded pink stucco job with a wooden porch and a shabby square of grass divided by a concrete walkway in front of the porch.

There was a beat-up Camaro in the driveway; a wiry man stripped to the waist was leaning over the hood. I walked over to the side of the car.

"Dennis Bigelow?" I asked.

He looked up from the open hood of his car. His arms were covered with grease but he had that well-kempt look that some men retain no matter what. His pants would have retained a crease in a cesspool. He didn't say anything.

"Lettitia Lorimar gave me your name."

Bigelow nodded with what appeared to be a trace of amusement in his eyes.

"That dumb twat?"

"The very one."

"She tells you she can put you on Donahue, don't give her five grand see if she does it."

Bigelow picked up the towel on which he had been leaning and begin to strip some of the grease from his hands.

"That what she nicked you guys for?"

"Hell, no. That's what she nicked *each* of us for. Be more'n twenty-five thousand and counting before we figured that pissing in a hole be about as likely to get us a shot on Donahue."

I was amazed. "Let me get this straight. You guys paid twenty-five thousand upfront to Lettitia Lorimar and she took the money and ran?"

"She got us a date doing protection for a 4-H fair in Olema."

"A 4-H fair?" I was almost sputtering. "You mean cows and bunnies?"

Bigelow nodded again.

"Pigs, too. Don't want to forget them porkers. One of them bust loose, Sonny had to tackle it out in some field."

"You guys have a reputation. How come you didn't go down there, stamp on her face with hobnailed boots or rip out her fingernails with pliars?"

"Yeah, well, we wanted to. Damned if just before we set off she wouldn't call, tell us about some terrific thing going to happen faster than you can spit. I mean, if it wasn't a shot on Donahue then Jack Nicholson himself was going to come up the Bay Area, play Sonny in some terrific feature film. One time she told us wait by the phone for a call from Hef, invitation to the Playboy Club. We figured we'd ride down LA, pussy be hanging off our noses. By the time we figured out Jack wasn't about to play Sonny and Hef wasn't about to call, Sonny was doing dark time, Frankie had open-heart surgery, the rest of us just let it slide."

I let the mystery and wonder of it all wash over me.

"So you come out here, tell me I'm a jerk for pissing away my money. I know that already."

"You still riding?"

"Does it look like I'm riding? I got a wife. I got two kids. I got a dog thinks food just sort of grows out the bottom of his bowl. I got an '82 Camaro. I'm lucky end of the month I can open up a can of suds watch pro wrestling. The fat guy, Dr. Doom, he used to ride with the Diablos. You know that? Anyway, I got time for riding? You tell me."

"I guess not."

A chubby woman with startlingly pale skin opened the screen to Bigelow's house and stood by the door, resting her hip against the frame. She was dressed in shorts and a short white sweater. She cupped her hands to her mouth.

"You coming?" she shouted.

"Innasecond," Bigelow shouted back, reaching up to close the hood of his car.

"You want you should come in, have a beer?"

"Why not?"

We walked up to the front porch. "Honey," Bigelow said, "this is some fella walked off the street tell me how dumb I am to piss my money away."

Honey gave me an absolutely gorgeous smile—the thing was like a sunburst. I could see why Dennis Bigelow might have given up riding with the Angels just to see that smile.

"I know who you are," she said. "You called an hour ago."

I smiled at the two of them; it wasn't hard. "Aaron Asherfeld," I said.

We sat in the kitchen of the little house; Honey got us both beers. I noticed that Bigelow, who had been covered with grease when I first saw him, now seemed almost clean sitting at his kitchen table. It was a gift.

A golden retriever with an angry bald patch on his back wandered into the kitchen to sniff me and pay his respects. Bigelow scratched him behind the ears; the dog stood there, appreciating the attention, and then wandered off and sank into a corner of the kitchen with a whoosh.

The three of us sat sipping beer from the cool bottles.

Honey finished hers up with a long swallow, exposing her white neck as she drank.

"I'm off," she said, placing her bottle down emphatically on the table.

She reached over to kiss Bigelow on the top of his head, flashed me her sunburst smile, and walked out of the kitchen in that self-satisfied way satisfied women have of walking.

"I can see why you quit riding," I said.

"Yeah," said Bigelow agreeably.

I took out a copy of Richard Montague's file folder picture and placed it on the table. The copy was less vivid than the original, but it was still clear.

"This someone you remember?" I asked.

"Sure," said Bigelow. "One of the wannabes."

"Wannabes?"

"Wannabe tough, wannabe righteous, wannabe an Angel. You'd be surprised how many wannabes used to hang around Oakland weekends, some weekday nights. Had a state supreme court justice one time, damned if he didn't try to go on a ride down to Monterey. Put his machine down on the Bay Bridge. Wasn't wearing a helmet. Hear he gorked out."

"Probably still on the bench," I said.

"Probably," said Bigelow, tapping the picture of Montague.

"Your boy was some sort of professor and all. Thought he was hotter'n pistol martial arts expert. Black belt in aikido or some such shit like that. Told Sonny he was super deadly, Sonny told him he wouldn't last a minute against Frankenstein."

"What happened?"

"Shit, what do you think happened? Frank comes out, pushes this little twerp over and sits on his chest. Montague, he's lying there, trying this kick and that kick and poking at Frankenstein with his fingers, only thing is you can't do much martial artsing you lying on the ground with three hundred pounds on your chest. Didn't hear much from him after that about no black belt."

"You guys ever handle any trade with him?" I asked casually.

Bigelow looked up toward the porch.

"What kind of trade?"

"I hear he was dealing on campus."

Bigelow said: "Not that I know of. Had a chemist riding with us for a while. Got himself shot by some kid taking target practice from an overpass."

"Lot of occupational hazards, riding."

"Tell me about it," said Bigelow, taking a swig.

"Let me ask you something," I said tentatively. "You ever hear of Montague involved with any of the Angels?"

Bigelow looked up alertly.

"Involved how?"

"Involved so that they're doing more than comparing crankcases."

"You shitting me?" Bigelow asked. The warmth had gone out of his voice.

"It's not my idea," I said quickly. "That's the rumor. Supposed to be a stash of videos, too."

"What kind of videos?"

"S and M. One of them's supposed to show Montague's death."

"Sort of stuff is disgusting," Bigelow said. He was genuinely offended.

"I'm not arguing with you," I said.

We sat there for a while longer, drinking our beers.

After a few moments, Bigelow said: "Frankie be the one to know. He was kind of bent himself."

"Know where I can get in touch with Frankie?"

"He's in the hospital, Pacific something medical center, in the city," said Bigelow. "Waiting for a new heart."

"What's the matter with the old one?"

"Rust," said Bigelow pleasantly.

I reached the Bay Bridge as the rush hour traffic was building to a peak. I tried listening to the radio: it didn't do any good. It never does. Someone was singing Guatemalan folk songs on KPFA and after she got through with them, someone named Chewy translated them into broken English. Afterward someone else began a complicated pitch for money. She had a flat uninflected bitter voice. The only thing good about the radio is that you can't see the performers.

The long line of cars waiting to get onto the bridge snaked its way along as the sky filled up with gashes of gold and pink. I opened my window despite the smell of the freeway and let the cool air wash into the car. A large bus maneuvered next to me, the thing ungainly as a dinosaur; on the side of the bus it said Department of Corrections in black letters. I looked up. The men staring back at me had the patient vacant expression of men for whom time no longer matters. One man caught my eye and solemnly lifted his arm, letting his hand flop in the Italian gesture of regret and disappointment.

I crossed the bridge before the light had completely burned itself out of the western sky and got off at the earthquake ruined exit that drops traffic onto city streets south of Market.

I was trying to make sense of what Dennis Bigelow had told me; but *trying* to make sense of something is like trying to sneeze. The more you do it, the less it works.

The California Pacific Medical Center takes up most of a block in Pacific Heights. I parked on Broadway in front of the ornate and gorgeous building that houses the Italian consulate and walked around the corner to the hospital. The information computer at the entrance to the center obligingly told me that coronary care was located in the Dorothy and Edgar Shumlowitz Memorial Pavilion. Unbidden, the silent machine then floated a map on its screen, complete with a large *you are here* arrow and a series of short arrows leading from the center of the building to the pavilion. In 1974, as associate at the firm where I was working told me he was chucking it all to join a couple of oddballs trying to market a personal computer.

I told him he was nuts.

From time to time, I see his yacht in the bay; its home port is Nice.

I crossed the tiled marble floor of the Dorothy and Edgar Shumlowitz Memorial Pavilion to the main admitting desk and asked for Frank Smith.

"You wan' spell tha' for me?" asked the Hispanic receptionist.

"S-m-i-t-h," I spelled. "It's kind of a tricky name."

"They all tricky," said the receptionist glumly. "He's in critical care. I don' think you can go there now."

"I'm his spiritual adviser," I said.

"Thas different," she agreed. "Those people, they need help from Awmighty God."

"We all do," I said.

Critical care was actually the second of two wings devoted to very sick cookies; the first was emergency care. That's where they brought the heart attack victims, fibrillating out their lives with weak disorganized cardiac rhythms, and heart transplant cases right after they sewed in the baboon's heart. Critical care was pretty much the holding tank for people who were going to get well or were going to die, but weren't going to do it right away.

It was still light outside, but the reception area had the cold feeling of any white space illuminated by fluorescent lighting.

The duty nurse was a prim, no-nonsense woman. She sat on a stool at the nurse's station; she was marking entries on a chart. I asked for Frankenstein's room; she gave it to me without looking up. She would have passed through a Mafia hit team. They couldn't have done any more damage and they might have done some good.

I knocked on Frankenstein's door and entered his room without waiting for a response. The room was dark, except for the flickering of a television. The sound was down. Even lying in bed, it was clear that Frankenstein had been a powerful man; he still looked massive. He turned his fully bearded face toward me; a oxygen tube ran from his nostrils to a tank.

"Frankie," I said. "How you feeling?"

He must have thought I was a new resident: he launched into his complaints at once.

"How'm I feeling? I can't breathe, I can't feel my feet, I can't eat, I can't drink and I can't piss. That answer your question?"

"That bad?"

"Worse."

"I'm sorry to hear it," I said. "But listen Frankie, I was talking to Dennis Bigelow today—"

Frankenstein cut me off: "I don't know you," he said. There was nothing wrong with his memory.

"No, you don't," I agreed. "Talk to me anyway."

"Why should I?"

"You have something better to do?"

Frankenstein turned his face back toward the television.

"You got that right," he said. "I got nothing to do except lie here and wait. So you were talking to Dennis Bigelow."

I took out Montague's picture and held it up; Frankenstein looked at it briefly.

"Tell me anything about him?"

Frankenstein turned his massive head toward me again.

"Suppose I tell you to piss off."

"I'm not with the police, Frankie," I said. "I'd piss off."

Frankenstein's dark brown eyes held the clouded obscure look of someone counting out his life in hours.

"Who you with then?"

"Twentieth Century Fox," I said.

"That a fact?" he said. "Dumb cunt finally came through with something."

He meant Lettitia Lorimar; there seemed to be rare unanimity of opinion among the Angels as to her proper designation.

"Studio sent me up check out some rumors."

"What kind of rumors?"

"Rumors he was bent," I said, making a hole with the thumb and forefinger of my left hand and slipping the index finger of my right hand through the hole.

It wasn't a terrifically elegant gesture.

"Supposed to be some videos out there, sort of thing that might embarrass the studio."

"Never heard of no videos," Frankenstein said, closing his eyes. He seemed uninterested in the whole idea and too tired to lie about it.

"One other thing."

"What's that?" he mumbled.

"You guys ever do any protection work for Chinese in the city, run illegals, that sort of stuff?"

There was a long pause; I thought Frankenstein might have drifted off.

"Oil and water," he mumbled obscurely, his heavy eyes closed.

The door opened silently and a young physician stepped into the room; he paid absolutely no attention to me as he checked Frankenstein's chart.

"How's he doing?" I asked when we were out in the hall.

The physician shrugged. "We find a seven-foot gorilla driving fast on one of the freeways, he'll be okay."

I didn't know Marianne Omo, but it wasn't hard to find her once I set my mind to it. She was featured almost every other day on the society page of the *Chronicle;* she was a chair something of this and a coordinator of that; she liked to throw intimate little parties for darling French diplomatic couples. She dressed in dresses by Versace. She kept a home in Pacific Heights and a home in Cap Ferrat. She was as busy as a beaver and chirpy as a woodchuck, and looked like a cross between the two, judging from her pictures.

Her own telephone was unlisted, of course, but her social secretary, Susan Ginsburg, had a number all her own. I called her up and told her I was thinking of doing a profile of Marianne Omo for *Vanity Fair.*

"I'm talking about a very authentic honest piece," I said. "I don't do puff jobs."

"Oh, of course, Mr. Asherfeld," said Susan Ginsburg. "I'm sure Marianne wouldn't be interested in any other kind of piece."

I told the secretary that I'd be in town for the day; I told her I was flying to Los Angeles to speak with Ronald Reagan about *his* biography; I told her that I could give Marianne Omo half an hour.

"Her schedule is simply impossible, Mr. Asherfeld. She's redecorating the kitchen again, wouldn't you know, but I can get you in right now if you hurry."

I said I'd hurry.

Marianne Omo lived on the end of Broadway in an enormous red brick house that faced the open woodlands of the Presidio. There was a black wrought iron fence that ran around the small front lawn and two gigantic clipped and trimmed evergreens on either side of the front door.

I rang the doorbell and waited. From far away, someone shouted "Darnkey, the door" in a languid voice. I rang the bell again.

The young man who finally opened the door had sleep-puffed eyes and a debauched air. He wasn't hung over if only because he wasn't entirely sober. He peered at me and said: "Why didn't Darnkey get the door?"

"No idea," I said. "He's probably in the pantry practicing his curtsey."

"Probably," said the young man. "He never gets it right."

He peered at me some more and then said: "You're here to see Muffy, aren't you? She's doing something virtuous in the sun room. You know these commercials, the one where they show an egg and someone says this is your brain and then they show the egg scrambling and this same person says this is your brain on drugs? I've been up all night testing whether it's true."

"What you discover?"

"Oh, it's true all right."

He weaved slightly at the door and then said "See you," and wandered back into the house, leaving me at the front door.

I found Muffy in the sun room: I just followed the thumping beat of an exercise routine from the hallway back through the cool and somber gallery and out onto a beautiful atrium; the thing was entirely enclosed by the house itself but filled with light that flooded through the elegant cut glass panels in the ceiling.

I stood by the door for a moment. Marianne Omo was pedaling away furiously on an exercise bicycle, the music blaring from four speakers set up in the corners of the atrium. I was surprised it didn't shatter the glass. She was dressed in a grey one-piece leotard. She saw me standing there, wiped a trickle of sweat from her face, and got off her bike. The moment her rump left the seat, the music stopped.

She walked over and shook hands with me firmly. She was a tall rangy woman with a young woman's thinness, but without any curves, her body all long lean sad muscles and bony hips and knees. Her face had wonderful sculpted features and the deep coloring of years spent in the sun, but the skin had been stretched tight by plastic surgery. She had great hair, though, an enormous brunette mop of the stuff.

She looked me over closely.

"*You're* Aaron Asherfeld?" she said dubiously.

"The one and only."

"I'm sure that's true," she said, "but a writer? I think not."

"I'm not here to do a piece about you, Mrs. Omo," I confessed. "I wanted to ask you a few questions about your husband."

"Odo?" said Marianne Omo, wiping her face with the towel she had draped over her leather exercise belt. It was the same gesture that Odo Omo had employed. "Whatever for?"

She seemed amused. She motioned me to one of the elegant iron chairs with the floral pattern on its back; there were half a dozen or so scattered around the room. "Do sit, Mister One and Only. I make it a point never to sit or recline unless I'm exercising or sleeping. Seats are death to the derriere."

I sat gratefully on one of the chairs. Marianne Omo stood in front of me and began stretching herself, bending over from the waist and clutching at her ankles, and then touching her right elbow to her left knee and her left elbow to her right knee.

"Ask away," she said imperturbably.

I decided that this was not a woman who would appreciate indirection.

"What's your husband got to hide?" I said.

Marianne Omo stopped stretching and put her hands on her hips.

"Whatever do you mean?"

I told her about the coach house and the camera and the security guard. Then I said: "He had two thugs go to the trouble of warning me to mind my own business."

"That sounds like perfectly good advice to me, Mr. Asherfeld."

"I get a lot of good advice, Mrs. Omo. I don't generally get it from people prepared to enforce their views by working me over."

Marianne Omo resumed stretching; she was now loosening her hamstrings, holding her leg up against the back of the chair next to mine, and leaning into the muscle.

"That should tell you something," she said. "That should tell you of the importance my husband attaches to his privacy."

"It tells me a lot," I said. "But it doesn't tell me *why* he attaches so much importance to his privacy."

Marianne Omo straightened herself up; her eyes were flashing.

"Mr. Asherfeld," she said. "If you knew *that*, his affairs wouldn't be private, would they?"

It was a good answer. I said: "I suppose not."

Then Marianne Omo added: "If you're here to suggest that my husband keeps some little bimbo down at his ranch, I am not interested."

"I wasn't going to suggest that at all," I said. "And as far as I know, it isn't true."

"Good," said Marianne Omo decisively.

I was mystified; my expression must have shown it.

"Don't frown, Mr. Asherfeld," said Marianne Omo. "It leads to lines." She paused in her stretching to look at me critically. "Although in your case I'd say good advice comes too late."

"It generally does," I said.

Marianne Omo continued stretching and I continued sitting.

Finally, I said: "You've been so helpful, tell me one other thing."

"Yes?"

"What kind of tattoo is it your husband wears?"

"Tattoo?" she asked, her leg in front of her. "Don't be absurd. My husband has never worn a tattoo in his life. I wouldn't allow it."

I sat there flustered, Marianne Omo standing in front of me. She was bending over from the waist, trying to place her palms on the floor. When she had gotten all the way down, I got up, scraping the metal struts of the chair against the tiled floor of the atrium.

"I'll let myself out, Mrs. Omo," I said.

"Yes, do," she said from her bent-over position, her head between her knees.

My Way

THE CHINESE GIRL standing demurely by the reservation desk could not have been older than fourteen. She was beautiful beyond belief, with translucent skin, absolutely straight, lustrous oiled hair, and an unmoving face of such purity of line that I kept looking to make sure that I was not being deceived by my lying eyes.

I had told her who I was. She tried pronouncing my name; it was hard going.

"A-un Ash-fed?" she said hopelessly, allowing herself to display the faintest of faint hints of a smile.

"It's very hard, I know," I said.

"I tell Jimmy Joy you here," she said and slid out from behind the lectern. She was dressed in a green and black high-necked Chinese hostess gown; the gown hung straight down from her frail collarbones. She had no curves, but she walked in a way that suggested an austere, an unfathomable, sensuality.

Jimmy Joy's was one of those very expensive Chinese restaurants that were popular in the fifties and that are still popular with tourists. There are leather banquettes in the main dining room and soft lighting and muzak and efficient classy waiters; the food is strictly Cantonese. At other Chinese restaurants in Chinatown you got sweet and sour pork in one of those bowls with a stainless steel top; at *Jimmy Joy's,* you got a little portion of fresh minced noodles with peanut sauce served on a large shiny plate.

I looked around the dark restaurant. There was a large picture of Frank Sinatra in the lobby: it had obviously been taken many years ago. It showed Sinatra standing next to a beaming Jimmy Joy; he had pencilled in the words: "To my good friend, Jimmy Joy, and signed himself "Frank." There were smaller framed pictures of Sinatra mounted on the walls of the hall leading upstairs; and still more pictures of Sinatra over the banquettes of the dining room itself.

Sinatra was singing "My Way" on the stereo.

Jimmy Joy glided down from the stairs leading to the upper dining room. He was a small man, with a careful face. He wore an iridescent grey silk suit and highly polished pumps. His gold watch with its dull gold band was the sort of thing sold to people who think they're being elegant because their jewelry doesn't actually flicker at night.

"Mr. Ash-fed," said Jimmy Joy dispassionately, extending his hand; he swept his other hand toward the walls.

"You may observe that my estabishment has been honored by the presence of Mr. Fank Sinatra."

"Hard not to," I said.

"Mr. Fank Sinatra, he eat here every time he in town," said Jimmy Joy proudly.

"How often is that?"

Joy pointed to the large picture.

"1957, he here last."

Jimmy Joy's English was fluent; it was just incomplete.

"Good year, 1957," I said.

"The best," said Jimmy Joy, leading me upstairs. "Private dinner," he added mysteriously.

The little banquet room on the second floor had just enough room for a large elegantly appointed table surrounded by a set of eight high-backed red chairs. The walls were covered in a deep purple crushed velvet. The large picture of Frank Sinatra beaming at Jimmy Joy in the lobby had been reproduced so that it was proportional to the smaller size of the wall.

The exquisite child who had greeted me at the reception counter flowed into the room and stood demurely by Jimmy Joy.

"This Nancy Sinatra Joy," said Jimmy Joy proudly, inclining his head in one of those culturally curious gestures Asians make from time to time.

Nancy Sinatra Joy allowed her delicate face the slightest suggestion of a smile and then glided from the room.

"Nancy Sinatra Joy?"

"Everyone in my family, they name after Fank," said Jimmy Joy. "He the inspiration of my happiness."

"I can see that. You have a lovely daughter."

"Nancy Sinatra Joy not my daughter," said Jimmy Joy gravely. "Wife."

I must have looked flabbergasted.

"Old wife too old," he said. "Trade in." He laughed uproariously. "It's what Fank do."

The bamboo curtain parted and Wah Gee slipped into the room; he nodded to me and nodded deferentially to Jimmy Joy. He was accompanied by a heavyset Chinese of about thirty. Despite his features, he carried himself in that relaxed way that indicated that he was American born.

Jimmy Joy stood up formally. "My eldest son," he said proudly, "Fank Sinatra Jr. Joy."

"How you doin'?" said Frank Sinatra Jr. Joy.

I said I was doing fine; we all sat down at the table again.

"I arrange dinner," said Jimmy Joy.

"You're in for a treat my dad arranges dinner," said Frank Sinatra Jr. Joy.

As if on cue, a diminutive waiter slid into the banquet room and removed our covering plates; almost immediately he was followed by another waiter, serving the first course.

We ate in almost total silence for the next hour or so: course after course of Cantonese dishes. Frank Sinatra Jr. Joy was right. The meal was extraordinary.

176

It was not until the last dish had been cleared and the table-cloth changed that Jimmy Joy leaned back, cigarette in hand, and looked discreetly at me over the half-spectacles he had worn throughout dinner.

"So," he said emphatically.

"My dad says you have a problem," said Frank Sinatra Jr. Joy. "I'd like to know about it."

I looked closely at Jimmy Joy's eldest son. His face was plump and somewhat pitted, and he had small, hairless hands. There was something compact and brutal in the way he held himself.

Wah Gee looked over the table. "Fank," he began apologeti-cally, but Frank Sinatra Jr. Joy cut him off with a hard glance. "I want to hear about it from Asherfeld over here," he said evenly.

"Me? I don't have a problem," I said. "The only problem I have is probably that I ate too much. Good food, though. I can see why Frank comes here."

Jimmy Joy positively beamed. "Best in San Francisco," he said. "Best Chinese food in San Francisco, that why Fank come here."

"Dad," said Frank Sinatra Jr. Joy, a note of exasperation in his voice.

"You don't have a problem," said Frank Sinatra Jr. Joy, "how come you're shaking down my dad?"

"I never met your dad before tonight, Frank. You know that."

"Wah Gee, then. He works for my dad. He tells me that you're over his office, trying to put the bite on him."

"Fank," said Wah Gee hopelessly.

Frank Sinatra Jr. Joy cut him off again, with another hard look.

I pushed my chair back; Nancy Sinatra Joy slipped noiselessly into the room. She stood directly behind Jimmy Joy and began sedately to massage his temples with her fingertips. Her face did not move; her carriage was entirely erect and yet relaxed.

"I looked up Wah Gee in order to get some more informa-tion about a client of his—Richard Montague. I'm checking out some leads, that's all."

Frank Sinatra Jr. Joy snorted derisively.

"Material like that's confidential. You know that, Mr. Asherfeld. It's like a priest. You go up to a priest, ask him what happened in confession?"

"Fank," said Jimmy Joy, leaning his head back to be cradled by the square of his wife's arms. "We not getting anywhere."

I said: "Look guys, let's put our cards on the table. I met the *Marquess de Camellia* last Tuesday night. I know what was on the ship. I know what came off the ship. I know where it went to. What I don't know is how Richard Montague fits in all this. You want to tell me, fine. If not, that's fine with me, too. I can always speak to the INS."

It wasn't a very elegant speech, but I thought it might get the job done.

Jimmy Joy looked at me for a long moment and said: "What you know about suffering?"

I said: "I was married three times."

It was a stupid thing to say, and I was sorry I said it.

Jimmy Joy said: "I born in Fujian. You know where it is?"

I shook my head.

"I no think so," said Jimmy Joy. "My mother, she spend life in water. Rice grow in water. Every day, she stand in water, bending over. I have six brothers and sisters. She lose them all. My mother, old woman at thirty."

Jimmy Joy ran his hands backwards against his cheeks to simulate sagging skin.

"Thirty! Old woman. One day, warlords come, bang, bang, everybody they shoot. What you know about any of this? You big fat and dumb, you come here make trouble for Chinese."

"What would Frank Sinatra say, he knows you're part of a slave trade?"

"Fank, he have big heart, big as all outdoors. He understand, Chinese people help Chinese people."

Jimmy Joy stood up; he was shaking with indignation.

His son and Wah Gee stood up as well. I thought the party might be over.

Jimmy Joy exited from the banquet room followed by his elegant young wife.

Frank Sinatra Jr. Joy said: "You've gotten him all upset."

"And just when he was going to tell us how he met Frank Sinatra, too," I said.

For Your Eyes Only

I DIDN'T HAVE EVERYTHING in hand, but I thought I had enough to talk with Dreyfus at the Federal Building.

"Hey, the wise guy," he said jovially when I telephoned. "I had this feeling you'd call. My horoscope it says I should expect the unexpected."

"You're reading horoscopes now, Dreyfus? Pretty soon you'll be dating a sex therapist."

Dreyfus chuckled his fast nervous chuckle; he told me to come by at noon; he said he'd round up Manny to sit in on the meeting.

It was only ten in the morning; I had time to kill. I turned on the little television that I kept on the kitchen counter. Someone with a voice with a lot of vibrato was singing a love song to a vacuum cleaner: "Hoover," she kept wailing as the camera followed a curiously self-animated vacuum around a wall-to-wall carpet, "it's got to be you."

There may be a more debased culture on the planet than ours, but I wouldn't bet on it.

I made sure my living room windows were closed and stood by my front door for a moment to look over my apartment. It was a small compact space. I owned everything in the apartment—the couch with the small checked red and white pattern that I had gotten at Wonderama, the bookcases, the furniture and the odds and ends; but the apartment and what was in it didn't belong to me: it wasn't mine. Maybe it had never been.

Dreyfus was waiting for me on the tenth floor of the Federal Building.

"So you been a busy boy?" he said, slapping me on the back.

"Busy enough."

"That's what I said to Manny. I said 'Manny, Asherfeld's been hustling for us out there.' "

Manny Edelweiss was waiting for us in Dreyfus's office; he was sitting at Dreyfus's desk, but his shirt collar was open and he wasn't wearing a tie. He looked relaxed and contemplative.

"How you doing, Asherfeld?" he said, rising in a half crouch from the desk.

It may have been the light, it might have been my mood. I didn't have the feeling that either Dreyfus or Manny Edelweiss were sitting on tenterhooks, waiting to hear what I had to say.

"So what you got, Asherfeld?" said Dreyfus, standing, as usual, with his back to the window. A rubber band had materialized between his stubby thumb and forefinger.

I told Dreyfus and Edelweiss how Montague had used affirmative action to hide CSR.

Dreyfus and Manny Edelweiss whistled the same sour note simultaneously.

"One smart cookie," said Dreyfus.

I told them about the tip I had gotten from Dee Dee Frobenmyer; then I told them about Neava Climax. "Montague was friends with two other members of the department, Bulton Limbish, Mike Dottenberry. They used to ride together. A week or so after I speak to Neava Climax, Limbish is busted by the Palo Alto police. It could be a matter of bad luck. Or it could be something else."

"What?" said Manny Edelweiss.

"Neava Climax trying to cut her losses," I said.

"Limbish came to me, asked for my help with the Palo Alto police. It didn't take him long to put the finger on Mike Dottenberry."

"Not much honor among these thieves," said Dreyfus.

I was going to put Dreyfus and Manny Edelweiss in the bigger picture. But I didn't.

Dreyfus waved his hand to stop me. "Doesn't matter, Asherfeld," he said. He turned to Manny. "Isn't that right, Manny? It doesn't matter anymore."

I was surprised.

"Why's that, Dreyfus?"

Manny held up a small accountant's ledger. "On account of this," he said.

I could see from across the room that the ledger was entitled "Commercial Scientific Research."

"Came in the mail the other day. Books are up to date, not a penny missing. Me and Manny, we checked the accounts ourselves over at the B of A in Oakland. Money's right where it's supposed to be."

"When was it posted to the account?"

"I know what you're thinking, Asherfeld, but that's not our problem. Money's where it's supposed to be. If it got there late, well, better late than never."

"And this business with affirmative action. You figure that's all right, too?"

"Asherfeld," said Dreyfus in a kindly voice, "between you, me and the lamppost, affirmative action's just a way to keep the monkeys quiet. I don't like it any more than you do. But hey, I work for the government. The government tells me to go look for the money, I figure when I find it I'm ahead of the game. *Capisce?*"

I didn't see any point in starting a fight with Dreyfus.

"Sure," I said. "Why make work for yourself when you don't have to?"

"Exactly," said Manny Edelweiss.

"There you go," said Dreyfus in his new kindly voice.

"Who sent you the books, by the way?"

"Montague's lawyers. We ask, they're here."

I got up heavily and prepared to go; Dreyfus held up his hand.

"Got something for you, Asherfeld," he said.

He walked over to Manny Edelweiss's desk and picked up a red folder stamped on its cover with the great seal of the State of California.

"Autopsy report," he said. "For your eyes only."

I walked from the Federal Building over to Powell and took a cable car to the top of Russian Hill. Sometimes on a cable car, when the sun is just right, you see the city the way it was in the old days: Arnold Genthe is photographing Chinese mandarins in Chinatown and well upholstered women in low-cut gowns are entertaining fabulously wealthy mining magnates in those magnificent mansions that long ago shook to pieces or were burned to ashes.

Cutting Classes

I DIDN'T DO MUCH OF ANYTHING for the rest of the week. I took in a movie about some dippy young woman who had come to the conclusion that Robert Redford with one million dollars represented a better investment of her time than her husband, who looked like a schnook and had no money. It didn't seem like a rough choice to me, but I've never been good at figuring out what women want. I took my shirts to the cleaners. One day I took a ferry over to Sausalito just because I felt like taking a ferry over to Sausalito. I watched a lot of TV and read a book about the future called *The Devil's Hand,* by an Indian economist who figured that five years tops and the world economy would come crashing down.

I thought that the dean might need a few days to figure out what was going on. He called on Friday morning.

"What's up?"

"You tell me, Asherfeld," he said evenly.

I told the dean that everything was copacetic; I told him not to worry; I said I'd be down after lunch.

"Asherfeld," he said, "this can't wait until after lunch."

"Sure it can," I said. "You'll see. Whatever problem you got now, it'll still be there this afternoon. Trust me on this."

"Asherfeld," said the dean, "don't underestimate me."

He hung up without waiting for an answer.

I dawdled around my apartment for another hour, and then got dressed and wandered down toward Columbus. I had coffee and a cruller at Gino's and spent some time looking at the pornographic magazines at the Magazine Emporium at Columbus and Broadway. The owner was a dishevelled Jordanian refugee with a conically shaped head and an unkempt beard. He had opened the Emporium just when the topless craze hit North Beach and discovered to his delirious surprise that he could safely stock journals that would have gotten him a public flogging in the Middle East. Each year, he pushed the margins of permissibility; now he stocked magazines of absolute depravity

182

and an assortment of bizarre sex toys: inflatable sheep, plastic blow-up women, enormous dildoes. He was a devout Moslem. Five times a day he spread a prayer mat on the floor between his cigar counter and the pornographic magazines and offered up his prayers in a thin tenor.

"You buy or what?" he asked me after I had leafed through the latest issue of an English publication called *Whips and Garters*.

"Me? I figure on standing here and going through your entire stock. Of course, if it bothers you, I could cut down to the next twenty minutes or so."

"It bother me," said Abdul sourly.

After I finished up, I headed back to my apartment and got myself showered and shaved. I thought the dean would appreciate the extra effort.

It was a little past two when I got to the university. I parked behind the dean's office in the dean's parking lot.

The dean ushered me into his own office without saying a word and sat himself at his desk, his elbows resting on the desk top.

Molé Anbisol was seated in his gleaming wheelchair; he had placed the thing next to the dean's desk so that the two of them were facing me.

I sat myself down and said: "What's up?"

"Why don't *you* tell us what's up, Asherfeld?" said the dean. "You're the one didn't make the drop."

"Sure I did," I said. "I just didn't make the drop into the accounts you gave me."

"What?" The dean almost rocketed from his chair. "What're you talking about, Asherfeld? Those instructions were specific. You were supposed to drop the money into those accounts. You've screwed up all my arrangements."

Molé Anbisol cocked his head to regard me better; he looked like a bright little bird.

"Calm down," I said. "I haven't screwed up anything. I had dinner with Wah Gee and Jimmy Joy. They wanted the money delivered in cash. That's what I did. I gave it to them in cash."

"Asherfeld," said the dean, his face reddening with fury, "we don't even *know* that these are the people asking for the money in the first place."

183

"That's true," I said. "They were pretty happy to get five hundred thousand dollars, though. Said thank you and all."

"Asherfeld," said Molé Anbisol somberly. "I can't believe you took it on yourself to change settled arrangements."

He withdrew his head backwards by a bit and looked at me along the corridor of his nose.

"I've got to tell you what's running through my mind," said the dean. "It's not pretty, but I've got to tell you."

"No need," I said. "You're wondering whether I might not have helped myself to that money, stuffed it in an old sock, sent it to the Canary Islands for safekeeping. You're absolutely right. It's the sort of question I'd be asking, too, I were in your shoes."

"If we both know the question, Asherfeld, what by you is the answer?"

I spread my hands apart.

"It's not my problem," I said bluntly, "you guys start wondering at two in the morning where that half million dollars went to."

Molé Anbisol said: "You know that that is an unacceptable response."

He hitched himself up slightly in his wheelchair by pushing down on the armrests with his elbows.

"This institution is not without resources of its own, Asherfeld," he added.

"Sure," I said. "I don't watch my step I could wind up in a room with Gordon Wooper."

"Asherfeld," said the dean, "you don't watch your step you could wind up facing some very serious criminal charges."

"Name one," I said.

"Defalcation of funds."

"You guys give me half a million dollars in cash and tell me to go pay off some blackmailers and you think *I'm* running the risk of being charged with defalcation of funds? Get serious. The money is gone. There's no way to recover it. But look on the bright side. You got what you paid for."

"Explain yourself, Asherfeld," said Molé Anbisol.

"What you wanted was silence, what you got is silence. Sounds like a K-Mart Special to me."

"What are you talking about, Asherfeld?" said the dean.

"I don't think Jimmy Joy and Wah Gee were holding up the university. They're not going to embarrass you. They were happy to get half a million dollars, but they didn't ask for it. Money's well spent even if you didn't have to spend it. As I say, you got what you paid for."

Molé Anbisol placed a long finger alongside his nose and said: "Let me understand this, Asherfeld. Your view now is that Jimmy Joy and Wag Gee were *not* responsible for the tape or for the unpleasant package the dean received? Do you have a reason for saying this?"

"Sure," I said. "I asked them about it. They said they had no idea what I was talking about. Denied knowing anything about Montague's death, any blackmail attempt."

"Asherfeld, that's exactly what you'd expect them to say if they knew something."

"It's also exactly what I'd expect them to say if they didn't," I said.

"This is crazy," said the dean. "If you thought they had nothing to do with this Montague business why'd you give them half a million dollars?"

"You told me to," I said.

The dean's forehead was now covered with perspiration.

"Why they take the money then, they're not involved?" he asked.

"What would you do if someone offered you half a million dollars in a brown paper bag?"

"Yes," said Molé Anbisol suavely. "I dare say we'd all do the same thing. Now that you've boisterously given away half a million dollars of the university's money, are you going to tell us what changed your mind about things?"

"Sure," I said. "You've earned it. I don't think CSR had anything to do with illegal immigrants. For one thing, Montague didn't need the money. He was living off a trust. He didn't need to dirty his hands."

"Why'd he bother with that whole affirmative action business?" asked the dean.

"It was elegant, it was clever. That's the sort of man he was."

"That is fairly conjectural," said Molé Anbisol.

"There's more," I said.

I reached into my briefcase and withdrew two red folders. I tapped the top one.

"Copy of CSR's quarterly audit," I said. "I got it as sort of a gift. Makes for interesting reading. For one thing, the books zero balance."

"But that's what you'd expect," said Molé Anbisol. "If CSR was just being used as a conduit, the books *should* zero balance."

"It's also what you'd expect if CSR wasn't being used as a conduit."

"That's it?" said the dean, spluttering. "What about everything else, Asherfeld? You come in here talking about tattoos, tongs, god knows what. What about Omo's ranch? What about watching the dock at night and the bus?"

"What about it?" I shrugged. "Less than meets the eye," I said. "The business about Violet, for example. Why should she have to leave that coach house every couple of weeks?"

"You tell us, Asherfeld."

"It made sense at first. Nights that Omo's expecting a shipment, they *need* the coach house. That's why Montague had Dottenberry arrange things in the first place. But there's a better explanation. Montague was having an affair with Zoe Dindle and who knows how many other women. He wanted a place to go, someplace convenient. Same thing with Odo Omo. His thugs track me down in San Francisco, I figure the man has something to hide. *Of course* he's got something to hide. It was staring me in the face all along. He's got a harem of ball boys up there on the ranch and doesn't want his world to think he's an imbecile. Odo Omo was doing exactly what he said he was doing. He was protecting his privacy. He didn't want to be outed."

"How do you know this?"

"I talked to his wife. *She* was worried that he was down there with some little bimbo."

"This is crazy," said the dean. "I can't make heads or tails of what you're saying. First you tell us this Omo's busy receiving illegal immigrants. Now you tell us you made a mistake. He's just up there on his ranch communing with the great outdoors. Then you tell us that Wah Gee and Jimmy Joy are smuggling in illegal immigrants. Now you tell us that these are classy citizens, they've got nothing to do with anything illegal."

"No," I said. "I'm not saying that at all. The part about Omo is right. I think Wah Gee and Jimmy Joy *were* involved with illegal immigrants."

"There you go," said the dean.

"I just don't think they were involved in holding up the university."

"Who sent the tapes then?" Molé Anbisol asked in a calm even voice.

"The Dean did."

Molé Anbisol sat back in his wheelchair.

The dean flushed deeply and said: "That's outrageous, Asherfeld. It's in terrible taste."

He began angrily stuffing papers into a briefcase. Abruptly he stopped what he was doing and bunched his fists by the sides of his cheeks.

"How did you know I hadn't used your drop?" I asked.

The dean lifted his head from his bunched fists.

"I told you. They called me."

I shook my head. "Couldn't be," I said. *"They* had the money already. Why would they call you?"

"You tell me, Asherfeld. We're going around in circles."

"No, we're not," I said. "You're lying."

The dean lowered his hands to his desk and sat straight up in his chair. He looked at me steadily through narrowed eyes.

"It wasn't their drop," I said. "It was yours. It's the only way you could have known that I hadn't used the accounts."

"What are you saying?"

"I'm saying that Richard Montague didn't owe Wah Gee or Jimmy Joy anything. I'm saying that they never threatened the university. I'm saying they never asked for payments of any kind. I'm saying they had nothing to do with Montague's death, didn't know about it, couldn't have cared less. I'm saying there was no video of Montague's death because Montague didn't die in any kind of an orgy."

There was a moment of tense silence in the room. The dean

kept his bunched hands on his desk; Molé Anbisol continued to look at me with his malignant spider's eyes.

"It was you," I said to the dean. "You're the only one who knew enough to make it work. I kept you posted myself, every step of the way. You pumped up Rimbaud and Hectorbrand with rumors. You knew the university would pay up."

"You can't prove any of that, Asherfeld."

"I'm not a policeman," I said. "That's not my job."

There was another one of those uncomfortable deep and somber pauses.

Then I said: "There's one more thing."

I opened the second manila envelope I had brought with me and withdrew a thick folder stamped with the seal of the State of California.

"Richard Montague's autopsy report," I said, opening the folder to the first page. There was a full-length forensics photograph of Montague lying on a hospital gurney; he was nude. I pushed the open folder toward the center of the table so that both Molé and the dean could see it.

"Montague's body wasn't mutilated," I said.

"What does that mean?" said the dean defiantly.

"It means you have to answer for UB," I said.

Molé Anbisol shifted in his wheelchair; he gasped. He understood.

Time to Die

DEE DEE FROBENMYER came to see me at Mike Dottenberry's office that afternoon.

He stood tentatively by the door, a big good looking kid with a toothy smile.

"Speak to you for a moment, sir?" he asked.

"Come on in, Dee Dee," I said.

"Matter is confidential," he said, discreetly tipping his head toward Mike Dottenberry.

I got up and walked over to the door.

"Alpha Tau's on suspension," he said. "Dean Climax, she put us on suspension."

I realized that the boy was close to tears. I looked at him for a long moment. He stood there, baffled and confused. He was still young enough to be unable to hide his feelings.

"Blackmail's a tricky thing, Dee Dee," I said. "You'll get the hang of it."

The telephone rang. Mike Dottenberry was sitting placidly at his desk. He picked up the receiver and held it from his ear for a moment and shrugged in perplexity. Then he motioned me to pick it up.

It was Violet calling; she was gasping, crying and wheezing simultaneously.

"Please do something, Mr. Asherfeld," she gulped. "Please come quickly, do something."

"Violet," I said sharply, "where are you?"

"At Donald's. Please do something."

"You call 911, Violet?"

"Yes," she gasped.

"I'll be right there," I said. Then I said to Dottenberry: "Call the Palo Alto police. Get hold of a man named Dulpstrindle. See if you can get him to go over to Dindle's place ASAP."

I tried to rush up Old La Honda Road, but I wasn't driving a Porsche and I didn't have a police escort, so I had to poke behind a moving van struggling slowly up the first part of the hill and a fat waddling Volvo lumbering up the second part.

Even so, I beat 911. Violet was standing alone in front of the Dindle's ranch house; she had been crying hysterically. Now she looked fat and stunned and deeply shocked. She stood on the gravel driveway, her face streaked with tears and her eyes red-rimmed.

"You all right, Violet?" I asked.

She nodded.

"What happened?"

Violet said nothing for a moment and then lifted her head and gave out a loud disorganized cry; it was a waste of time talking with her.

I could hear the wail of a police siren far away ascending Old La Honda Road. I didn't think it would do any good to go into the house alone. I walked over to Violet and put my arm around her shoulder, feeling her blubbery body beneath her blouse, and more or less maneuvered her to the little wooden bench in front of the house. I had her sit down.

The police siren drew closer and closer. I stood there in front of Violet, looking out at the gravel driveway.

A dusty tan and white police car pulled into the driveway and squealed to a halt, the siren abruptly coming to a stop.

Dulpstrindle got out heavily from the driver's side; he nodded curtly to me.

"They patched your man into me down by Page Mill Road. Lucky thing I was close. You go on in?"

I told Dulpstrindle I had just arrived.

"What about her?" he asked, noticing Violet. "She looks pretty shocky."

"I'll be all right," said Violet from somewhere far away.

Dulpstrindle nodded severely and said: "Paramedics on their way. They're taking care some guy got stung by killer bees down at a nursery."

He stood there for a moment, a large competent man.

"Might as well come with me, Asherfeld," he said.

Violet had left the door of the house ajar; Dulpstrindle pushed it wide open.

The house looked normal, but there was a thick cloying smell in the air.

Dulpstrindle pointed silently to the hallway floor. There were drops of what looked like blood glistening on the tiles.

We walked stiffly to the staircase. There was a long wet red streak above the red line that someone had used to separate the two sides of the house and there was blood on the stairs.

Dulpstrindle nodded heavily and began walking downstairs.

At the downstairs landing, the blood widened to a sticky pool.

Duplstrindle braced as he turned from the landing to look at the studio.

Donald Dindle was sitting in the green felt easy chair; Zoe Dindle was in his lap. Her head was slumped against his chest; his head was thrown backward. For a moment they looked like lovers.

Zoe Dindle's black cashmere sweater was matted with blood.

A knife had been buried in her chest below her bosom; I could see the handle, pearl white against the black sweater.

Donald Dindle had blown out the back of his head with the large automatic pistol that now lay a few feet from the chair. There was an elegant pigskin briefcase at his feet.

Milk and Honey

I HAD TOLD THE DEAN that I had hand-delivered half a million dollars to Wah Gee and Jimmy Joy, but, of course, I hadn't. I was pretty sure that if anyone asked, Wah Gee and Jimmy Joy would deny knowing anything, which is pretty much what they would have done if I *had* given them the money.

I went down to the B of A on the corner of Columbus and Union; it was the bank I had used to set up the dean's accounts. I asked to speak with the manager. He was a smooth-skinned Filipino with a lilting accent. I told him I wanted to close each of my five accounts and convert the money to fifty cashier's checks. He looked at me skeptically over his thin-framed gold spectacles and then punched in the accounts on his desktop computer.

"These funds were deposited with us just last week," he said.

"I'm fickle."

He resumed looking at his screen.

"I'm not sure the checks have cleared," he said lamely.

"The law gives you three business days to float my money," I said. "*I* gave you a week."

He shifted uncomfortably in his leatherette seat; he knew something was odd. He just couldn't figure out what.

"Any transaction over ten thousand dollars," he said, "I have to report to the IRS."

"No you don't," I said. "You've got to report any *deposit* over ten thousand dollars. This is a withdrawal."

"I'll need a few hours," he said dubiously.

I said that that would be fine.

When I came back that afternoon, the money had gone out to sea and come back; the manager had the cashier's checks waiting for me. There was nothing else he could do.

"A considerable sum of money," he said.

"You think so?" I asked.

He nodded shyly.

"It depends on what it's buying."

I stood for a long while at the little desk they have in banks for customers to fill out deposit slips. I addressed the plain manila envelope the bank had given me to Mrs. Ami Goode; I didn't know what to say and I didn't want to send the checks without saying anything.

Finally, I wrote: "Milk and Honey."

I mailed it from the mailbox at the corner of Columbus and Green.

Except for Violet, I never saw any of them again; I never wanted to.

I went down to the university in order to let her know what really happened.

It was a calm clear day.

Violet met me in her office. She was sitting placidly at her desk, her hands folded in front of her. She smiled her pretty smile at me.

The door to the chairman's office banged open and a tall woman with a long sad stupid face emerged. I recognized her right away.

"Aaron Asherfeld," said Violet miserably, "this is Naomi Lipscombe Griller, the new chairperson of the department?"

Naomi Lipscombe Griller gave me a quick savage look and turned back to re-enter her office.

I said to Violet: "Come on. We'll get coffee."

We walked together toward the Union. Violet told me that she was moving: Omo had asked that she vacate the coach house. I thought he might. She said that Mike Dottenberry was helping her find a new place.

"He's been so wonderful," she said.

We sat on the terrace at the Union and looked out at the silent campus, the light brilliant now in the noon-day sun.

Violet was munching an enormous jelly donut and sipping from a latte.

"No more Jennie's?" I asked.

"No more diets," she said defiantly. "I've joined this support group FATT? Fighting Against Trendy Thinness. It teaches me to accept who I am."

I nodded. "Probably something we should all do, Violet."

"I'll always be fat," she said. "And no one will ever love me."

After she got through with her jelly donut, Violet asked: "How did you figure everything out, Mr. Asherfeld?"

"Sometimes there's less to things than meets the eye."

"I don't understand."

I waved my hand vaguely in the air; I didn't want to explain everything to her.

"Odo Omo had a tattoo," I said. "I thought it might be a tong mark, something sinister. Turned out to be just a fake tattoo, something silly he pasted on. I thought that Neava Climax might have been involved with CSR. It turned out she wasn't. I thought that Bulton Limbish might have been more than a foolish idiot. It turned out he wasn't. See what I mean. Less than meets the eye."

Violet nodded her fat head. "I think I understand," she said. I didn't tell her that Zoe Dindle had killed George Epinall. There was no reason to.

Violet sipped at the rest of her latte and pressed a few crumbs from her plate with the tip of her index finger.

"Do you know how he died?" she finally asked in a small voice. "Do you know how Richard died?"

"It was an accident," I said. "That's all it was."

"Please," she said. Tell me."

"He choked to death, Violet. He was alone and he choked on a bite of pepperoni pizza. He couldn't swallow the pepperoni. The medical examiner thinks preservatives in the meat caused an allergic spasm. He tried to perform the Heimlich maneuver on himself and bruised his own throat. That's why it *looked* as if someone might have strangled him."

Violet took a moment to absorb the information and then giggled.

"And he was always so thin," she said triumphantly.

* * *

It was a good time to leave. I made my goodbyes and headed off down the sun-washed walkway toward the bookstore. I had parked illegally in front of the university.

Tiny Face and Miss Piggy were manning a table just beyond the fountain. I walked over. They had propped up two signs on a pair of artist's easels on either side of their table.

"What's it all about?" I asked.

"It's about smashing stereotipifying symbols," said Tiny Face.

"It's about symbols that are used to define us," said Miss Piggy.

She pointed to the signs. One showed the outline of a woman in red, the other showed an outline of a man in black. They looked for all the world like signs used to identify male and female bathrooms.

"What about them?" I asked.

"These signs perpetuate sexist stereotypes in restrooms," said Miss Piggy.

"This is like a passive woman in a dress," said Tiny Face, tapping the woman's sign, "and this sign is all I'm this macho broad-shouldered dude in pants."

"I can see how it's a problem," I said.